THE FORGOTTEN LORE

Book 1

DIANA PETERFREUND

RP|TEENS
PHILADELPHIA

Running Press Teens
Hachette Book Group
1290 Avenue of the Americas, New York, NY 10104
www.runningpresskids.com
@runningpresskids

First Edition: April 2026

Published by Running Press Teens, an imprint of Hachette Book Group, Inc.
The Running Press Teens name and logo are trademarks of Hachette Book Group, Inc.

The Hachette Speakers Bureau provides a wide range of authors for speaking events. To find out more, go to www.hachettespeakersbureau.com or email HachetteSpeakers@hbgusa.com.

Running Press books may be purchased in bulk for business, educational, or promotional use. For more information, please contact your local bookseller or the Hachette Book Group Special Markets Department at Special.Markets@hbgusa.com.

The publisher is not responsible for websites (or their content) that are not owned by the publisher.

Illustrations by David De Las Heras
Print book cover and interior design by Mary Boyer
Ellen Poe created by Ryan Wiesbrock

Library of Congress Cataloging-in-Publication Data
Names: Peterfreund, Diana author
Title: Ellen Poe : the forgotten lore / Diana Peterfreund.
Description: First edition. | Philadelphia : RP Teens, 2026. |
Audience: Ages 13 & up | Audience: Grades 7-9
Identifiers: LCCN 2025032375 (print) | LCCN 2025032376 (ebook) |
ISBN 9798894141688 trade paperback | ISBN 9798894141695 ebook
Subjects: CYAC: Mystery and detective stories | Poe, Edgar Allan, 1809-1849—Fiction |
Ability—Fiction | Ghosts $ Fiction | LCGFT: Detective and mystery fiction | Novels
Classification: LCC PZ7.P441545 El 2026 (print) | LCC PZ7.P441545 (ebook)
LC record available at https://lccn.loc.gov/2025032375
LC ebook record available at https://lccn.loc.gov/2025032376

ISBNs: 979-8-89414-168-8 (trade paperback), 979-8-89414-169-5 (ebook),
979-8-89414-330-9 (hardcover, library edition)

Printed in Indiana, USA

LSC-C

Printing 1, 2026

DEDICATION

1‡(08‡ 9: 16(); (85†8(5*† (8)85(-4 .5(;*8(

It is nearly a mon
, requesting an in
–, I placed it ("
swered letters". Thi
seeming discourtes
answer.
I have now to
you at any time
adway. You will
the morning befor
Very Respy.
Yr. C

CHAPTER 1

Breakfast with Dead People

I'VE BEEN STAYING WITH MY AUNT FOR NEARLY TWO weeks, and in that time, I've had thirteen nightmares. Aunt Marie said that's what happens when getting used to sleeping in a strange place.

Emphasis on the *strange*.

I woke up gasping from the latest, my hands in a white-knuckled grip on the silken purple covers of this ridiculous bed. There was light coming in through the blinds, but I couldn't shake the stifling darkness from my dream. I couldn't forget the eerie, pale faces of the people. Even now, I felt their cold fingers reaching for me.

I shuddered and gulped in grateful breaths of fresh air. I was fine. It was a dream. I wasn't in that hot, dark place with those silent, dead people.

I was just . . . here. In this bizarre bed, in this silly room, with the broken fireplace and the crates stacked four feet high along the wall. And, of course, the raven.

I glanced above the door, where, naturally, he was still there. A stuffed raven doesn't tend to move. He was perched on the little plaster head, still staring down at me with his beady glass eyes.

I'd like to think he was looking after me, but that's not how the poem goes.

"Morning, Chip," I said to the raven as I threw back the covers. I figured if you were going to have a dead bird staring at you while you slept, got dressed, and did your homework, you might as well have the decency to give it a name. Chip's name was in honor of the tiny little piece missing from his beak.

What, were you expecting "Nevermore"?

After getting dressed in my school uniform, I opened the door and carefully edged my way down the hallway toward the stairs. Raven's Rest has been in my family for generations, and boy, can you tell. Nearly every square inch of living space is stacked, floor to ceiling, with artifacts my family has collected over the years and remnants of businesses they failed to get off the ground. The dark, narrow hallways are tricky to navigate, given all the boxes and crates. Technically, Aunt Marie and I were cleaning everything out. But it was a slow process.

Chip and the rest of my bedroom's unfortunate decor were the result of my aunt's attempt to turn this Baltimore townhouse into the world's most elaborate Edgar Allan Poe–themed bed-

and-breakfast. But until she managed to clean out some of this junk, it was also the world's most *unsuccessful* Edgar Allan Poe–themed bed-and-breakfast.

My room—in case you hadn't guessed—was supposed to be themed like Poe's most famous poem, "The Raven." It was the least offensive of the choices available. I couldn't imagine how bad my nightmares would be if I were staying in "The Pit and the Pendulum" or "The Tell-Tale Heart."

I followed my nose to the kitchen, where I found Aunt Marie frosting a fresh batch of cinnamon buns and crooning along to Stevie Nicks. I didn't think much of the beds in this place, but the breakfasts couldn't be beat.

Now all we needed was paying customers.

The kitchen has large windows that let in a lot of morning light, though some of them are blocked by stacks of crates filled with decades' worth of what Aunt Marie calls history—and what any rational person would call junk. One whole wall of the kitchen is devoted to broken appliances of yesteryear, hunching there like a hoarder's hobgoblins.

Aunt Marie was so intent on piping frosting on the buns that she didn't notice me at first, but Cattarina—her slender tortoiseshell cat—picked her way across the floor between crates to rub her furry, multicolored cheek against my knee socks. I reached down to give her a scratch behind her ears. Before coming to stay at Raven's Rest, I never thought of myself as a cat person, but Cattarina was growing on me.

If nothing else, she was the tidiest living thing in the house.

"Ellen!" Aunt Marie looked up from her pastries and pressed a hand to her chest. "You startled me, standing in the shadows like that. I thought you were a ghost!"

Of course she did. Raven's Rest, you see, was said to be haunted by none other than the ghost of Edgar Allan Poe.

Should I have been offended that she thought I, a sixteen-year-old girl in a school uniform blazer and a plaid skirt, looked like a two-hundred-year-old, dead, alcoholic poet? I say yes.

But I didn't say it out loud. Instead, I pulled up a barstool to the kitchen island and grabbed the coffee pot off the warmer. I never used to drink coffee, but the nightmares have been doing a real number on my sleep schedule, so I was in desperate need of some caffeine.

Aunt Marie watched me add four heaping spoonfuls of sugar and half a cup of milk to the mug. "I'd be concerned about letting you drink coffee in the morning," she said, "but honestly, I don't know how much you're actually getting when you dilute it like that."

I rolled my eyes and kept stirring. The resulting concoction was pale gray in color, like the skin of the people in my dreams. I pushed it away.

Aunt Marie handed me a cinnamon bun. "More nightmares?"

"Yeah." Then I took a huge bite of the bun, because if my mouth was full, I couldn't very well answer any more questions, could I?

Aunt Marie didn't press; she just went back to frosting. When she didn't have other guests to feed—which was always—she sold her baked goods on the ground floor of the townhouse, out of a storefront that has been at least five different businesses run by various members of my family that I can remember. There was the bar my grandfather ran before they lost the liquor license. The corner store managed by my grandmother before she died. The short-lived record store, which was my father's baby. And the coffee shop and "art space" my aunt kept trying to make happen.

Her coffee was terrible, but she got by on pastries.

The silence stretched between us, and I could not think of another thing to talk about. Was there weather today? Did sports teams even exist?

All I could think about was the people from my nightmare. Their black, pitted eyes; their long, unhinged mouths.

Last night was the worst to date. Even the cinnamon-infused sugar currently making a beeline for my bloodstream did little to dispel the chill.

Fine, Aunt Marie. You win.

"I was in total darkness, and I couldn't breathe," I said all in a rush.

"Hmm." Aunt Marie considered this, then turned to the stove and ladled out a mug of something steaming. She placed it in front of me. Apple cider.

That actually did sound really good right now. I took a warming sip. Better than the ghostly coffee.

"Buried alive?" she asked, the way some grown-ups ask if you have homework.

"No—I was wandering around, in the darkness. I wasn't trapped."

She tapped her chin thoughtfully. "Could be immurement instead of burial. You know, being entombed? Bricked up inside the catacombs, like in 'The Cask of Amontillado.'" She sounded almost excited about the idea.

I blinked at her. "Explain to me how that's better."

"Oh, it's not. But it does support my theory."

Aunt Marie believed dreams were trying to tell you something. Oh, I forgot to mention her short stint as a psychic doing tarot readings on the ground floor. That was after her band broke up, though.

Anyway, her theory was that all my nightmares could be traced back to stories by Edgar Allan Poe. "The Cask of Amontillado" was a typically gruesome Poe yarn in which one Italian nobleman lures another into an underground burial vault with the promise of wine, only to lock him in there to die and rot.

Fun times. Poe also loved writing stories about murder, torture, houses collapsing, and corpses being reanimated, so that's something I apparently had to look forward to. I'd just love to be finished with all the horror stories and on to the other, nicer things he wrote about—like finding buried treasure, or arranging furniture.

Yes, arranging furniture. The man was pretty prolific for a guy who died at forty.

For generations, my family has been obsessed with Edgar Allan Poe. According to family lore, we're his direct descendants, thanks to a fling my five-times great-grandmother supposedly had with Poe a few days before his untimely death here in Baltimore in 1849.

This house was a tavern back then, and the story goes that he was as enamored of the barmaid as he was of the drinks she poured.

Thanks to that little accident, everyone in my family possessed the following: one, the middle name of Poe, and two, a positively encyclopedic knowledge of the poet and everything he ever did. My grandmother used to recite "Annabel Lee" to me as a lullaby when I was still in my crib. The very barstool I currently occupied was supposedly the one Poe sipped his last drink on.

At least, that's what they say.

Dad and I didn't believe it, though. We left Raven's Rest and all the Poe stuff behind ten years ago. Our apartment across town had not one single Poe reference. Our clocks had no pendulums, and the only birds we discussed were the Orioles.

But Aunt Marie believed that now that I was back living here, it would all start coming up again. Every ill-fated Poe reference from my childhood, dredged up from my formative memories and reconfigured as a series of unavoidable nightmares.

Not even old Edgar could come up with something so horrific.

"I'm in 'The Raven' room, not the 'Cask of Amontillado' room," I pointed out.

"We don't have an Amontillado room." Aunt Marie brightened. "But maybe after we clear out the basement, I could make one. I'm thinking wine cellar-slash-boudoir . . ."

All of a sudden, being bricked up and left to die sounded somewhat appealing.

You'd think so too if you saw the state of that basement. We'd spent all weekend down there, and most of our efforts were still stacked in crates on this very kitchen island.

We were never getting anywhere with this project before Dad came back to fetch me. I was only staying with Aunt Marie for a couple of months, while he was out of town on a construction job.

"So, basically you think that the nightmares will stop as soon as I move out." It was a small comfort.

"Or," Aunt Marie continued, "we could redo one of the guest rooms. De-Poe it, for the sake of your unconscious mind? What do girls your age like? Rainbows? Robots? Strangely beautiful K-pop stars?"

"Don't worry about it. I won't be here that long." Dad said he'd be back as soon as he cashed out this gig. We'd get a new place. A bigger place, closer to my school. Maybe something with a backyard, so I could finally have a puppy.

"I don't want you suffering," Aunt Marie insisted. "And I don't want you feeling like you have to drink the worst coffee in Baltimore to stay awake for school, either."

We both examined my abandoned coffee mug and its pale, ghostly contents.

Here's why I know I wasn't dreaming about "The Cask of Amontillado." The victim in Poe's story was chained to the wall and left alone to die. But I wasn't alone in that stifling darkness. There were others there with me—sickly, glowing people with skin somewhere between smoke and parchment, their features oddly stretched, like reflections in dark glass. They reached for me with long, spindly fingers. They clutched at their necks. They screamed with no sound.

The dreams were horrible, like the stories of Edgar Allan Poe. But it wasn't *Poe* dreaming them up. It was me. The edges of the people I saw were blurry, watery, like their souls were being drained away, but I could still make out the details.

The woman in leggings and a T-shirt. The man wearing headphones. The boy in the hoodie. They weren't the nineteenth-century creations of a genius literary mind. They were people like I'd see on the street every day. They were all of them suffocating, just like I was in the dream.

They were all of them dead.

"It was just a dream," I said aloud, as much to convince myself as to inform Aunt Marie. "It's no big deal."

Dad and Aunt Marie didn't really look that much alike. Dad was kind of rough around the edges, with the full sleeves of tattoos and the shaved head, while Aunt Marie had this whole flowy earth-mother thing going on. But when they gave me the look that meant they weren't buying a word I said, you could absolutely tell they were brother and sister. And Aunt Marie was totally giving me that look now.

"Okay," she said. "But don't be in such a rush to move out. You know I'd hate to lose my decluttering buddy."

I'd been here for two weeks and we'd barely made a dent, mainly because Aunt Marie insisted on going through all my boxes after I was done and *de*-decluttering the things I chose to throw away.

Even if I did ask her to redo my room, I doubted we'd ever get around to it. She still hadn't finished "The Bells" room, mainly because she couldn't find a way to make it both authentic and quiet enough for anyone to sleep in.

"It's fine," I said. I went back to stuffing my face with cinnamon roll, and she went back to frosting the rest of the batch. Cattarina found a ray of sunlight to sit in and bathe her ears. For a moment, we could pretend this was a normal household having a normal breakfast.

"Everything going well at school?" Aunt Marie asked, somewhat awkwardly. "All your . . . homework done?"

It was actually kind of cute how she was learning to parent a teenager in real time. The first week I was here, she operated on memories from my childhood, when I last lived in this house. She bought me chicken nuggets shaped like dinosaurs and thought I needed little star stickers to encourage me to finish my schoolwork and brush my teeth.

I had to admit, those nuggets were still pretty good. But I didn't need stickers to remind me to get my homework done. Getting good grades was vital to keeping my scholarship at Evergreen Prep.

Which reminded me, I'd better get a move on if I wanted to make it to school on time. Thanks to my new living arrangement, I needed to take two different buses to get all the way across town.

"Thanks for breakfast," I told Aunt Marie, and grabbed my backpack.

That's when disaster struck. Somehow, the fabric of my backpack caught against a frayed piece of wood on the nearest crate, and when I went to yank the strap over my shoulder, everything went flying.

Including me.

The next thing I knew, I was splayed out on the linoleum of the kitchen floor among the contents of my homework binder and at least a decade's worth of Reynolds family basement junk. Old newspapers, broken knickknacks, some bronzed baby shoes, at least three books, and—oh, ick. Were those *mouse droppings*?

"Ellen!" Aunt Marie stood over me, the bangles on her wrists clanging as she leaned down to help me up. "Are you okay?"

I brushed her off, then I did the same with the mouse droppings. "I'm fine. I'm fine!" I was going to be late, was what I was. I reached over to gather up my schoolwork among the detritus.

And that's when I saw it. Or rather, *him*.

There, in the shadows of the corridor. I blinked and he was gone, but—just for a second—I thought I saw him.

Him-him.

Mr. Edgar Allan Poe.

It is nearly a mon

, requesting an in

, I placed it (

swered letters". Th

seeming discourtesy

answer.

I have now to

you at any tim

adway. You will

the morning befor

Very Resp.

CHAPTER 2

Textbooks About Bloody Murder

NATURALLY, I DID NOT OPEN MY MOUTH AND SAY anything as dumb as "Hey, Aunt Marie, I think I just saw the ghost of Edgar Allan Poe in the hall." I'd never hear the end of it.

Instead, I shoved all my junk back in my bag, made sure every light in the hallway was on, and sprinted as fast as I could down the hall and out the door. I didn't even lock it behind me.

But that was surely just because I was running late. I didn't really think there was a ghost lurking in the hall. That would be crazy, right?

Outside, the sun glinted on the damp cobblestone streets, the air smelled like the harbor, and the very idea of ghosts—in dreams or otherwise—seemed kind of silly. The morning was still warm, with none of the autumn chill I knew was due around the corner, and there were already people out, setting up their café tables, walking their dogs, jogging, or heading out on their commute. Normal, living people doing normal, living things.

I took a deep, cleansing breath.

Maybe Aunt Marie was right about one thing. Moving back to Raven's Rest was causing all kinds of things to get stirred up.

I hurried several blocks and just managed to flag down the bus before it pulled away. My school doesn't provide transportation, so now that I live down here, I have to take two public buses to get across town and up to the campus. Mr. Sousa, the bus driver, likes to keep an eye out for me—not only because he knows I take this route every day, but also because there can sometimes be weirdos on board.

Today, though, it was the usual mix of commuters wearing headphones or catching up on their sleep . . . or sometimes both. I reached into my bag for my own earbuds.

Which is when I realized two things. One, they must have fallen out along with my school stuff when I fell in the kitchen and are probably lying among mouse droppings on the linoleum back at home. And two, there was a strange book in my backpack.

The cover was made of cracked leather, with embossing worn so smooth by the passage of time that I couldn't make out what it said. When I opened it, the first pages cracked and crumbled to dust right before my eyes.

I sneezed, which quickly obliterated two more. I clapped my free hand over my nose and mouth in mortification.

"Bless you," said the little old lady across the aisle.

I turned to thank her, but the words died on my lips as I took in the man seated behind her.

It was *him* again. Edgar Allan Poe. Riding the City Link bus uptown in a three-piece suit, his cravat jauntily knotted beneath his pale, mustachioed face.

Quickly, I whirled back around in my seat, my heart pounding.

This was not like the dead people in my nightmares. Poe didn't look menacing. He didn't even look dead. Okay, maybe he was a bit . . . *translucent* around the edges, especially where the sunlight hit him.

I sneaked another look. He nodded politely, in greeting.

I spun back around. What was happening?

I needed to get a grip. There was an obvious explanation. He was probably just an impersonator, riding the bus to a gig. This city was full of Poe stuff. Poe museums, public housing, memorabilia, a brand of craft beer . . . They even called their football team the Ravens, for heaven's sake. This was just some guy, on his way to an acting job.

Except . . . real people didn't tend to be see-through.

I braved one more peek. The old lady across the way was giving me a weird look. If she thought I was odd, she should check out the dead person behind her.

The bus traveled through an underpass, momentarily plunging us into shadow. The figure of Edgar Allan Poe flickered in the changing light. His lack of substance didn't seem to bother him at all, though. He glanced my way again and smiled.

You have never seen a smile on the face of Edgar Allan Poe. Trust me, you can't even imagine what that looks like.

Not that it was a bad smile. In fact, it was kind of nice. Friendly, even.

"Ellen!" I turned around. It was Mr. Sousa, the driver. "Hon, this is your stop."

"Oh, sorry." I'd been so distracted by Poe I hadn't even noticed. I slid the mysterious book back into my bag.

When I stood up to leave, I took one last look around, but he was nowhere to be seen.

❁ ❁ ❁

There was no sign of Poe on the next bus, and I didn't see him as I headed up the long, tree-lined lane from the bus stop to the school. I spent the walk convincing myself he was just an impersonator, and that I probably needed glasses.

Evergreen Prep is usually a relief after all the clutter of Raven's Rest. The school is stuffed with history too, but the pristine, moneyed kind—polished floors and giant libraries where none of the books get taken out because we all have top-of-the-line laptops. There are two main school buildings. The New Building is all sleek glass and non-right angles, and houses the gym, the math and science departments, the black box theater, the cafeteria, and the hall of lockers. And then there is the Old Building, which I think was some mansion once owned by a Victorian-era shipping millionaire, and holds the administrative offices, the library, and a few low-tech classrooms. All the rooms in the Old Building are cramped, with high ceilings covered in elaborate plaster figurines. Even the railings of the stairs are carved to look like fantastic beasts.

I think I'm the only student here who prefers the New Building. But I have a raven staring at me while I sleep, so I don't need a gargoyle watching over my shoulder in history class, too. Also, my favorite classes are math and computer science, which are both in the New Building. Numbers are way better than poetry. They're neat and orderly, and they always make perfect sense.

English is in the Old Building, mostly, I think, because we don't need any specialized equipment or electronics in the room. I had it second period after computer science, so after a peaceful, entirely spirit-free hour of learning about developments in cybersecurity, I dashed across the green into the Old Building and ascended the polished staircase to my dreaded American Literature seminar. English class was never my favorite, and this year was proving to be particularly bad.

I slid into my seat along the wall just as our teacher, Ms. Morris, began handing out our new texts. Ms. Morris likes us to read on paper—she says we're more careful than when we read on a screen.

She obviously didn't see me disintegrate that antique volume on the bus. It was still sitting in the outer pocket of my bag, hopefully not getting crushed by my binder.

Ms. Morris passed by, and a creased paperback landed on the surface of my desk. I stifled a groan as I saw *his* stupid face staring up at me from the cover. I recognized this particular portrait of Poe. It was the Thompson daguerreotype, and I hated the fact that I could identify it on sight.

Daguerreotypes were a kind of old-timey photograph, and Poe took several after he became famous. This one was the last-known portrait before his death. The picture showed the writer staring at the camera, his eyes haunted, his hairline receding, his odd little mustache covering a mouth that seemed about to speak.

Honestly, he looked way better on the bus this morning, even with the pallor and the whole being a little bit see-through thing.

Below the portrait was printed the title *The Complete Works of Edgar Allan Poe.*

This was definitely not my week.

Ms. Morris began her lecture on our new unit, and I tuned right out. She wasn't going to say anything I hadn't heard a thousand times before. The good news was, no homework in English class this month. They'd all be reading "The Tell-Tale Heart" or "Annabel Lee" for the first time. I got those as bedtime stories in preschool.

"Ms. Morris?" One row down, Rebecca Lambert primly raised her hand. "I object to studying this author. He was incredibly problematic."

"Yes, Miss Lambert. He was a very complicated man—"

"He was a creep!" Rebecca insisted. "He married his thirteen-year-old sister."

"Cousin," I corrected, and immediately regretted it. All eyes in the room slid toward me. "Virginia Clemm was his thirteen-year-old *cousin.*"

"Like that's any better?" Rebecca sneered.

“Well, it was at least legal to marry your cousin,” I offered, which was yet another mistake. How had I somehow put myself in the position of *defending* Poe’s marriage to his teenage cousin? It was creepy. Rebecca was right.

And the look she was giving me now was pitched somewhere between disgust and pity. I realized I would probably never have someone to sit with at lunch again if I didn’t shut up.

Though I never would have won any popularity contests last year, I wasn’t the pariah I’d been lately. I’d always had some classmates I would consider friends. Sure, they had big houses and nice cars and at least two parents, but I didn’t really feel the differences between us. I’d had partners for school projects and friends at lunch.

But everything changed last summer. We were supposed to go on a trip to Ocean City, but I had to bail at the last minute because my dad got that job out west and I had to move in with my aunt. Can’t really drop everything to spend a day at the beach when you’re busy shoving all your worldly possessions into a few suitcases. I don’t remember exactly what I told the other girls—that week was mostly a blur, to be honest—but they were not amused. After a string of super angry texts, most of them from Rebecca, I got deleted from the group chat. I guess when they move, their mommies or their maids do all the packing for them.

Even worse, when school started back up, it was obvious that I was not forgiven. Rebecca and the rest of that group have all been treating me like some kind of criminal.

I'd like to think that this whole thing is just temporary, like staying at Raven's Rest, but who was I kidding? I was doomed.

While Ms. Morris danced around the unsavory facts of Poe's life, I tried my best not to listen, just in case I was compelled to offer any more corrections. Besides, I knew all this stuff already.

Poe was born in Boston into a family of stage actors, and his suffering began early. His dad abandoned them, and his mom died young. The kids were all split up, and Poe was taken in by a rich, childless couple in Richmond, Virginia, named Allan. The Allans raised him but never formally adopted him. After dropping out of both the University of Virginia and West Point, Poe was disinherited by his foster father and moved in with distant family here in Baltimore. Including the aforementioned teenage cousin.

After that, his life was a series of more tragedies: He traveled around the country, in and out of work, always desperately poor. His sketchy marriage to his cousin was supposedly happy, but then she got sick and died. He achieved fame in writing but never really made any money from it. And then, his mysterious death at only forty left behind a legacy of haunting stories and poems, mostly about beautiful dead women.

Speaking as someone with more than a passing familiarity with dead people, they weren't very beautiful at all. At least, not the ones in my nightmares. The details from last night's dream were already fading for me. This morning, it all felt so clear, but now it was like a reflection in water, bubbling away.

There were three of them, I think, or maybe four. Their eyes glowing pits, their mouths open in screams I couldn't hear. Their too-long arms reaching toward me, their fingers clawing against some barrier I could not see. And that last ghost, the boy with the blond hair. The one who flew right at my face.

They'd all been terrifying, but they'd also been *dreams*. It was weird those scared me so much more than the sudden appearance of Edgar Allan Poe on the bus. Seeing dead people in your dreams could be explained. But up and about and walking—er, *riding*—around?

Was I going crazy?

"Wasn't he crazy?" one of my classmates asked, and I stared at him wide-eyed for a second before I realized everyone else was still talking about Poe.

"No, he was a drunk," said another.

"It's hard to say what was the root cause of Poe's health problems," Ms. Morris explained. "There are accounts of him drinking too much, or getting fired from jobs for being drunk. It's also true that he suffered from bouts of hallucinations, even what doctors today would call mania or psychosis. And he was able to write very honestly and genuinely from the perspective of psychotic narrators, like the murderers in stories like 'A Tell-Tale Heart' or 'The Black Cat.'"

If you were crazy, did you know you were going crazy? Did you know that the things you saw that weren't real . . . weren't real?

"But," Ms. Morris went on, "back then, they didn't have the kind of medications we have for people who are suffering from mental health crises. It's possible Poe's difficulties with alcohol were a form of self-medication. It's just impossible for us to know."

Don't worry, Ms. Morris, I'll ask him on the bus home, I wanted to joke.

I looked down at the book on my desk. Poe's face stared up at me, rumpled and haunted. I wondered what his dreams were like. Did he have nightmares like mine?

The door to the classroom opened and in walked the principal, leading another student. From my spot against the far wall, I couldn't quite see the new kid, except to note that he was tall and apparently hadn't gotten the memo about not being allowed to wear hoodies over your uniform. Maybe he didn't have all the pieces yet.

"Ms. Morris," said the principal, Ms. Engle. "We have a new addition to your class."

The two adults remained in hushed conference for a minute while everyone else in the class openly gawked at the new kid like sharks sensing feeding time in the tank.

Rebecca was practically breaking her neck two rows over trying to get a glimpse of him, but I had already decided that I was profoundly uninterested. Instead, I read the opening stanza of "The Raven" just in case—I don't know—it could have changed since I last recited it from memory.

Nope. The midnight was still dreary, the narrator was still weary, and he was still whining about his poor deceased girlfriend, Lenore.

"—a seat over there by the wall" was all I heard Ms. Morris say. As the new boy passed my desk, I casually glanced up, determined to be the one person who didn't have an entire fit over something as mundane as a new student.

Unfortunately, I was extremely wrong about that.

Because what I saw was the dead boy from my dream. The ghost with the glowing eyes. It was impossible, but I'd know the blond hair and that face anywhere.

In my shock, I must have knocked the Poe book off my desk. I leaned over to pick it up, at precisely the same moment as the new boy. Our heads cracked together.

"Ow," he said.

Our eyes locked and his pale, grayish-blue eyes looked nothing like the scary pits I'd seen last night.

"You're dead!" I blurted, way too loud.

His mouth dropped open. "Excuse me?"

"Um, Ms. Engle?" said Rebecca, somewhere above. "Ellen Reynolds just threatened to kill the new kid."

It is nearly a mon
requesting an in
, I placed it (
swered letters". Th
seeming discourtes
answer,
I have now to
you at any time
adway. You will
the morning befor
Very Respt.
H. C

CHAPTER 3

The Principal's Office of DOOM

I AM NOT THE TYPE OF KID WHO KNOWS WHAT THE inside of a principal's office looks like. I'm the kind who hides the bumper stickers that say things like "My Child Is an Honor Student at Evergreen Prep" before my dad can do anything so embarrassing as put them on his laptop sleeve. The kind whose report cards state "is a delight in class" and for whom teachers scramble to find more work so I don't grow bored waiting for the other kids to finish. The kind who secures fancy scholarships to private prep schools where the tuition costs more than anyone in my family makes in a year.

At least, I used to be.

Now, apparently, I'm the type that's hauled into Ms. Engle's office. She's sitting on the other side of a desk that's probably a century old and made from the hull of a sunken Confederate warship or something, and she's looking at me as if I've suddenly morphed into some kind of disappointment.

I've always liked Ms. Engle—the little I've interacted with her. She's young and seems to really care about the school. She was always at lacrosse games last year, she goes to the plays, and she even handed out certificates after the intramural coding challenge last spring. While I don't have a ton of experience with the disciplinary side of the school, I haven't heard any horror stories either.

But maybe that's just because the kids who get in trouble don't live to tell the tale.

How did this become my day? Literally the only thing that has gone right this morning was Aunt Marie's cinnamon roll. The rest of it has been all nightmares and mouse droppings and seeing dead people around every corner.

Or . . . not-so-dead people.

When most people have bad days, they wish they could have just stayed in bed. But my bed was designed to look like a creepy poem, complete with a dead bird staring at me. It's not my bed, not my room, not my home. School is supposed to be my escape.

And now Poe and my nightmares are haunting me here too.

But I couldn't even worry about that now. First, I needed to avoid getting expelled.

I've already tried all the usual excuses. The Seven Stages of Getting-out-of-Trouble Grief.

Stage One, Shock: "Wait, what?"

Stage Two, Denial: "No I didn't!"

Stage Three, Anger: "Shut up, Rebecca." (This was the point where I was kicked out of class.) The last thing I saw was the not-so-dead boy's surprised face.

Stage Four, Bargaining: As I was marched toward the principal's office, I tried to talk my way out of it. "Rebecca misunderstood. She's had it in for me since school started. Please, just let me explain."

Stage Five, Guilt: Ms. Engle was stone-faced the entire trip downstairs to the administration suite on the second floor of the Old Building. She wasn't going to listen to me. Even worse, there were other people in the hallway staring at me as I followed behind. I cast my eyes at the thick carpet. Would they call Aunt Marie? Would they call my *dad*?

And so here I sat, deep in Stage Six: Depression.

"I honestly don't understand, Miss Reynolds," she was saying. "This kind of outburst is completely unacceptable in this institution. You threatened another student—"

"This is all a misunderstanding," I argued. I was startled. The dead boy from my dream showed up in my English class. And he was so much more solid than the Edgar Allan Poe sitting on the bus.

Ms. Engle was giving me the same look that Aunt Marie and Dad do when they don't believe a word I'm saying. Do grown-ups learn it in a class or something?

"We expect a higher standard from students at Evergreen Preparatory School, particularly scholarship students such as yourself—" Ms. Engle went on, as if I hadn't said a word.

Ah, there it was. I was under suspicion because I wasn't one of the rich kids. Obviously, I was violent and untrustworthy. Obviously, Rebecca was absolutely right about what she heard and I would, out of the blue, threaten to unalive a perfect stranger.

Only I couldn't think of what innocent thing I might have meant by saying "You're dead" to the new kid instead, and I couldn't very well tell the principal the truth.

"—no way to welcome a new student into your classroom—" she was saying.

There was a knock on the office door, and the administrative assistant poked his head in. "Ma'am? The new student is outside, and he says he needs to speak to you urgently about the present matter."

Engle blinked in confusion, then looked at me, her mouth pinched.

I raised my hands in defense. "I have no idea. Like you said, I've never seen that boy before in my life." Well, other than in my dreams. Where he was very much dead.

It was him. How could I possibly forget his face when the nightmare was so fresh in my mind?

Ms. Engle stood, straightened her skirt, and stepped outside. I leaned all the way forward in my seat, trying to see what was going on behind the door. Darn these thick, historic walls and fluffy carpeting. I couldn't hear a thing.

After what seemed like forever, she reentered her office, followed by the not-dead boy.

Now that I was over my initial shock, I could assess his appearance more fully. He was actually kind of cute, when he wasn't getting his soul sucked out through his eyeballs. I probably only came up to his shoulder, and he was thin and lanky, his hands shoved in pockets of baggy pants that weren't uniform standard. His pale blond hair was as long as my own neat, chin-length bob, but fell in a tousled shag with ends that curled around his jawline and disappeared into the top of his hoodie.

Why was he here? To witness my execution?

I must have looked confused, because instead of returning to her desk, the principal positioned herself between us. "Let's try this again, shall we?"

I scrambled to my feet.

"Ellen Reynolds," she prompted, "meet our new student, Gus Davenport." She nodded pointedly at my hand, which I stuck out like a marionette on strings.

Gus slipped his hand into mine, his expression amused, his smile kind of crooked. His skin was warm, thank God, and, unlike in my dream, he did not look like he was about to reach for my throat.

"Gus," Ms. Engle went on, "this is Ellen, one of our brightest and *most responsible* students." All this with a very knowing, meaningful glance in my direction.

Note that she did not say *most popular*. Because who are we kidding here?

"Ellen, do you have anything to say to Gus?"

"I'm really sorry for earlier," I said dutifully.

"And?" she prompted.

"And . . ." I looked at her. "I . . . um . . ." *I didn't threaten you? I didn't actually think you were dead?* Only I *did.* I *had.* He *was.*

"And I'm glad to meet you too," Gus said quickly so I could stop fumbling for words that wouldn't come. I'd known this guy for ten minutes, and he'd already saved my butt twice. I wasn't sure what to think about that. "I really appreciate you volunteering to show me around the school."

"I—" Realization hit me. I wasn't getting expelled or suspended or apparently even being given detention. I might survive this incident with nothing more than a tour guide gig.

Relief rushed through me. I hadn't realized how scared I'd been that the principal was going to call my father out west. What if she made him come back for a meeting and he ended up losing the job? We'd never get a new apartment without his completion bonus. I'd be sleeping underneath that stuffed raven for the rest of the year.

Time to make nice with the new kid.

"Yeah. Well, no problem. Happy to." What was I even saying? I felt like a keyboard where all the letters were stuck down, spewing nonsense onto the screen.

"Wonderful!" Ms. Engle clapped her hands together. "Now, why don't you two go do that right now, and leave me to the rest of my work?"

Gus turned and sauntered to the door. I followed him, still feeling a bit topsy-turvy from the whiplash. What had Gus said to the principal to get her to do such a complete one-eighty?

“Oh, and Miss Reynolds?” Ms. Engle’s voice stopped me right before I escaped. I looked back at her. “If I hear even a whisper that you aren’t acting as an Evergreen Prep student should, I will not hesitate to enact serious consequences.”

A chill washed over me. She meant my scholarship.

“Yes, ma’am,” I said, and nearly ran from the office.

Gus waited for me in the hallway, his hands back in his pockets. I hadn’t realized how strange it was to see a kid in these halls in street clothes. The other students flowed around us in their dark green and navy uniforms, but Gus looked like he hadn’t a care in the world.

Maybe the first thing I should acquaint him with was the school dress code.

“You’re welcome,” he said to me.

“What?”

“You’re welcome,” he repeated. “Now, about ‘showing me around.’” He removed his hands from his pockets to make the little air quotes with his fingers. Now that I’d heard him speak more, I detected a slight Southern accent. “It shouldn’t take too long. This school’s microscopic compared to my old one. Football field’s the one with the grass, little boy’s room is the icon of the stick figure without a dress on? Do I have that right?”

“Something like that. Basically, any class that needs equipment is in the New Building across the green. Science, computers, art, PE . . .”

“English needs equipment,” he says. “Books. And apparently protective headgear.”

Very funny. And since he was in the mood to chat, I simply had to know.

"I'm sorry about that. But . . . what did you say to her back there? She was ready to suspend me before you stepped in."

"I told her it was an accident," Gus said, as if it were the most logical thing in the world. "Why would you, a complete stranger, threaten me?"

"That's what I said!" I insisted. "But she didn't believe me."

"Well, she thought you were trying to get out of trouble. When really, I was."

"What? What trouble were you in?"

"I don't want to make an enemy here on my very first day," Gus said with a shrug. "Especially one who's psychic."

That brought me up short. "I'm sorry, what?"

"You apologize a lot—anyone ever tell you that?"

"Well, people keep taking everything I say the wrong way!"

He laughed again. "That sounds like a them problem, to be honest."

"Not when I'm the one getting in trouble for it."

"Well, I took care of that for you." Honestly, he seemed awfully smug about it. Every inch of this boy screamed money. I was used to that by now—nearly everyone at Evergreen but me was rolling in it—but his casual "took care of it" made it sound like a debt he'd paid off. I wanted to know what he wanted in return.

"You did." I regarded him carefully. "What did you mean, psychic?"

"You know, like you have a sixth sense or something." He looked friendlier when he wasn't haunting my dreams, but I still wasn't sure what Gus Davenport was up to. "No one else saw your face when you said that to me. I know you weren't threatening me. I just want to know how you know."

I didn't understand. "Know what?"

"That I was dead."

It is nearly a mon

, requesting an in

–, I placed it (

swered letters". The

seeming discourtes

answer,

I have now to

you at any tim

adway. You will

the morning befor

Very Respy.

W. C

CHAPTER 4

Home Sweet Tomb

BEFORE I COULD STOP MYSELF, I REACHED OUT TO touch Gus. His faded black cotton hoodie felt solid enough under my fingers. I poked him on the shoulder and felt his flesh, firm and substantial.

I was just remembering the boy from my dream, and the see-through man on the bus. Gus wasn't see-through, but after the morning I'd had, one could never be too sure.

Gus seemed highly amused by my exploration. "If you're trying to take my pulse, you're going about it all wrong."

"You're not dead," I said.

"I'm not," he agreed. "Not anymore. But I was—for two and a half minutes." He said it matter-of-factly, like other people might tell you they went to the dentist last week. "And now I'm dying to know how you could tell."

No way. I barely wanted to tell Aunt Marie about my creepy dreams. I was not about to have a sharing session with the new kid so he could tell the rest of my classmates what a freak I was and seal my fate as a social outcast.

At Evergreen Prep, the end of each class period is marked by the sound of a large bronze gong some well-heeled alumnus donated. They wouldn't ever disturb our academic flow with anything so disruptive as a jangling bell or buzzer like a normal high school. Instead, discreet speakers pipe the mellifluous clang all over campus. I heard its music now.

Saved by the bell.

"I've gotta go," I gasped. "See you around—" not-dead boy "—Gus."

I started back up the stairs toward English class.

Gus leaned jauntily on the carved wooden gargoyle that served as the newel post at the base of the stairs. "Oh no," he said loudly. "I'm *lost*."

For real? What was this guy's deal?

He flailed his fingers at a nearby janitor's closet clearly marked for the purpose. "Is this the way to gym class? I don't know. Wow, I bet Miss Engle wouldn't like it if she heard I lost my tour guide."

"*Ms.* Engle," I corrected, because apparently I have a terminal case of correcting people when I should really be keeping my mouth shut.

Students flowed into the hall around me. They were staring at both of us, and I tried to tell myself it was because Gus wasn't in a uniform and not because word had already spread of our little incident.

I sighed. "Fine. I'll take you to your next class. Just let me get my stuff from English first."

He bounded up the stairs behind me, like some overeager golden retriever. As we walked down the hall, I pointed out various rooms—the music studio, the yearbook office, the entrance to the library.

The library—it must be said—was the most beautiful room on the entire campus. The ceilings were painted with murals of philosophers and mythological figures. The shelves went all the way to the twenty-foot ceilings. They even had those rolling ladder things, though all the books the students actually used were at eye level and below.

Old-timey millionaires, apparently, really liked their books.

Gus remained unimpressed with his surroundings, which made me wonder exactly what he was used to wherever he came from.

Or maybe, if you died for two and a half minutes and came back to life, everything else paled by comparison.

"So . . ." I said, by way of conversation. "When did you . . . die?"

"Recently." He didn't elaborate, but instead began peppering me with questions. Which was fair. "Why did you poke me back there? You didn't *really* think I was a ghost, did you?"

Way to change the subject, Gus.

"No," I lied. I was not, it must be said, a great liar.

"Because that would be ridiculous," he said.

"Yeah," I echoed. "Ridiculous." It *was* ridiculous. Nearly everything that had happened to me since moving into Raven's Rest could be categorized under that label.

"The first thing that happened when we met was cracking our heads together. So obviously I'm substantial."

I stopped in the hall and stared at him.

"I—" I wasn't sure what to say. "I beg your pardon?"

Gus stopped and turned around. "Substantial," he repeated. "Solid. Corporeal. Made of flesh and blood. Not a ghost."

Why was I having a discussion about ghosts with a total stranger? Why was he discussing whether or not he, personally, was a ghost as if it was some kind of science experiment? How had my life turned into a ghost story all of a sudden?

"I mean, think about this rationally . . ." he started to say.

Enough was enough. I was not having this conversation. I started walking again, and threw "Ghosts aren't rational!" over my shoulder after him. Who cared if people stared? I was obviously well on the way to my reputation at Evergreen moving from "scholarship kid" to "certified freak."

Gus caught up too quickly, thanks to his long legs. "No, but you can try to figure out whether or not they exist using rational means. You had plenty of evidence that I wasn't a ghost. Would we have banged heads if I were a ghost?"

Nothing about this was remotely rational, and I was done playing whatever game this was.

"Thanks for clearing that up," I said as we walked into Ms. Morris's classroom. My belongings were still sitting on my desk—thank goodness—my book bag hanging from the chair.

"Is everything okay, Miss Reynolds?" Ms. Morris asked from her spot at the front of the room.

"It's great!" Gus called. "Couldn't be better. Just a misunderstanding. I don't hold a grudge at all."

Ms. Morris, to her credit, looked mildly scandalized by Gus's enthusiasm.

"What he said," I added, shoving my books in my bags. "I'm—uh—I'm really sorry for causing a disruption in class." I checked the front pocket. The leather journal was still inside.

Up at the front of the room, Ms. Morris was getting Gus set up with a syllabus and his very own copy of *The Complete Works of Edgar Allan Poe.* When I turned around to rejoin them, I saw the man himself—Mr. Edgar Allan Poe—standing behind them.

I stopped dead in the aisles between the desks. Ms. Morris was showing Gus the pages he'd have to read before the next class. Edgar Allan Poe was peering down at it thoughtfully, as if he, too, were listening to the assignment.

He was still a bit blurry and translucent around the edges, as he'd been on the bus earlier. Insubstantial, as Gus would say.

"We'd better go," I choked out. "We have to get all the way across the green to PE."

"I'm glad you two have worked everything out," Ms. Morris said. "And welcome to Evergreen, Mr. Davenport. I think you'll find no better guide to what this school is all about than Miss Reynolds."

Behind her, Edgar Allan Poe smiled and nodded.

I had to get out of there. I tugged on Gus's sleeve. "Let's go."

I practically sprinted into the hall, and despite Gus's far-longer legs, he had to hurry to keep up with me. I took the stairs two at a time, as if hell was on my heels.

Or at least a very persistent ghost.

❁ ❁ ❁

Thankfully, PE was the last class that Gus and I shared, and I was able to point him in the direction he was supposed to go from there and forget about him for the rest of the school day. Even better, it was the last I saw of anyone who had ever been dead—well, except for the photographs of historical figures my government teacher used in his lecture that afternoon.

The bus ride home proved similarly uneventful. I finished my chemistry homework along the way, and, for a while, I could almost forget that any of this had happened.

From outside, Raven's Rest looked like any number of historic brick row houses in Baltimore. The shop on the ground floor was closed up for the afternoon, which meant Aunt Marie had sold out of pastries already. No one came in just for the coffee.

I unlocked the front door and opened it, peering carefully inside in case any dead poets felt like jumping out at me.

"Hello?"

Not even Aunt Marie answered.

I took a deep breath. Ghosts could not hurt me. They couldn't even touch me. They were scary things in my dreams, but—as my new best friend Gus Davenport had so helpfully explained at school—they were non-corporeal. Insubstantial. No more dangerous than air.

Of course, air could be poisonous.

Wait, could you breathe in a ghost? Ugh.

Stop it, Ellen, I told myself. Ghosts are not real.

But, just in case, I shut my eyes and felt my way down the dim entry hall by touch and memory and climbed up the stairs to the second floor.

It didn't take long before I banged my shin against a stack of boxes, and then my shoulder against another. This was getting ridiculous. I told myself to get a grip and opened my eyes. No sign of any ghosts.

"Hello?" I called again.

"Up here." My aunt's voice drifted down from the third floor, where most of the bedrooms were. Cattarina appeared on the landing at the top of the stairs and gave me her meowed greeting.

I dropped my backpack off in my room, double-checked to make sure Chip hadn't moved since this morning, and followed Cattarina down the hall to the "Pit and the Pendulum" room.

It wasn't that Aunt Marie's idea for a Poe-themed hotel was a bad one. Spooky tourism was totally a thing, and if there was anywhere tourists would want to soak in the ambience of the world-famous horror writer, it would be the city of his death. She just wasn't great at follow-through.

Like the coffee shop that didn't sell decent coffee. The band that broke up. The hotel where none of the rooms were ever really finished.

"The Pit and the Pendulum" is an Edgar Allan Poe short story about a guy being held in a torture chamber. It wouldn't be my choice for a room to sleep in, but I'm obviously not in charge of the design. In the story, the poor narrator was condemned to death in the Spanish Inquisition or something. I had no idea if the real Spanish Inquisition ever got so imaginative in the way they killed people. Anyway, he was put in this giant, pitch-dark room with an immense pit in the center that he had to keep away from. Later in the story, he was tied to a plank with a huge sharp blade swinging like a pendulum ever closer at him. He had to escape by encouraging rats to come chew on the ropes binding him, and was eventually pushed nearly into the giant pit when the walls of his prison became red-hot and began to close in.

Obviously, creating a real room of this nature would be an absolute feat of technical engineering, in Spanish Inquisition times and even in the modern era. Plus, it would probably get Aunt Marie arrested.

But she did the best she could. The walls of the room were painted with undulating red waves that looked like flames thanks to a panel of flickering red and orange LED lights placed along the floorboards. There was a large, round black rug in the middle of the room to approximate the pit, and one wall was dominated by an immense, industrial-style clock with a large, brushed-nickel pendulum the size of my head swinging underneath. Aunt Marie got one of her artist friends to make it for her.

It was super cool, don't get me wrong. But it took a special person to be able to sleep in here. Or even to want to. So, no wonder we'd never booked it.

The "Pit and the Pendulum" room, being reserved for our hypothetical guests, was always the tidiest room in the house. So, it was weird to come up here and see it strewn with all the junk Aunt Marie had been trying to get rid of for the last few weeks. She'd also brought up a bunch of extra lamps and things.

She was seated in the middle of the "pit" carpet, a comfortable, plush shag, which unfortunately had a tendency to show every speck of dust that the vacuum failed to catch. Her ancient laptop lay open next to her, and she was surrounded by stacks of papers and objets d'art.

"Are you making changes to the room?" I asked her.

"Not exactly," she grumbled. "How was school?"

Oh, fine. Made a friend—I think. Saw some ghosts—maybe. Might be going mad.

I settled on "Oh, fine." I was much more interested in whatever was going on here, though. Ever since I'd moved in, we'd spent my afternoons supposedly "decluttering"—which usually took the form of me going through boxes and trying to throw most of this junk away, and Aunt Marie coming behind and putting the vast majority of it back in the crates. Now, all that stuff was lined up against the walls.

I sat down across from her on the rug. "What's going on?"

Aunt Marie sighed. "Guess there's no point in hiding it from you anymore. I'm trying to sell some of this junk online—but you know me. All this computer stuff is so complex."

Computer stuff I could handle. "Wait, you're selling things? Why?"

"Because we don't have any guests. Still. And—well, hon, they raised the taxes again. It's great that the neighborhood is doing well, but not so great if we want to keep the house."

She handed me a slip of paper with a scary-looking red stamp on it saying *2nd Notice*. I looked at the total, and my breath caught in my throat.

All of a sudden, the rug I sat on felt like an actual pit, and I was falling into it.

Here's the thing. Yeah, I moved in with Aunt Marie, and yeah, my dad was out west working. But that wasn't the whole story. The reason all of that was happening was because Dad got behind on rent—by a lot—and we had to leave our apartment. The beach trip I missed with those girls at school? Our move wasn't remotely planned. Instead, the landlord was throwing our stuff out on the lawn. How was I supposed to tell the other girls at school *that*?

I know Dad will fix it, but he needs a few months to save up the money. You need a lot of extra money to rent an apartment. Two whole months of extra cash on top of whatever the rent is, and probably even more because of what happened with our last lease. So that's what we were doing. I was living at Aunt Marie's for free and the company that hired Dad was providing him housing while he worked for them, so he could save up all the money we needed to get a new place.

But the only reason that was even possible was because we had Raven's Rest to fall back on. Raven's Rest was the only home I had. The only home that Aunt Marie, at least, has ever known. And if that went too, I wasn't sure what was left.

CHAPTER 5

Not Remotely Homework

OF COURSE, AUNT MARIE HAD AN IDEA. ONE THING about the Reynoldses is we always bounced back. No matter how many jobs we'd had, how many businesses we'd started, how many failures we'd faced, we always made it through.

But we'd always had Raven's Rest too. This house had been in my family for more than a hundred and fifty years. Baltimore had changed a lot, but our home was always here, always ours. A long, unbroken line of Reynoldses all the way back to—well, back to the time of Edgar Allan Poe.

Aunt Marie believed the hotel would be great, but we needed money faster than it would take to make this business profitable. So her plan was to sift through the things in the crates and see what could be sold. Sometimes antiques went for big money, and no one had more of those than us. That's the real reason why we'd been on this so-called decluttering kick for the last few weeks.

The "pit" carpet, with its deep-black coloration, was supposed to be the backdrop for her staging photos, but she was struggling with the tech aspect of it all. That I could handle.

I had my doubts about the plan as a whole, though. Valuable antiques were things like paintings, silverware, or jewelry. Most of what we'd found was junk like old bronzed baby shoes and broken umbrellas. The old furniture here was stuff we still sat and slept and ate on. Our dishes were chipped, but we used them. And I don't think any Reynolds ever had jewels to speak of. We were tavern-keepers, not pirates.

"Well, we have to find something," she said. "Or a lot of little somethings. Honestly, it's better to sell my bed than the whole house."

Aunt Marie showed me a list of potential items of value that she'd printed off the internet. I looked it over. To be fair, there were apparently valuable items I had no idea were worth anything at all. Stuff like old toys, old fountain pens, antique military medals, and—wow, seriously? Vintage coffins?

I was absolutely positive we possessed at least one vintage coffin in the basement. But how valuable was valuable? Five hundred dollars? A thousand? We didn't have a whole cemetery. I read on.

Rare books, historical documents, and old maps.

That's when I remembered the book from this morning. The one I'd accidentally picked up in the kitchen. It was in terrible shape, but maybe that didn't mean anything to collectors.

After I helped Aunt Marie navigate the set-up page of the online auction site, she went to start dinner and I headed to my room to change into street clothes. Usually, this was the time I'd be doing homework, but there was only one book in my bag that I was interested in.

I was careful when I removed the old leather volume from my bag, regretting how I'd allowed it to jostle around in there all day. Now that I realized it might be worth some money, I needed to be more careful.

While setting up Aunt Marie's account, I'd clicked over to a site where they were explaining how to determine the value of old books. I needed to look for the title, and something called a colophon, which would explain who had printed it.

I brought the book over to my desk and turned on the lamp. The leather embossing of the cover had worn almost smooth. Just like on the bus, I could see tiny indentations in the surface, which could be letters, or it could just be that this thing was ancient.

I held my breath and opened it again. The first page was soft, gray, and crumbly, with no discernible marks on it at all. I turned that page and saw not the freshly typed print of a title or printer's marks, but instead, handwriting. At first glance, it looked like an accounting book of some sort, just rows and rows of numbers and nonsense letters in a neat black script.

How disappointing. I'd been hoping for a first edition, instead I got someone's budget records.

Carefully, I turned another page. The paper was dry and brittle, but if I moved slowly, and didn't press each leaf down as I turned it, I could manage to look at each page without it crumbling into dust.

For several pages there was nothing but these rows and rows of numbers. Sometimes they went across the entire page, and sometimes there'd only be three or four on a line. There didn't seem to be any rhyme or reason to them, and I couldn't understand what it was they were counting up. There was no summation line or any other calculations that I could understand.

I used to think numbers always made sense. Maybe I was wrong.

Three pages in, the numbers gave way to a sketch, and my heart dropped into my stomach.

The picture was of a man's face. Or at least, what used to be a man. Because there was something very wrong with this guy. It wasn't due to the artist's lack of skill—whoever it was had clearly meant to draw the image in this bizarre, monstrous way. The man's brow and nose were nearly normal, but his jaw stretched unnaturally, almost as if it was unhinged. And his eyes did not have the normal arrangement of pupils, irises, and whites, but instead yawned black and deep, like the hollows of a skull, with glowing centers.

I'd seen faces just like that before. But only in my nightmares.

Suddenly I didn't care anymore how old the book was. I slammed it shut and pushed my chair back from the desk. My pulse raced, my breaths were coming short and fast.

Why were *my* nightmares drawn in this weird old book?

Maybe they weren't as unique as I thought. Maybe they were just some universal human fear, like how lots of people hate snakes or how toddlers are afraid of monsters under their beds.

I should check, I thought. I should do an internet search on creepy ghost dreams and see if everyone had the same kind. Though if that were the case, why hadn't Aunt Marie ever mentioned that when we were talking about my dreams?

And even if it were a common occurrence, it still didn't explain the starring role Gus Davenport—who clearly wasn't dead—had served in the nightmare I'd had last night.

None of this made any sense. I glared at the book, sitting innocently on the desk in the slanted light of the lamp.

And that's when I saw it.

I blinked and shook my head, as if the impression would vanish as easily as the appearance of Edgar Allan Poe on the bus this morning. But it didn't. I looked up at Chip, who still sat on that plaster bust of Athena, staring down at the proceedings in silent interest.

If you've read "The Raven" you'd know that shadows are very important to the poem, so this room, lovingly arranged by Aunt Marie, was designed to cast as many as possible. There was an electric space heater in one corner that, when turned on, had a little fake fire effect. There was a tiny light behind Chip that I never used because it made a huge raven-shaped shadow on the floor. All the lighting in here was mood lighting. RIP my eyesight.

And the lamp on the desk was casting some very interesting shadows on the cover of the book. Regular indentations, a shape that looked almost like a word.

I leaned forward, and the effect vanished. I leaned back and saw it again. Three regular, even marks that were definitely letters.

But I couldn't read them—the leather had deteriorated far too much with age, and if I leaned closer to try to get a better look, the shadows were not at the right angle. I tried twisting and turning the book under the lamplight, but I still couldn't make out what it said.

I had an idea. I retrieved a slip of loose-leaf paper and a pencil from my desk drawer. I placed the paper on top of the journal and rubbed the pencil back and forth over the paper, hoping to make an impression of the shape of the letter beneath it. Slowly, the letters came into focus, in a formal, block script.

E. A. P.

The pencil nib broke off, and I stared at what I'd done in a mix of shock and horror.

E. A. P.

It couldn't be.

Okay, Ellen. Calm down. Remember how everyone in the family was completely obsessed with that man? Remember how they all had been for more than a hundred years? Those initials meant nothing. Two-thirds of them were the same as my own. The journal could belong to anyone. Absolutely anyone.

And then I thought about the numbers inside. All those neat rows of weird symbols.

Poe wasn't *only* a poet. He wasn't *only* a genius writer of tales of the macabre and the spooky. He was also obsessed with codes. He put them in his stories. He published essays on the nature of cryptography. He hid notes to women he admired in poems that seemed to be something else entirely. He had whole magazine columns on codebreaking, some of which people didn't manage to solve until the twenty-first century.

His love of coding was practically the only thing the two of us had in common.

If this journal really did belong to Edgar Allan Poe, it had to be worth millions. Forget about the back taxes—Aunt Marie and Dad and I would never have to worry about money again.

I lifted the paper and looked down at the little journal. Now that I knew what it said on the cover, it was easier to see the faded letters embossed in the leather. The strong right angles of the E. The triangular A. The tall, rounded P.

And there, just next to the last letter, two other little indentations. Small and round, like a pair of hollow eyes.

I didn't need my paper or my pencil marks. I knew what those were: o and e.

"E. A. Poe," I said aloud.

"Through all, I—wrote," said a man's voice at my back.

I whirled around in terror, and there he was again. The man from the school, from the bus, from the hallway.

Edgar Allan Poe.

He was dressed in the same three-piece suit he wore in those old-timey photographs, but he looked way better than he did on the cover of my English book. And he looked almost normal—not distorted and scary like the figures in my dreams. Just a bit . . . see-through around the edges.

He sat on the edge of my bed and looked at me with an expression akin to relief.

"Through joy and through sorrow, I—wrote," he said. His voice was strong, commanding, with a slight Southern lilt. "Through hunger and through thirst, I—wrote. Through good report and through ill report, I—wrote. Through sunshine and through moonshine, I—wrote."

Weirdly, I wasn't scared. It was almost—almost as if I'd been expecting him. All day long, weird things had been happening. Bad dreams and unexpected drama and money troubles. Somehow, the fact that there was a dead poet sitting in my bedroom talking to me seemed—well, if not normal, at least not a huge problem.

"Look at me!—how I labored—how I toiled—how I wrote!" He raised his hands and gestured past me, at the journal.

"So, this is yours," I said. "You're—you're Edgar Allan Poe."

He made a face at the name. Too late I remembered that Poe did not like the name Allan. It was the name of his foster father, who had raised him and then abandoned him in his early twenties. Even though most people call him Edgar Allan Poe now, he never signed his name that way. He published his work as Edgar A. Poe.

I had to say, I knew the feeling. I never used my own middle name either. Though I probably wouldn't tell him that. After all, my middle name was Poe.

"Your own Eddy," he corrected.

"Eddy?" And *my own*? What in the world was that supposed to mean?

"Poor Eddy," he sighed piteously, his suited shoulders heaving.

He should talk. He was dead. His problems were over. Mine were obviously just beginning.

All those years, the folks in my family said this house was haunted by the ghost of Poe. Dad and I didn't believe it. We thought it was just another one of the wild family legends. But what if it was all true? His ghost was standing in my room, after all this time.

What if we really *were* the poet's descendants? After all, he'd just called himself my own. What was that supposed to mean if not that we were related?

I gestured at the journal. "So, this is yours?"

He nodded.

"And what—it's in code or something?"

Poe—Eddy—nodded again.

I frowned. On one hand, this was great news. That had to be worth a fortune. On the other hand, it wasn't like I had concrete proof. I couldn't very well say, "This journal definitely belongs to Edgar Allan Poe. His ghost told me so."

A ghost. Standing in my room. Shouldn't I be screaming and bolting? Shouldn't I be fainting to the carpet in dead shock?

Instead, I was thinking about my options. Selling the journal might be tricky. It would have to be verified and authenticated by historians or something. I had no idea how long something like that could take, but Aunt Marie was already on her second notice about the bill. How long did we actually have?

"Ellen!" Aunt Marie's voice came floating up the stairs. "Are you done with your homework? It's dinnertime."

I gave Eddy a guilty shrug. "I—uh, I have to go to dinner. Are you coming too?" I wondered if Aunt Marie would be able to see him.

Eddy sighed, his chin hanging down. Why would ghosts sigh? They didn't have to breathe. Or maybe he was sighing because I was eating dinner and he was not.

Eddy may not be as terrifying as the ghosts in my dream, but he was still just as bad at communication.

CHAPTER 6

A Conversation, Kinda

AT DINNER, I TRIED TO GET AUNT MARIE TO GIVE me a little background information about the history of Poe hauntings at Raven's Rest. Fortunately, asking a Reynolds to talk about Edgar Allan Poe was a bit like asking a toddler to tell you about his favorite dinosaur.

The real trick was getting them to stop.

"Well, I've certainly never seen him," Marie said with a laugh, serving me a portion of her delicious, flaky-crusted pot pie. "Can you imagine? On one hand, it would be great for business. On the other hand, how could you sleep at night with a poet roaming the halls?"

"Yeah," I said weakly. Wait, how *would* I sleep tonight?

"But my grandmother said she saw him regularly her whole life. She talked about him like an old friend, you know?" Marie smiled softly. "She used to tell me about him when I was little, like I'd be able to see him too, only I never did. Disappointing, really. Our own Eddy."

I stilled, my fork halfway to my mouth. "Our own Eddy?" I whispered.

Aunt Marie shrugged and took a sip of iced tea. "That's what she called him. Eddy. I guess that's what family and friends always called him. He would sign his letters like that. Edgar was his full name—his professional name—but Eddy was his nickname."

Our own Eddy was currently chilling with Chip in the Raven room. I couldn't even imagine what he thought of what Aunt Marie had done to the place. Actually, maybe he liked it. He had, after all, published whole essays on the proper way to arrange furniture.

"So do you think he was real?" I asked. "Like really real, or just another story that Great-Grandmother told?"

Aunt Marie chuckled. "I'm a Reynolds, hon. I'm contractually obligated to think he's real, to think all of it is real. If I don't believe it, how am I supposed to get the potential guests of this hotel to buy into the idea?"

But if Aunt Marie thought it was real, then why wasn't Eddy's ghost appearing to her? Wouldn't he rather haunt someone who believed all this stuff, instead of me?

Or maybe that's why I saw him. People like Aunt Marie and my grandparents believed all the Poe stories without question. They didn't need any proof that it was real. But Dad and I didn't buy it. And now I had a ghost in my bedroom.

When I'd told Aunt Marie about the dreams, I'd gotten hours of lectures about Jungian dream analysis. How much Poe trivia would I be subjected to if I told her I was seeing visions of the dead poet himself?

I thought about it while I ate my pot pie. Like everything Aunt Marie baked, it was delicious. The crust was buttery and flaky, the gravy rich, the chicken and vegetables tender and full of flavor. Aunt Marie was good enough to work at a restaurant, but her few attempts had never lasted longer than a couple of months. She said she didn't have the stomach for the food service industry, and that ten years of playing at bars and restaurants in her band had taught her enough of that business to stay far away.

Sometimes she catered parties for extra cash, but that required her to do things like make what the customers wanted instead of what she felt like making, and she wasn't necessarily great at that. Her coffee disasters alone had ruined more than one gig.

But if this journal was really Poe's—really *our Eddy's,* or whatever—then all our financial woes were over. Aunt Marie could spend the rest of her life baking just the things she wanted for just the people she wanted to.

I decided to change the topic. "What if we find something really valuable? Not like, old jewelry or something, but something with actual, historical significance? How will we know what it's worth?"

"If I think something has real worth, then I'll take it into an antique store to do an appraisal."

"But how will we know?" I asked. "We're not experts. What if we throw something away, thinking it's junk, but it turns out to be worth a lot of money?" Like, I don't know, an old accounting book that was secretly the coded journal of Mr. Edgar A. Poe.

Aunt Marie winked at me. "Ah, I see you're coming around. Now you know why I've been so hesitant to throw things away the last two weeks. Even old newspapers can be worth something if they are from an important date in history or have something memorable in them." Then she started telling me about how some guy in Ireland just discovered a forgotten story by Bram Stoker—the man who wrote *Dracula*—published in a moldering old newspaper at a library.

"If there's unknown stuff by Stoker out there, then doesn't it stand to reason that there might be unknown work by Poe too?" Aunt Marie asked. "Maybe right here in this house?"

I thought about those pages, about all those lines of numbers. What if they were more than Poe's diary entries? What if they were actual unpublished work by the writer himself?

"May I be excused?" I barely waited for her answer before I dashed from the dining room and back up the stairs, two at a time. The Raven room was just as I'd left it—still full of shadows, still featuring a stuffed black bird standing guard over the door. Eddy had disappeared, somewhere. But maybe he'd only been there to confirm for me that the journal was in fact his? Was, in fact, valuable?

That would be wild. All this time, Dad and I had been denying the family legends, and had been struggling. But maybe we had a way out of this mess once and for all. The journal was the answer to all our prayers. Aunt Marie and I could split the proceeds of the sale. She could pay off any bills the house had left and spend the rest of her life making music and cinnamon buns. Dad and I could buy our own house somewhere. I could start a college fund, like a normal kid.

MIT, here I come.

I grabbed the journal from the desk and turned to bring it to Aunt Marie.

Eddy stood between me and the door.

I stopped dead. He held his hand up—not reaching for me, like the freaks in my dream, but almost as a warning.

"There are some secrets which do not permit themselves to be told," he said to me, quite seriously. He pointed at the journal and shook his head.

Oh no. He had to be kidding.

"Out of my way," I said to the ghost. I know Gus said ghosts weren't substantial, but that didn't mean I wanted to try walking through one.

But Eddy did not move. Instead, he said, "Not in knowledge is happiness, but in the acquisition of knowledge."

"No," I replied. "Happiness is in the acquisition of *money*. Do you know how much this book could be worth?" I waved the journal around in the air.

But Eddy just shook his head again. "You will observe that the stories told are all about money-seekers, not about money-finders."

But I didn't care anything about stories. I just wanted to save the house. "Are you saying you don't think this is worth anything?"

He shrugged. "I have made no money. I am as poor now as ever I was in my life—except in hope, which is by no means bankable."

"That's where you're wrong," I told him. It's true that Poe was always poor. After his rich foster father disowned him in his early twenties, he lived in poverty for the rest of his life. He was always asking people for money or complaining that they lived on nothing but bread and molasses, which I bet tasted even more gross than it sounds.

Even "The Raven," his most famous poem, only made him nine dollars when it was printed. In fact, Poe probably made more money by going around reciting his work in performance halls than he ever did having it published.

But everything was different now. Lots of artists who never made a dime while they were alive have turned out to be worth millions in the modern era. Vincent van Gogh, Emily Dickinson, our own Eddy... I wasn't going to take the word of a two-hundred-year-old ghost about the modern market value of artifacts he left behind.

Still, Eddy didn't move from in front of my door. It was fitting, I supposed. After all, we were in the Raven room, and the narrator of that poem couldn't get the bird to budge, either.

I put the journal back on the desk and flopped into the desk chair. "Well, if I can't show Aunt Marie the journal, what do you want me to do with it?"

Eddy straightened and pronounced, in his soft Southern lilt, "When the proper time arrives, all that the gentleman intended, and all that he did not intend, will be brought to light."

I groaned. "You want to wait? That's not profitable. We could go sell it to a collector. An expert. There are people who have devoted their entire lives to studying you. Whole Edgar Allan Poe societies!"

"Human ingenuity could not construct a cipher which human ingenuity could not solve," Eddy said, as if that was the answer to everything.

Was that it? Maybe there was a reason Eddy didn't want this journal made public. After all, he'd obviously been very concerned about keeping its contents a secret—he'd even written the whole thing in code.

What if I broke the code first? Then I could see if there was something really damaging in there, some secret that Eddy was right in wanting to take to the grave. And if not, well, I could always sell it then.

But, honestly, did I actually want to know? Poe was famous for writing about psychopaths and murderers. Even the facts that we did know about him were—as Rebecca had so helpfully pointed out in class—"problematic." The whole world knew he'd married his thirteen-year-old cousin. Did I really want to know the truths about his life that even Poe kept secret?

"Why me?" I asked him now. "Even Aunt Marie would be a better choice. She's your biggest fan, honest. Look at how she designed all the rooms in this place. Not me. I don't even believe half the stuff my family says about you."

"From this purpose nothing shall turn me."

I was getting nowhere with him. It was as if we spoke two completely different languages. Everything he said was in this stilted, formal, old-timey speak. Was that what people really sounded like in the 1800s, or was Eddy just annoying like that?

"Maybe you'll listen to me if I talk to you in iambic pentameter," I grumbled.

Eddy appeared amused, as if the idea that I'd compose so much as a haiku was hilarious.

And he was absolutely right. I was never any good at creative writing. Or English, really. My skill was in numbers.

Oh. Right. Well, put like this, the whole endeavor started to make a bit more sense.

I didn't know that much about Poe's secret codes, only that he was obsessed with them. He wrote poems in code and published stories about codes. There were even some people who believed there were codes in his writings that had never been solved, even to this day.

And if that was the case, there was no way I'd be able to manage it.

Eddy came closer. It would be a stretch to say he walked, as it was more fluid than that. Drifted, maybe, in a way that was both deeply unnerving and not precisely scary. His expression was a comforting one, almost pitying.

Poor Eddy? How about poor Ellen?

"It appears almost an impossibility to unriddle what has been put together by so complex a method," Eddy said, gesturing at the journal. "To some persons the difficulty might be great; but to others—to those skilled in deciphering—" he smiled at me "—such enigmas are very simple indeed."

"You *want* me to solve the code?" I asked him.

He nodded eagerly.

I stared down at the journal. For more than a century, it had been gathering dust in the basement of Raven's Rest. What possible secrets could it hold?

"Okay," I said to Eddy. "I'll break the code in your book—or at least try to. But then I'm going to sell it. You of all people know what it's like to need money."

"My friend, thy beau, hath made a settled matter." Seemingly pleased by our bargain, Eddy settled himself in the corner on some kind of invisible ghost chair. He crossed his foot over his other knee and clasped his hands before him, as if waiting. "Let my heart be still a moment and this mystery explore."

Wait a second. That line I knew—that was from "The Raven."

"If we're going to do this," I said to him, "you're going to have to stop quoting poetry at me."

This time, Eddy's smile looked almost devious, as if he had zero intention of following that instruction.

I sighed. This was going to be a nightmare.

[I]t is nearly a mon[th]
[,] requesting an in[terview]
—, I placed it (
[an]swered letters". The
seeming discourtesy
[a]nswer.
I have now to
you at any time
[Bro]adway. You will
the morning before
Very Resp[ectfull]y

CHAPTER 7

The Father of Cryptography

SPEAKING OF NIGHTMARES, IF YOU THOUGHT THAT the arrival of the walking, talking ghost of Edgar Allan Poe in my waking life was going to supplant the scary creatures invading my dreams, you would be wrong. Sleep was as restless and disturbing as ever.

The good news—such as it was—was that at least it was the same dream this time. The same freaky dead people, Gus Davenport included. The same hot, choking darkness. The same sense of unending terror.

Okay, I guess it wasn't very good news, after all.

Possibly better news was that Eddy did not choose to hang out in my room all night like some kind of creep. I put the journal away in my desk drawer for the night and Eddy vanished along with it, which was a major relief. If he really had spent time with my great-grandmother when she was young, I hoped that he was just as considerate with her. I had a raven staring at me while I slept. I didn't need a ghost.

The best news of all is that when I did wake up, gasping, from that ghostly nightmare, I wasn't alone in the room. Cattarina had come to sleep at my feet, but she woke when I did, padding with her soft little paws across the covers and pressing her furry little head against my hand. Long after my breathing and heart rate had returned to normal, she stayed by my side, purring, warm and solid and thankfully real.

I started wondering if I should ask Dad for a cat instead of a dog when we got our own place.

In the morning, I outlined a plan of attack.

Step One: I'd read everything I could by Poe about secret writing and codes. I knew that his story "The Gold-Bug" was about people who had solved a code that led them to a pirate treasure. Maybe the code in Poe's book would do the same.

But probably not. After all, Poe had been as broke as we were.

Step Two: I'd read up on the codes that other people had found in Poe's writing. I knew he was known for publishing coded poems in magazines, especially addressed to other writers or women he admired. Most of these were pretty easy, things like poems where a single letter in each line spelled out the recipient's name or contained riddles that spelled out their own answer.

Step Three: I'd try to get Eddy to give me a straight answer himself.

After I'd gotten up, gotten dressed, and convinced myself I wasn't opening a can of worms by pursuing this, I removed the journal from the desk drawer. Sure enough, as soon as I did, Eddy appeared, casually leaning against one of the four carved posters of my bed.

Cattarina, who'd been snoozing in a beam of sunlight on the purple silken covers, started up in shock.

Eddy gazed lovingly down at the kitty and held his hand out for her to sniff. She proceeded to rub her cheek against—well, I wasn't quite sure what, exactly, because Gus said ghosts were insubstantial.

Maybe cats don't think so.

Still, if Cattarina noticed his presence, then he had to be more than just a hallucination, right? Crazy wasn't contagious.

"You're a cat person?" I asked the ghost.

"There is something in the unselfish and self-sacrificing love of a brute," he said thoughtfully, gazing down at Cattarina with love, "which goes directly to the heart of him who has had frequent occasion to test the paltry friendship and gossamer fidelity of mere Man."

Well, okay then. Maybe the straight answer thing was asking too much.

"Did you hear that, Cattarina?" I told her. "He called you a brute."

Cattarina glared at me, unimpressed. So did Eddy.

So much for my new understanding with the cat. Here, I thought we'd bonded in the night. As the two of them got better acquainted, I went to work.

First things first. The journal was far too delicate to carry around in my backpack. If I hoped to get money for it, I had to make sure no more pages crumbled into dust. Comic books and things got more money for being in mint condition. I had to make sure the journal survived.

I opened the cover carefully and took pictures of every page with my phone. When I got to the one with the ghostly sketch on it, I paused.

I'd nearly forgotten about it in all the excitement of seeing an actual ghost. But it was strange that Poe had drawn the very same images I saw in my dream, only hundreds of years ago.

"What are these?" I asked him. "Why did you draw them?" There were more every few pages. Different figures, in different poses, but all with that same eerie otherworldliness.

Eddy came closer to peer over my shoulder at the drawings, his movements the same drifting non-walk I'd noticed yesterday, as if he moved on an unseen track.

He reached toward the page, but his fingers hovered close without making contact. "The wild ideas of the land of dreams became, in turn,—not the material of my every-day existence—but in very deed that existence utterly and solely in itself."

Here we go again.

"What does that even mean?" I begged him. You'd think I'd have a better understanding of old-timey speak, since I'd heard so much Poe growing up. But it all sounded like nonsense to me. Like a string of junk code that didn't do anything in the program but make it longer and more unwieldy. Select and delete, dude.

Eddy looked pained. "In visions of the dark night I have dreamed of joy departed," he said, almost helplessly.

I groaned. "I know. You were super depressed. The whole world knows how sad you were. But that's not what I'm asking. Did you see these ghosts?" I pointed at the page. "Did you see them in your dreams too?"

"In dreams," he echoed.

Well, now we were getting somewhere. "And?" I pushed him. "Do you know why? Did it ever stop?"

He looked at me, his expression grim, and then that dumb, dead poet had the absolute gall to say:

"Nevermore."

Hilarious. A real riot act. But that did not explain a thing. I closed the book and placed it back in the drawer.

Eddy's mouth opened as if to protest.

"You think about it while I'm at school, okay?" I said to him. Maybe, with some extra time, he'd be able to dredge up some quotations that could be a little more helpful to my cause.

He clasped his hands together, fingers entwined as if to beg, but I shut the drawer.

Eddy promptly vanished.

What? He couldn't possibly think I was going to take him back to school.

❁ ❁ ❁

On the bus that morning, I read through "The Gold-Bug," which was a story about some people looking for a buried treasure and breaking a code to learn how to find it. The code in the story was called a substitution cipher, and it was one of Poe's personal favorites.

According to Poe, it was an especially hard one to solve because each letter of the message was substituted with another letter, number, or symbol based on a particular key. This key could be anything—a code word, a string of numbers, an arrangement of letters, or even a saying that was only known by the people who had created the code.

If you didn't have the key—like the people in the story who did not have the pirate's—then the only way to solve it was by figuring out the frequency of letters used in any language and slowly, methodically going letter by letter through the encrypted message and breaking it down. For instance, in English, the letter E was the most common one.

Of course, that only worked if it was a simple substitution. Ciphers could get a lot more complex than that. According to the note in the back of the story, Poe had even written an essay about these types of codes and how to solve them, and he had published many examples he claimed his magazine readers had sent him—but most people think Poe made them up himself. Some of these codes were so hard to crack that they hadn't been solved until the end of the twentieth century.

I was still thinking about the possibilities as I walked up the drive toward the school, so engrossed that I didn't even see him until I'd almost passed the gate.

Gus Davenport was seated atop the broad stone wall right above the sign that read *Evergreen Prep*. He was dressed again in street clothes, and he didn't seem to notice or care. Today, he wore a pair of nonregulation cargo pants in faded black and a charcoal button-down shirt open over a plain black tee. His blond hair was tousled and shone brightly in the morning sunlight.

He looked way better now than he had in my dream the other night. His eyes were bright, his face was normal, and he was very much alive. Someone inform my subconscious.

As I approached, he made an impressive hop down and fell into step beside me. Like we were friends.

"Do you need directions again?" I asked him.

"Good morning to you too," he replied. "Hey, what do you have for first period? I have advanced Latin."

Seemed fitting. Dead boy, dead language. "Computer science."

"Ah, darn," he said. "So, I'll see you at English?"

"Guess so." I took in his outfit. "Still waiting on your uniform?"

"My what?" He grinned at me and sauntered off. I watched him go, somewhat mystified. I admit I was a bit rusty on the punishments for dress code offenses, never once having violated the guidelines myself. Scholarship kids don't have the luxury of breaking rules like that. I had five uniform shirts, three skirts, a blazer, and a vest, and when the weather got cold, I wore sweatpants underneath them, but so did everyone else.

I just hoped that if Gus was getting dress-coded, it wouldn't reflect poorly on me as his orientation tour guide.

Computer science was primarily a self-guided class—every student was going at their own pace in learning coding language. Today, however, my focus was on *de*coding.

My suspicion was that the codes in the journal were some kind of substitution cipher, like in Poe's story. But I didn't want to do all the work that the characters had. Thank goodness for modern technology. A simple internet search revealed a website that would encrypt and decrypt Poe's Gold-Bug code at the press of a button.

I pulled out my phone and dutifully typed a bunch of the numbers from one of the diary pages into the text box on the decryption website, then pressed Submit.

It came back as gobbledygook.

Well, at least I'd tried.

"Cryptography, huh?" I turned to see my computer science teacher, Mrs. Sakai, standing behind me and checking out my work. Busted.

"Yeah," I said sheepishly. "Well, kind of. I found this old book in my house with secret messages in it, and I was trying to figure out what it says."

"Cool." Mrs. Sakai gestured at my phone. "Can I see? I used to love this stuff when I was a kid."

I showed her the photographs. She studied them for a minute.

"You know, it's funny. In the olden days, ciphers like this used to be the gold standard of secret codes, because unless you had the key, they were pretty tough to crack. The only way to do it was brute force, which would take—oh, ages." She gestured to my computer. "May I?"

I rolled my chair to the side and gave her access to my computer as she navigated to another website, one I'd never seen before.

"But then computers came along," said Mrs. Sakai. "One thing they can do much better than us is run through the algorithms for this kind of decryption at lightning speed. That's why we don't use that kind of encryption anymore. It's too easy for computers to solve."

Ah. Well, that explained why people were finally able to solve Poe's codes in the twentieth century. They used computers.

She straightened. Before me was another website with a generalized decryption program. "There you go. This one will decipher pretty much anything people can hand code in seconds. By the way, this is all in our cybersecurity unit, next semester. This program here? It's just Python. Another month and you could code it yourself."

I wonder what Eddy would think of something like this. All those long explanations in his story on how to hand-decode instructions to find buried treasure, and now it was all available at the push of a button.

Actually, he'd probably be shocked about a lot of things in the twenty-first century. After all, one of the characters in "The Gold-Bug" was enslaved, because again, Poe was from the time before the Civil War.

I typed in the numbers I'd photographed from a page in Poe's journal, and pressed Submit.

And thanks to living in the future, the program returned results in seconds. It even properly formatted the date.

September 30, 1848

Ever true, this heart so beats
All for the one my young soul claimed
Admired, relinquished, but not released
Admire, still—it never waned
Admire forever, if you so please
Your hand to give, my world to gain.

Is it bad to say I preferred the numbers to poetry? Don't mind me, I always found his poems kind of sappy. This one, at least, was not about a dead woman.

Even more interesting, I don't think it was one I knew.

Could this be an unpublished poem by Edgar Allan Poe? And if so, how much would a discovery like that be worth?

I jotted down the translated version of the code and was about to flip to the next photo, when the sound of the gong piped in over the speakers installed in the walls.

That was okay—these codes and this website weren't going anywhere. And at least now I had something to work with.

I was going to save Raven's Rest.

CHAPTER 8

Poe-ish

IN ENGLISH CLASS, WE WERE COMPARING THE PIECES by Edgar Allan Poe we'd ostensibly read for homework—"Annabel Lee" and "Ulalume"—two poems about death, despair, and beautiful, dead young women that I'd unfortunately been familiar with since kindergarten. Instead of participating, I flipped through *The Complete Works of Edgar Allan Poe* looking for the poem I'd decoded and tried to ignore the fact that Gus Davenport was sitting behind me.

The problem with paperbacks is that they are so hard to search. I couldn't just type in a word like I could on a computer file and hope for the best.

The poem I'd decoded didn't have a title, just a date, but our textbook wasn't arranged chronologically, so that wasn't much help either. And I couldn't even tell if the poem was short or if it was part of a longer work on another diary page I hadn't been able to decode yet.

"Miss Reynolds?" asked Ms. Morris. "We haven't heard from you yet."

Her words cut through my concentration. "Sorry?"

"We're discussing the tools that Poe used to create atmosphere in his work."

"Repetition," I said, almost automatically. "He repeats words and phrases like an echo. It's . . ." *Boring? Lazy? Cheating?* "Hypnotic," I finished at last, because I supposed that was what he meant it to be.

"Can you give us some examples?"

Boy, she wasn't letting me off easily today, was she?

"Sure," I said, closing the book and sitting up in my seat. "In 'Annabel Lee' he keeps going on and on about the *kingdom by the sea* and his *beautiful Annabel Lee.* It's a refrain he puts in over and over again. In 'Ulalume' he repeats multiple words in every line as part of the rhyme scheme. *Sere, tomb, weir, soul*—it's more like a chant, he repeats himself so much."

Ms. Morris's brow furrowed, then she opened her own book as if to double-check what I was saying. "Yes—yes, that's . . . right."

He repeated himself in the poem I'd decoded in comp sci too. *Admired, Admire, Admire* . . . three lines in a row started like that. Maybe his poems were so long because he kept repeating himself. If I tried that on my essays for English class, I'd flunk out.

"Is that because they were supposed to be read out loud?" Gus asked. Apparently, he neither wore the school uniform nor waited to be called on. "It's almost like a chorus in a song."

"You're right, Mr. Davenport," said Ms. Morris, instead of dinging him for not raising his hand. "And these poems were meant to be read aloud. 'Ulalume,' in particular, was written for a performance. Poe made a portion of his income from lectures and poetry recitations. Remember, his mother was a famous actor, and he probably inherited some of her talent."

That was apparently a good enough segue to talk about all the dead women in Poe's life that these poems could have been written about.

Which made me think. When Poe wrote about dead women, he made up names for them: Ulalume, Annabel Lee, Lenore. But when they were still alive, he was okay with using their real names, even if he hid them in secret messages in the lines of the poem.

That was the thing about Poe. He had a lot of female admirers, and he admired them right back. Even before his wife, Virginia, died, he'd had close relationships and even wrote love poetry about other women. In the year before he died himself, he'd been engaged to at least two other women—and that was not including my family's story about the Reynolds lady he'd supposedly wooed as well.

There was one woman, Sarah Helen Whitman, who broke up with him a year before his death, supposedly because he wouldn't stop drinking. And then another, Elmira Shelton, who was his childhood sweetheart in Richmond and with whom he reconnected the summer before he died.

The poems he wrote to his living lady friends weren't quite as famous. Possibly because they weren't as good as the poems about fictional dead ones.

Hey, I just call it like I see it.

And maybe that's all this poem was. A little ditty to some woman he had a crush on. Maybe it was even my great-times-five grandmother. But no matter how dumb it was, I was sure people would get excited about it if it was for real. Unfortunately, I wasn't finding any reference to it in the supposedly "complete works" textbook that Ms. Morris had given us.

Which meant one of two things: Either I was in possession of a previously unpublished work of poetry by Edgar Allan Poe, and thus a millionaire, or . . . the journal was garbage, "Eddy" was a hallucination, and I was about to be homeless—for real this time.

I'd far rather option A.

How would one go about authenticating something like that? It's not like they had Poe's fingerprints to dust the journal with. I didn't even know if fingerprints lasted hundreds of years. Maybe I should only be touching that thing with gloves.

Poe had a particular style of writing, but it had been imitated so many times it was almost meaningless. The journal could belong to one of my Poe-obsessed ancestors. I bet you could even ask some AI chatbot to write a poem like Edgar Allan Poe and get a nice one.

But not if Ms. Morris had anything to say about it.

Instead, she made us clear our desks and get out a piece of paper to compose our own poems. "Edgar Allan Poe used a pen, so you will too," she told us.

Yeah, right. She just didn't want anyone cheating and using AI. I've got your number, Ms. Morris.

We were to write a poem in the style of Edgar Allan Poe, utilizing at least three of the techniques we'd talked about in class.

The other students got to work, tapping their pens against their desk or their chins, scrubbing stanzas and crossing them out.

I usually hated these kinds of assignments. Sure, write a poem in half an hour. No problem! But I'd spent the last forty-five minutes staring at the same six lines. I had them memorized by now. And they weren't in the book.

Was it still plagiarism if no one knew the poem was by Poe?

I leaned over the paper and began to write.

Ever true, this heart so beats
All for the one my young soul claimed.

Well, there was one problem, I supposed. If Poe wrote this the year before he died, then he wasn't young at all. He was nearly forty. It would sound weird if I wrote about a lost love of my youth.

Wait a second. A lost love of his youth? That was Elmira Shelton, the woman he was possibly engaged to when he died.

Elmira was a weird name, and it reminded me of that repeated word in the poem: admire.

Admired, relinquished, but not released
Admire, still—it never waned
Admire forever, if you so please ...

Quickly, I wrote out the rest of the lines. I stared down at the poem. Poe liked to hide secret messages in his work. One poem he wrote, to a woman named Frances Sargent Osgood, spelled out her name in subsequent letters on every line—the first letter of the first line, the second letter of the second, et cetera.

Maybe this one did too. I began counting letters, my heart racing faster and faster as I got to each line and circled the letter I needed.

Ever true, this heart so beats
ALl for the one my young soul claimed
AdMired, relinquished, but not released
AdmIre, still—it never waned
AdmiRe forever, if you so please
Your hAnd to give, my world to gain.

I stared down at the words. *Elmira*! It must mean Elmira Shelton.

All the pieces fit. His special way of hiding names in his poem, a poem about a young love regained, and the actual name of Poe's final girlfriend, who he'd first loved long before his marriage.

The journal was real. It was Poe's. I knew it.

"What are you doing?" Gus whispered at my back.

"Writing a poem, what are you doing?" I hissed over my shoulder.

"Watching you circle letters."

"Ms. Morris?" In the next row over, Rebecca raised her hand. "Is this supposed to be a group project? Because Ellen and the new kid are talking and it's super distracting."

Gus turned to her, eyes narrowed. “What is your deal?” he asked. “Did Ellen steal your boyfriend or something? What’s with all the snitching?”

Rebecca let out a gasp of indignation.

“Mr. Davenport,” said Ms. Morris. “At Evergreen, we respect our classmates by allowing them to finish their work undisturbed. I’m sure you haven’t finished your poem yet, either.”

“Oh, but I have,” said Gus. “And so has Ellen. It’s not our fault this girl over here is a slowpoke.”

I wished, suddenly, to be in the torture chamber from “The Pit and the Pendulum” so I could throw myself to my death.

“You’ve finished?” Ms. Morris crossed her arms and gave him a doubtful look. “Already?”

“Yup.” Gus waved around his paper. From the vantage point of sitting right in front of him, I could see it was completely blank.

Did he honestly expect that to fly?

I wasn’t sure if Ms. Morris could see the page from the front of the room, but either way, I doubted this ended well for Gus.

She held out her hand. “May I see it?”

His eyes slid over to the blank sheet of paper. Uh-oh, dead boy. The jig was up.

“Actually,” he said quickly, “much like the poems that Poe wrote, I feel like this one is best recited. Aloud.”

Every eye in the room flipped back to Ms. Morris, who seemed entertained, if nothing else. “All right, Mr. Davenport,” she said. “Let’s hear it.”

Gus looked at the teacher. She did not blink.

Then he sighed, unfolded his long legs from where they were wrapped around his chair, and stood, holding the paper in front of him as if it really had words written on it. He flipped his hair out of his face. He cleared his throat.

"This ought to be good," Rebecca said under her breath.

And then in a commanding voice, he began:

There once was a pretty dead lady,
Who was buried in someplace quite shady.
She woke nevertheless,
And put on a nice dress,
To go out and party in Hades.

There was a ripple of laughter from the other kids, primarily the boys. You could tell Ms. Morris wanted to laugh too, but somehow she held it in.

I just stared at him in shock. It would take me easily an hour to whip out a poem like that, even if I wasn't copying.

But like everything else, Gus was going to get away with this too. Ms. Morris just shook her head in defeat. "You win, Mr. Davenport. Now," she added in warning, "write that down."

He grinned and sat, looking all too smug.

"Miss Lambert?" Ms. Morris turned to Rebecca. "Can you name the three Poe-ish elements in Mr. Davenport's work?"

"I—" Rebecca glared daggers at the new kid. "Um, beautiful dead women?"

"Yes."

"Uh—" She frowned. "Mythological references?"

"Very good."

Rebecca flailed. "I don't know."

"Anyone else?" Ms. Morris asked.

I raised my hand. "Premature burial."

"Thank you, Miss Reynolds," said Ms. Morris. "Now, would you like to recite your poem too?"

I'd rather be prematurely buried myself. "Pass. I'm still . . . working on it." I scrubbed my eraser over some of the circles, just for show.

Ms. Morris relented. Perhaps she even took pity on me. Which was good. I hoped she kept it up, especially as, a few minutes later, when the gong sounded, the poem I left on her desk was almost definitely copied from the journal of one Mr. Edgar Allan Poe.

As soon as class was over, I bolted for the door, taking the stairs down the exit two at a time in hope of escaping—

"Ellen."

I turned to see Gus easily keeping pace beside me. Darn his long legs. He didn't seem to have a backpack either. No uniform, no backpack—was he actually even enrolled in this school?

"What do you want?" I asked. "I assume you remember how to find your way to the gym."

"Everyone at this school is so friendly!" he exclaimed, spreading his arms in mockery. "You, that Rebecca girl . . . I feel at home already!"

I slowed down. Okay, he had a point. "That was pretty impressive, your little limerick."

"Oh, thanks," he said with an offhand shrug. "We did Poe last year at my old school. I'm shocked I even remembered it. When did you write yours?"

"What?"

"Well, you obviously copied it from somewhere. No one writes a poem with a secret message in it that fast."

I stopped dead on the green and turned to face him. "I'm sorry. How long were you staring at me?"

"Oh, the whole time," he replied, as if that was totally fine.

"The whole time?"

"Of course."

"Why?"

"I'm trying to figure out the extent of your powers. Or their origin."

"Sorry?"

"There you go apologizing again." Gus made a tsking sound with his tongue. "Every time I see you, you know something you're not supposed to. Like how I had a near-death experience. Or that we were going to be assigned poems to write in English class. So, either you're psychic, or you have a secret backdoor to school administrative files, and either way, I want to know more about it."

This guy was unbelievable.

"I'm not psychic," I insisted, which I thought sounded pretty convincing for a person who had recently had several conversations with a ghost. Then, I took off for the gym.

"So . . . a computer hacker, then," Gus said, falling into step beside me again. "That's fine. I can work with that. I don't love the invasion of privacy, if I'm being perfectly honest. But I'm sure we can come to a mutually beneficial arrangement—"

"If you're trying to blackmail me," I said to him through gritted teeth, "you're going to be super disappointed. I'm broke."

"No problem," Gus said, "I'm loaded."

I rolled my eyes. I truly hated the rich kids at this school.

"And what do you want from me, then? To go into your file and take away all your dress code violations? Put on a tie. This isn't rocket science."

"If you went in to look at my medical history, you can go in for everything."

Except I hadn't done that, and I had a sneaking suspicion that Gus Davenport knew it.

I just shook my head at him and kept walking.

This time, even Gus had to jog to keep up. "Okay, okay, okay. Just tell me one thing, then. Tell me one thing and I promise I'll leave you alone."

Now that was an intriguing offer. I slowed, stopped, and turned. "Okay."

He looked astonished by my sudden capitulation.

"But you have to be honest," he warned me.

Or what, he'd haunt me forever? Get in line.

"Okay."

"How did you know I was dead? For real this time."

All the humor had fled from his face. And there was something in his eyes—almost like the pleas I recognized in the terrifying faces I'd seen last night. This was more than mere curiosity. He truly needed to know.

I took a deep breath. “I’m not psychic,” I insisted. I wasn’t. That was for fortune tellers. Tarot card readers. Aunt Marie’s friends. Aunt Marie, if I was honest.

He didn’t reply. Just waited.

“But . . . I dreamed about you. You and two other people. And you were all dead.”

CHAPTER 9

The Outcasts Club

I WOULD LIKE TO STATE, FOR THE RECORD, THAT what happened next was *not* my idea. In fact, I'm not even sure precisely how it came about. But it wasn't like I could *stop* Gus Davenport from getting on the bus with me after school. It was a public bus, after all.

And Gus was absolutely amazed by its very existence. He found it delightful that he could just pay for the fare with his phone. He thought it extraordinary that Ms. Baker, the southbound bus driver, knew the names of all the regulars. And he was completely fascinated by the fact that you could just pull on the little wires to request a stop.

"Don't do that," I warned him. He frowned in disappointment.

So instead, he managed to fold up his legs enough to get into the bus seat, and he thoroughly enjoyed the view as the wide green lawns and boulevards gave way to a more urban landscape as we headed back downtown.

"And you do this every day?" he asked, as we stood to change to the second bus.

I ignored Ms. Baker waggling her eyebrows at me in approval and disembarked. "Have you never been on public transport before?"

"I've been on the U-Bahn in Berlin," Gus said thoughtfully. "And once I took the Fuji Excursion in Japan, which is really nice. But a bus? Never. I'm not even sure we had that kind of thing in my hometown. Our housekeeper had to have her son drop her off."

Oh, he was *rich* rich. I dreaded to imagine what he'd think of Raven's Rest.

"Well, you'd better figure out how you're getting home after this little adventure," I warned him as we boarded the new bus. "Aunt Marie is kind of . . . between cars right now."

He waved his hand dismissively. "No problem, I'll just call a ride service."

Oh. No problem. Sure.

Once again, I wasn't sure what Gus was doing here with me. Why wasn't he off chilling with Rebecca and the other rich kids? Who actually *wanted* to join the Outcasts Club?

"Don't you have anything better to do with your afternoon than discover the joys of public transport?"

He shook his head. "Not really. They've already cast the play this fall. They said if I wanted I could paint the sets, but"—he made a face—"seriously? No."

"Well, I'm sorry you can't be Romeo or whatever—"

"Romeo?" he scoffed. "When Mercutio is right there? Please. It's the best part in the show. He's so much cooler, and he has all the best lines."

"Doesn't Mercutio die?"

"They all die," he pointed out. "It's *Romeo and Juliet*."

Okay, he had me there.

Gus looked out the window for a second. "Do you think I'd be better at playing a death scene because I've done it myself?"

"I—I don't know," I blurted awkwardly.

"Because I don't remember it happening," he said in a rush. "I didn't see a light at the end of a tunnel. I wasn't greeted by angels or ancestors. My heart wasn't weighed on a scale by some Egyptian god. If you saw me when I was dead, then you know a lot more about whatever happened than I do."

I thought of the ghostly boy from my vision. The version of Gus with his life choked out of him and his soul being sucked out of his eyes. Was that why he was following me around? "I—don't know anything. I just—it was just a nightmare."

The bus was pretty empty this afternoon, but I still didn't want to talk about this in public.

Gus, however, had no such hesitation.

"Yeah, so you said. A nightmare you had about me and my parents."

That was who he thought the other two people in my dreams were. He'd told me just before we had to rush off for PE that his parents had died at the same time as he did, only they never came back to life.

I wasn't sure what he wanted from me. My nightmares weren't psychic visions from his dead parents. If so, why would he be in them too?

But I couldn't blame him either. If I were in his shoes, and some crazy girl said she saw him and his dead parents in a dream before they'd even met, I'd probably want details too.

"How—how did"—you—"they die?"

He fixed me with a look. "What, that wasn't included in your dream?"

"It wasn't like that," I said softly, remembering their distorted faces, their silent screams that I could somehow feel, even if I couldn't hear them. "It wasn't like I saw what happened to you either. You were like . . . ghosts or something. And I knew you were dead, but I just knew it the way you know crazy things in your dreams sometimes."

Like how not to open the door, or go down the stairs, or that the hamburger with shoes on was absolutely supposed to be Santa Claus in this bizarro-world projection of your unconscious mind.

"Hmm," he said, then looked out the window. "Ooh, bagel shop."

That's when I knew the serious conversation was over. The devil-may-care Gus Davenport was back in charge.

After the second bus dropped us off, I led him down the worn cobblestone streets of Fells Point. The rocky road was another detail that Gus was amazed by. He said it looked like Europe. I had never been to Europe, but I was still pretty sure it did not.

All too soon, we'd reached the storefront of Raven's Rest, which by some miracle was still open even this late into the afternoon.

I guess my aunt was serious about making money this time. We'd see how long that lasted.

The shop on the ground floor of my family's townhouse has been many things over the years. A tavern, a corner store, a fortune teller's, a music shop. Aunt Marie's current project was turning it into a coffee shop and "art space," which mainly meant very little in the way of decor except for the deeply terrible paintings some of her friends chose to hang up. It also featured wonderful pastries, bad coffee, and open mic nights a few times a month.

I bet Gus would like that. He could ply his limerick skills onstage.

Aunt Marie was against the far wall hanging a painting when we entered. I beelined for the food counter, where I saw there were a few of today's offerings—apple streusel muffins—still available.

"Be right over!" called my aunt, struggling with getting the picture straight on the wall. When she finally stepped back, I could see why. It was off-kilter in the frame too.

Eventually, she gave up and trotted over to the counter, brushing dust off her hands. She brightened when she saw us standing there. "Oh, wow, it's later than I thought. Hi, Ellen! How was school? Who's your friend?"

"Gus Davenport, ma'am," said Gus, holding out his hand.

"Marie Poe Reynolds," said Aunt Marie, because she's the kind of Reynolds to make sure she works her middle name into conversations. I am not that kind. At all.

But if Gus noticed she had the same name as the poet we were talking about in English class, he did not react.

Maybe it only meant something here in Baltimore too. The whole city was obsessed with Poe. Gus was a newcomer. He didn't get it yet.

"Gus is in my English class," I explained to Aunt Marie. "We have a project."

There. That wasn't a lie. Not exactly. I didn't say it was a project *for* English class.

"Great!" she exclaimed. "Is Gus staying for dinner?"

"Oh, I'd love to!" Gus said before I could decline on his behalf.

So that was that. Aunt Marie loaded us down with leftover pastries and sent us off into the house proper.

"I feel like I have to explain some things about my house," I warned him at the front door. "It's supposed to be a hotel. Kind of. A . . . theme hotel."

"Oh, this I've got to see," said Gus as he slid right past me and through the open door into the corridor.

I followed behind him, bracing myself.

Gus stood in the hall, his tall frame filling most of the available space. "Oh," he said, blankly.

Oh? Oh *no*.

I tried to see the entrance corridor of Raven's Rest through a stranger's eyes. Narrow and dark, it featured wrought-iron hall sconces, purple walls painted with ravens in flight, and scores of crates and boxes lined up against one wall. The staircase before us was similarly dim, with burnished wood newel posts and stairs that seemed to sag beneath the weight of centuries.

Slowly, Gus turned to look at me. "Is the theme of this hotel Moving Day?" he asked, with mock solemnity.

"I wish." I gestured for him to go up the stairs.

The second floor was homier, at least, with the sunny kitchen and a sitting room that was almost—but not totally—completed and ready for hypothetical guests.

Although today, I guess we had a real guest, at last. Not paying, but still.

Gus peered into the living room.

Poe once published an essay about his theories of furniture arranging, which was kind of ironic because people who actually knew him said he barely had any furniture at all in his own house, on account of being so broke.

Still, I get it. His theories were what he'd want his place to look like if he had the money for it, just like Dad and I like to talk about what we're going to do when we finally get our house.

Once I sold Poe's journal, I had all kinds of ideas about what I'd want our place to look like. Sleek, modern furniture, soft blue throw pillows. No taxidermy birds.

Anyway, the living room at Raven's Rest was designed exactly to Poe's specifications, which were probably super fashionable in the 1800s, but now it looked—well, kind of like it was designed by someone in the 1800s. Someone who was really obsessed with the color red.

The couches were red, the curtains were red, the wallpaper was silver, but Aunt Marie painted over it with little red decorations that Poe apparently called arabesques but just looked like curlicues to me. There was also an octagonal table in the center of the room that she painted to look like white and silver marble—though I think it was plain particleboard—because Poe was obsessed with octagonal marble tables.

For some reason.

There was even a print of a portrait of Poe on the wall, but most people didn't recognize that it was him. Mainly because he's really young in it and doesn't have his mustache and also, possibly, because the man who painted the original—Samuel Osgood—did not particularly like Poe very much, on account of the fact that Poe was writing love poems to his wife.

"Purple hall down there, red room up here," Gus observed. "Is the theme rainbow?"

"Nope." I was starting to get into this game. It wouldn't be fun with Rebecca or any of my old friends. But something about Gus made it okay for me to show him this weirdo house. It was like he was in on the joke too.

I led Gus into the kitchen, where Cattarina hopped down from the windowsill and came right over. Though instead of greeting me as she usually did, she flopped down hard and showed her belly to Gus.

"Cute cat," he said and reached over to scratch under her chin. "What's her name?"

"Cattarina. How did you know it's a she?"

"Calico cats are always female," he replied as if that made any sense at all. "Did you know they're also the state cat of Maryland? It's because their colors match the flag."

Wasn't he full of trivia?

"Do you have any pets?" I asked him.

He shook his head. “What do you think?” He smiled, as if with some private joke.

Honestly, I couldn’t decide. Gus was overly friendly and lacked boundaries, like a dog, but he was also sly and contrary, like a cat. And there was something unusual about him too. He’d be the kind of guy you found out later kept tarantulas or electric eels.

I grabbed some drinks from the fridge and put the pastries Aunt Marie had given us on a plate. “Come on,” I said, and led him up the stairs to the third floor. Might as well get this over with.

The third floor of Raven’s Rest is where the theme was really supposed to come into play, with every bedroom decorated to look like one of the writer’s famous works. Gus followed me up the stairs, Cattarina hot on his heels.

He paused to poke his head into the “Pit and the Pendulum” room, then gave me a quizzical glance. “Not rainbow?”

“Not rainbow,” I confirmed, then opened the door to my own room.

He followed me inside, taking in the four-poster bed, the purple, silken coverlet, the fake fireplace, the curtains printed with marble columns, and my overflowing suitcase sitting in the corner.

“This was not what I expected from you,” he said. “I’ll be honest.”

“Yeah, well, I only moved in a few weeks ago.”

“Ah.” He nodded in understanding. “I get it. Obviously, I just moved myself.”

I gestured toward Chip, positioned above the chamber door. "And that would be Chip."

"A crow?" Gus asked. "Like in the hall downstairs?"

Yeah, you could definitely tell this guy was not from Baltimore. "A raven, like in the hall downstairs."

"Ah." He examined Chip. "I hate to be the bearer of bad news, Ellen, but this is a crow."

"It is not."

"It is." He pointed at the bird's head. "Ravens have downward-pointing bills with a noticeable hump on them, and they also have big, ragged feathers on their throats, which might have been a mistake by the taxidermist, but you know how you can really tell?"

I blinked in astonishment. "How?"

"The size," said Gus. "Basically, if you think it's a crow, it's a crow. If you're wondering if it's a crow or a raven, it's still just a crow. But if the first thing that comes to mind is *dear God, what is that giant, monster bird?* It's probably a raven."

"Oh." Aunt Marie was going to be so disappointed.

Now Gus circled the room, as if cataloging all the other details. "So, you've got a crow, which you think is a raven, sitting on a marble bust above your door. It's a little on the nose, but I'll allow it. And your aunt—Marie?"

"Yeah."

"Marie *Poe* Reynolds." He turned to face me. "And this is a Poe-themed hotel."

I nodded. Whether it was cat gender or the difference between crows and ravens, this guy did not miss a beat.

“So, is she a *Poe* Poe?”

I shrugged. “Honestly? We don’t know. That’s the legend. But, technically, we’re all Poes. I’m actually Ellen Poe.” I took a breath. “Ellen Poe Reynolds.”

Gus considered this for a long moment. Then he went and sat down on the edge of my bed. Cattarina hopped up beside him, then climbed into his lap like she was his cat. I’d be mad but she’d pulled the same move on Eddy last night, so maybe she just liked people who had died.

He stroked her chin thoughtfully, and then he asked me a single question.

“Does Ms. Morris know?”

It is nearly a wom

, requesting an in

-, I placed it (

swered letters". The

seeming discourtesy

answer.

I have now to

you at any time

adway. You will

the morning befor

Very Respt.

Yr. O

CHAPTER 10

The Most Annoying Ghost in the World

THAT WAS THE MOMENT I DECIDED TO SHOW GUS the journal. I'd spent most of the afternoon worried that I had nothing to offer the not-dead boy, but I'd never considered how he might be able to help me. Gus was full of all kinds of information. He knew about cats and crows and the likelihood that a ghost would have physical mass. Maybe he knew about how to verify historical documents.

"Of course she doesn't know," I said. "No one knows. I didn't even believe the family stories until—" Well, until yesterday.

"Until—?" he prompted.

I went over to the desk, opened the drawer, and pulled out the journal.

When I turned around, Eddy was standing behind Gus, near the window.

I gasped and dropped the book.

It wasn't that I forgot about the ghost and his attachment to this old book. It's just, when a grown man appears out of nowhere, it's always a bit of a shock.

Not now, Eddy, I thought at him, but I had no idea if ghosts could read minds.

Gus leaned forward and swiped the book off the floor, dislodging Cattarina, who meowed in protest.

"Careful," I warned him. "It's very old and delicate."

He raised his gaze to mine. "You're the one who dropped it." And yet, with extraordinary tenderness, he carefully lifted the cover and looked inside.

"I found it the other day, in some old boxes of stuff from the basement. I think it could be hundreds of years old and very valuable."

He frowned and turned a page, then another. Eddy looked over his shoulder with interest, and I did my best to pretend that he was not there.

"It's in code," Gus said at last, and, honestly, I was impressed, as I'd first assumed it was just an accounting book.

I came and sat next to him. "That's what I thought too. And this morning, in comp sci, our teacher showed me how to decode it. There are websites where you can just plug the symbols in, and it solves it for you."

Behind us, Eddy let out a little gasp.

"I had no idea it was that easy to break a code," Gus said.

"Years of love have been forgot, in the hatred of a minute!" Eddy exclaimed. I sneaked a glance over my shoulder. On a living person, his face would be red with indignation. His remained pale and translucent, but it still managed to convey his anger.

But hey, he'd had a good run of it. Some of his codes hadn't been broken for over a hundred years.

"Well," I said sheepishly. "It is now. With computers. It was *extremely hard*—you know—back in the day." I gave the ghost an apologetic shrug.

"I blush, I burn, I shudder," Eddy raged through his teeth.

If that got him upset, wait until he heard about modern medicine. Poe's wife and mother both died of tuberculosis; now doctors could cure that with antibiotics.

"What does it say?" Gus asked.

"Well," I said. "You know that poem I was working on in English class?"

"Yeah."

"It says that."

"Huh." He studied the page for a minute. "So, there are Poe-style poems in this book."

"Yeah," I said meaningfully. "*Style.*"

Gus gave me a quizzical look. "You can't mean—you don't think this book actually belonged to Edgar Allan Poe, do you?"

I turned to Eddy, who folded his arms and lifted his nose in the air, obviously still miffed about the whole computer program thing. "Well, yes." I pointed at the cover. "Look, there are his initials, right there."

He examined the worn leather cover. "I don't see anything."

"Trust me, it says E. A. Poe."

"You just finished telling me everyone in your family is named Poe. This house is a whole Poe-themed museum. What if this is just one of the props?"

That would actually make a ton of sense—except for the matter of Eddy. Who Gus could not see.

"You have no problem believing that I'm psychic, but you're extremely skeptical that this diary belonged to a famous poet?"

"I didn't say that."

"Would it help some if I told you it was his ghost who informed me?"

Gus looked at me curiously. "Was it?"

I chanced another look at Eddy, who was now carefully watching the conversation. "The analytical power should not be confounded with simple ingenuity, for while the analyst is necessarily ingenious, the ingenious man is often remarkably incapable of analysis."

"No one asked you," I snapped at Eddy.

"Excuse me?" asked Gus.

It was hard to pretend that Eddy wasn't standing right there, looking over our shoulders and acting like a normal part of the conversation. But Gus couldn't see or hear him. If he was a figment of my imagination, he was a very good one.

However, my enthusiasm for telling Gus everything was fading fast.

I tried another tactic.

"When I broke the first code today, I saw a date—1848." I pointed at the relevant part of the code. "That was the year before

Poe died. And the poem I decoded had another code hidden inside it—it secretly spelled out the name of his fiancée at the time of his death. Poe wrote poems like that to his lady friends all the time, but that one was not in his complete works."

"Well, that's certainly more promising evidence than the fact that your family name is written on the cover. Does your family have any other of Poe's belongings? I mean, real stuff, not stuffed crows you call ravens."

"Not that I know of," I said. "But then again, I don't think Poe *had* a lot of stuff. He was famously broke. And most people think he was mugged or something before he died too. His luggage and his walking stick were both gone, and he wasn't even wearing his own clothes."

Gus carefully turned over another page, and his eyes widened at the gruesome sketch staring up at him. "Yikes. What's this? Did Poe do illustrations too?"

Not that I knew of. "I think—I think that's supposed to be a drawing of a ghost. Like the ones I see in my dreams."

Gus made a face. "That's what I looked like in your dream?"

"More or less."

Gus thought for a long moment. "I'm no expert in historical documents, but it strikes me that the most rational explanation is that this is just some book in your family's household. Maybe it's even one you saw a long time ago, and that's how you got the image of the ghosts in your head. If so, then it really is just a figment of your imagination, and the fact that one of them resembled me—is just a coincidence."

That would suck when it came to the journal being worth money. And, you know, my overall sanity. But if I was disappointed by the theory, Gus looked devastated.

"What do the rest of the codes say?" he asked.

I shook my head. "I didn't get a chance to input any of the others yet."

"Well, what are we waiting for?"

I retrieved Aunt Marie's laptop and brought it up to my room, then found the decryption site. Gus read out the symbols and I entered them into the text box, while Eddy watched the proceedings with a mix of intrigue and disgust.

"How can you!" he cried out to me. I ignored him. "How can you?"

Guess he'd see soon enough.

Seconds after I pushed Submit, another poem appeared.

A Gift, December 1848

Hearts that ever beat so bold
Need no base or material thing
No lock of hair, no glint of gold
Nor even that conventional ring.
Friends know a love no fortunes bring.

Another poem, another puzzle.

Behind Gus, Eddy was staring in open-mouthed fascination at the decrypted code. "Horrible!—wonderful!—outrageous!—hideous!—incomprehensible!" he spluttered.

Honestly, I kind of pitied him. Who knew how long he'd spent putting it together, only to watch it be broken by this machine in a matter of seconds?

"So, basically," I said awkwardly, because Gus definitely had not asked, "what the computer does is analyze all the options for these letters based on the idea that the message is in English, and decodes it according to the likelihood that certain letters appear with a particular frequency, or alongside other letters in the English language. It's kind of how large language models operate with chatbots. They predict words. This is just predicting letters."

"Cool," said Gus, still reading.

"Like in English, E is the most commonly used letter. And how there are only two words with only one letter."

"Like A and I?" Gus asked.

"Exactly. And a certain number of words with two letters, etc. Poe wrote a whole short story on how to decode messages using techniques like that. And the machine just does it super fast. Way faster than a human could."

Eddy's eyes got even wider.

"The *machine*?" Gus asked me doubtfully. "Don't you mean the website?"

Sure, but how was I supposed to explain what a website was to a ghost from the 1800s?

Gus, unbothered by the presence of a spirit in the room, was still staring at the screen. "The poem you plagiarized for English class—"

"Hey!" I said, with a guilty glance at Eddy, who was visibly reeling from the ease with which I'd broken his code.

"Well, you did," Gus said with a shrug. "Who was that poem about?"

I showed Gus the decryption from computer class that I'd photographed on my phone. "If you take the first letter of the first line, the second letter of the second, etc., it spells out 'Elmira.' That was the name of Poe's fiancée when he died."

Gus pointed at the date on the "Elmira" poem. "This says September."

"So?"

"Well, this new poem says December. And the name in the poem isn't Elmira. Look." He grabbed a sheet of scrap paper and jotted it down. H-E-L-E-N. "The first five lines spell out 'Helen.'"

I double-checked Gus's work; he was right.

"Helen is probably a reference to Sarah Helen Whitman," I told him. "That was Poe's other fiancée that year."

"*Other* fiancée?" Gus asked, incredulous. "Guy really got around, didn't he?"

I looked up at Eddy, who was studiously avoiding my gaze. "Yeah, well, that's apparently one of the reasons Sarah Helen Whitman broke up with him," I said. "That and the drinking."

In fact, Poe had proposed to both women that year. They were both rich widows, and Poe was in desperate need of money. There was also another woman, still married, named Annie.

"So which one of these ladies was your ancestor?" Gus asked me now.

"Neither," I said.

"I suppose her poem's a few more pages in?"

I stole another glance at Eddy. Was it?

The ghost at least had the dignity to look sheepish. "There are chords in the hearts of the most reckless which cannot be touched without emotion."

Oh yeah, because *that's* an excuse.

I think Eddy had expected me to be amazed by the cleverness of his codes. But now that the computer was solving them so easily, I was merely mortified by their contents.

"Let's do the next one," Gus said and began typing it in. Once again, modern technology worked its miracle, and another poem appeared.

This one, however, did not include a title or a date.

And yet if I may offer one
Which holds a puzzle in its grip,
Three orbits round of tiny moons
Reveal its inner workmanship.
A cosmic key concealed within
The domed dominion of this clip.
Three numbers which—their date divine—
A product sacred in our view
The very stars did thus align
To give our souls a mate so true.
And our tresses intertwined
Forever links both me and you.

Gus dutifully wrote down the letters again. "A-H-O-M-B—this is not a name," he reported.

I examined the poem. "It starts with the word *And.* Maybe it's just another stanza of the Helen poem on the previous page?"

We tried again to make words, this time with the sixth letter of the sixth line and the seventh letter of the seventh. Again, it was nonsense.

"I don't get it," I said, mostly to Eddy.

He seemed pretty pleased by that, nodding smugly. "The enigma seems still in as bad a condition as ever."

Very funny.

"It reads like a riddle or something," I said. "It could be an allusion to something we don't understand two centuries later. Poe loved to make clever references to current events in his work."

"Could this website solve that as well?"

"Not this one," I said. "It's a decryption program. It just does ciphers. For riddles or hidden messages, we'd have to try something else."

"Maybe an AI chatbot, like you said," Gus suggested.

"It may well be doubted whether human ingenuity can construct an enigma of the kind which human ingenuity may not, by proper application, resolve," Eddy scolded him. Gus showed no indication he had any idea.

I rolled my eyes. *Repeating yourself already, dude?*

"I don't think so," I said to Gus. "Any chatbot would have to know a lot of really specialized information. You could train one, I guess, to solve Poe-specific puzzles, but—" I glared at Eddy. "It's not really the *proper application.*"

Eddy beamed at me. “The solution is by no means so difficult as you might be led to imagine from the first hasty inspection of the characters,” he said, as if that was helpful.

I wondered if he was also so annoying when he was alive. Maybe that’s why his foster dad disowned him, and the reason he kept getting in fights with other writers in Boston.

“You know,” I said out loud. “I heard that Poe died with *very few friends*. I wonder why that was?”

“Huh?” said Gus, utterly clueless.

Eddy thought, turned to me, his expression pained, and exclaimed, “I fear you have been thinking everything ill of me!”

There was a knock on the bedroom door, and Aunt Marie poked her head in. “Hey, guys,” she said brightly. “Dinner’s ready. Are you at a good stopping point?”

“Sure,” I said, closing the laptop. We weren’t getting anywhere, anyway.

Aunt Marie stepped inside the room and shuddered. “The vibes in here are super weird.”

“Oh, now you notice?” I asked her. I had been sleeping with a stuffed raven—er, crow—for weeks.

She took a few more steps in, and Eddy drifted away from her.

“No, I’m serious,” Aunt Marie said and held out her arm. “Look, all my hair is standing up. Like we’re being watched.”

“That may be the taxidermy, ma’am,” said Gus.

Sure. Or the ghost.

“The spirits of the dead who stood in life before thee are again in death around thee,” intoned Eddy.

That was quite enough of that. I put the journal back in the desk drawer. Eddy, thankfully, disappeared.

"Dinner?" I asked the others.

"Do you ever feel like someone is walking over your grave?" Aunt Marie was saying to Gus.

"Every day," he replied frankly. "But then again, I've actually been dead."

CHAPTER 11

The Very, Very Long Con

UNSURPRISINGLY, GUS AND AUNT MARIE GOT ALONG great. At least there was one member of the family who had no problem with being thought of as a little bit kooky.

Well, one living member, anyway.

Because we had a guest, we ate dinner in our "The Masque of the Red Death" dining room, with its black paneling, red stained-glass windows, and black gothic furnishings. An enormous old grandfather clock, broken, stood against one wall. Above the table hung an elaborate black chandelier festooned with what appeared to be red, dripping candles. At one point, the fixture held scarlet-colored bulbs, but thankfully, Aunt Marie realized that it made everything look unappetizing, so now it just had regular light bulbs inside it.

While I ate two full bowls of Aunt Marie's homemade broccoli cheddar soup with fresh bread, Gus and Aunt Marie had an entire conversation about the reality of near-death experiences, and the supposedly special powers conferred on people who had them afterward.

"Connection to past lives," Aunt Marie suggested to Gus, gesturing with her spoon.

"No, nothing like that," he said.

"Intuition?"

"I've always been a pretty smart guy," he admitted, with little to no humility.

"Premonition?"

"Nope."

"Ability to see spirits?"

"Not that I know of."

"*Definitely* not," I added.

They both looked at me for a moment, but when I failed to elaborate, they moved on.

It wasn't my fault no one else saw Eddy. And how weird was it to hope that I was actually seeing Eddy, and not having some kind of wild hallucination?

More soup. Definitely more soup.

"How about dreams?" she asked now. "Have you been having odd dreams? Prophetic dreams?"

"Not me," Gus said, and pointed in my direction. "That's all Ellen's department."

Aunt Marie nodded sagely. "Yes, the dream of the people suffocating."

"What?" Gus sat up straight, his entire demeanor changing. "You didn't say we were suffocating."

"*We?*" Aunt Marie pounced on that. "What do you mean, *we*?"

Uh-oh.

"Gus bears a small resemblance to the dead boy in my dreams," I said softly, but I don't think either of them heard me, because Gus said, at the same time and much louder:

"Ellen's been dreaming about me and my dead parents." He turned his penetrating stare in my direction. "But she never mentioned the suffocation part."

"I asked you how they died!" I said in my defense. "I asked on the bus."

"Yeah, and I don't know if you noticed, but I was very determined not to give you any hints. I know how cold reading works. You secretly get me to give you all the information without realizing it and then you use it against me."

Cold reading? I almost spat out my soup. "Wait, you think I'm a *con artist*?"

"I'm still deciding on that part. It's a new angle, for sure. All the Poe stuff. Welcome to Baltimore, right? And you haven't asked for money—yet. Though I've been dropping lots of hints."

Yeah, he'd been super braggy about how wealthy he was. Still, that didn't make him an outlier at Evergreen. Lots of my classmates dropped heavy hints about their family trips to the French Riviera or their second homes in Aspen.

"I haven't asked for anything. You're the one who followed me across town, *to my house*!" I shouted at him.

"Playing hard to get is part of sucking in the mark," Gus replied, as if giving an oral presentation on the art of the con. "I've seen it before. It was important to figure out what your game was before my sister heard about you. She believes anything anyone tells her."

"Sister!" I exclaimed. There had been no sister in my dream.

Aunt Marie's gaze traveled back and forth between us, as if she wasn't entirely sure what to think.

"I'm having major doubts about this so-called English project," she said at last.

I could not believe I showed this jerk my journal. I couldn't believe we were giving him free bread and pastries. I could not believe I thought he was trying to be *my friend*.

"If you think I'm trying to take advantage of you," I said, "then why do you keep going out of your way to get me *out* of trouble?"

Gus ducked his head, guiltily. "Keep your friends close and your enemies closer?"

"Teenagers!" Aunt Marie gave a dramatic sigh. "Stop."

"Aunt Marie," I argued, "I did *nothing*!"

"And it's really offensive to reduce us to our ages," Gus pointed out.

But she just sighed again and directed her next words to the ceiling. "There's a reason I never went into teaching. There's a reason I never had my own kids."

Any other time, I may have thought she was just talking to herself, but I, too, had been having conversations with invisible entities lately, so you never could tell.

"Maybe I'm the one who did something terrible in a past life," she mused.

"Why did you say suffocated?" Gus asked her.

“Explain to me how a coded journal was part of the con in your twisted little imagination?” I asked him.

“Wait, what coded journal?” Marie asked both of us. Gus and I both started talking at once, and she held up her hands. “Let’s start over again, shall we?”

I batted some broccoli around in my soup. Gus tore a hunk off his bread and shoved it into his mouth.

Aunt Marie poured herself some more wine. “So, what’s all this about a coded journal?”

“I found a book in one of the crates the other day,” I said. I decided the skip the part about Eddy, for now. “And I think it belonged to Edgar Allan Poe.”

“Yeah, right,” Gus said with a snort, and ate more bread.

Marie gestured for him to be quiet. “Go on, Ellen. Why is that?”

I started listing off reasons on my fingers. “Well, it was in code, and he loved codes. And it was dated from 1848 and 1849. And when I decoded it in my computer science class, it contained poems holding hidden messages that spelled out the names ‘Elmira’ and ‘Helen.’ ”

“As in, Sarah Elmira Shelton and Sarah Helen Whitman?” Marie asked, her tone one of hushed excitement.

“Yeah,” said Gus. “He really had a thing for Sarahs.”

“More like a lot of people had the same name back then,” said Aunt Marie. “That’s why they went by their middle names.”

“But if you two did that, you’d both be Poe?” Gus wasn’t about to let us off easily.

I rolled my eyes. I was never going by Poe. "But if it is his book, it would be worth a lot of money, right? The lost poems of Edgar Allan Poe! That would be worth millions!"

"Ohhhhh," Gus exclaimed. "I get it now. You're trying to unload the journal on me."

"Why would I do that?" I asked him. "Are you an antique collector?"

Gus shook his head. "No, the scam is that you oh-so-generously 'let me have it for a good price' with the promise that I'll be able to resell it for much more."

"I thought the scam was I was a fake psychic connecting you to your dead parents?"

"I *said* I was still trying to work out your goals!" he cried.

"That's funny," I snapped back at him, "because I've been wanting to figure out what it was you were trying to get out of *me* all afternoon!"

"Ellen," Marie said, her voice one of enforced calm. "Please." She looked at Gus. "I can assure you, my niece is not a con artist. She's been complaining to me about her nightmares for weeks."

"Excuse me, ma'am," Gus replied. "But that's exactly what a con artist would say. I've met all sorts in the last couple months. My sister is completely obsessed with contacting my parents from *the great beyond*. I've been dragged out in front of every medium, psychic, ghost whisperer, and aura photographer in a hundred-mile radius, and it's all of it a scam."

This was probably not the time to tell Gus that Aunt Marie was also one of those fortune tellers he so despised. Let him think she just made muffins.

“It’s a pretty long game we’re playing, then,” said Aunt Marie, “to enroll Ellen in your school several years before you arrive there on the off chance that you’d have a near-death experience last summer.”

Gus stared at her, his eyes wide. “I didn’t tell you it was last summer.” He faced me. “And I didn’t tell *you* that we suffocated.”

“Did you, though?” I pressed. “I mean, did they?”

He frowned at his soup. “Kind of.”

Aunt Marie gasped, her hand pressed to her throat. “Oh, Gus, I’m so sorry.”

“It was carbon monoxide poisoning. The air we were breathing was no use to us.” He pushed his bowl away. “But I don’t remember it happening. We were all asleep. They never woke up, but I was revived by paramedics.”

But I remembered it. I remembered it all too well. The hot, cloying darkness. The figures scratching at their throats.

I couldn’t think of a single sentence to say in response to him. How could you put words to such impossible circumstances and horrific feelings? What would I do if I woke up one day and my dad didn’t?

“I don’t know how you know these things,” Gus said.

“I don’t know anything,” I whispered. “I don’t even know why I dreamed about you.” And, even worse, I worried that learning the details wouldn’t make my nightmares go away—they’d just transform them into something more specifically terrifying.

I looked at Aunt Marie for help, but clearly, interpreting my dreams for me and interpreting my dreams for the strange kid who showed up at her house and called her niece a scam artist were two very different things.

If we were con artists, this was the point where we'd tell Gus we'd have answers for him—for a price. But I had no answers. No one did.

"Whatever." He crossed his arms. "I don't even care."

Aunt Marie cleared her throat. "Okay, now, what about this journal? Can I see it?"

"Uh . . ." I flailed. "I'd rather not."

"And why is that?"

Because this dinner was already awkward enough without adding the world's most annoying ghost to the mix.

"We've only decoded a few of the poems," I said instead.

"I have them," Gus said, producing the pages he'd been writing in my room. I gave him a furtive look. *I* was supposedly the sneaky one?

"You were going to take them with you?" I asked him.

"I hadn't decided what I was going to do," he admitted. He unfolded the sheets and showed them to Aunt Marie.

She looked over the three poems. "I don't recognize any of these."

And if Aunt Marie didn't recognize a Poe poem, that meant no one had ever seen them before. "That's what I mean!" I said. "I think the journal might be Poe's—might be full of unpublished poems from the final year of his life."

"That *would* be something," said Aunt Marie. But she didn't sound convinced.

"If Poe really had something to do with our ancestor—here at Raven's Rest—in the days before he died, wouldn't it stand to reason that he might have left something here? He didn't have any of his belongings on him when he was found. They had to have gone somewhere!"

"I'm the first to admit we have a lot of junk in our basement," said Aunt Marie, "but actual Poe artifacts? Surely someone would have donated or sold them a century ago. There were times when our ancestors tried to prove our heritage, our connection—but no one believed us. We weren't part of literary high society like Sarah Helen Whitman or anything like that."

"That's who the second poem is for," said Gus. "Or at least, that's what Ellen thinks."

"Could you sound any more doubtful?" I asked him. "Look, it spells out 'Helen.'" I pointed to the relevant letters.

But Aunt Marie looked more interested in the third poem—or at least, the second part of the second one. The one that talked about cosmic keys and such and didn't spell out anything at all.

"This reminds me of something," she said.

Gus agreed. "It reads like a riddle."

"It reads like a description," Aunt Marie replied. She tapped the top of the page. "'A Gift, December 1848.' So, Christmas?" She looked at me. "Where was Poe in December of 1848?"

"In Providence, Rhode Island, with Sarah Helen Whitman," I supplied dutifully.

Gus stared at me in astonishment. "How do you *know* that?"

I shrugged. Because I was a Reynolds? Some families drilled their kids on multiplication tables. I'd learned Poe trivia. "It was a famous moment in his life."

"And it makes sense," said Aunt Marie. "We know he was with Whitman, and this poem has her name in it. Maybe the poem is the gift, but . . . look. If you read the two pieces together, he's saying something different."

"He says he doesn't need to get her jewelry," said Gus, "but then, in the very next line, he says 'and yet.'"

"Exactly," said Marie. "And then he proceeds to describe some jewelry."

"Poe didn't have jewelry to give his girlfriend," I said. "He was broke."

"Maybe he was broke because he had too many girlfriends he was giving jewelry to," Gus pointed out.

"Oh, so now you think it really was Poe?"

"*Teenagers,*" Aunt Marie warned. "And you know, it is true that Poe gave jewelry to Elmira Shelton. The engagement ring he gave her is down in the Poe Museum in Richmond."

"What did it look like?" Gus asked. "Was it carved with little moons and included a lock of his hair?"

Aunt Marie laughed. "No, it's a tiny metal band with his name engraved on the inside."

I frowned and studied the words of the poem again.

"But it doesn't say he gave Helen a ring," I pointed out. "It says 'clip.'"

"Like a money clip?" Gus asked. "A tie clip? A *paper* clip?"

“Think nineteenth century, dead boy,” I said to him. “It’s jewelry. Like a brooch.”

“Dead boy?” Gus repeated. “*Dead* boy?”

Oops. Was that out loud? I was ready to apologize, then I saw the look on his face.

A sly, cunning little smirk. The one he wore whenever he was about to get the better of someone. The one that made me instantly aware how much I was going to regret this.

“Whatever you say, Ellen *Poe*.”

It is nearly a mon
, requesting an in
–, I placed it (
swered letters". The
seeming discourtesy
answer.
I have now to
you at any tim
adway. You will
the morning befor
Very Resp.
W. C

CHAPTER 12

Victorian Goth Freaks

GUS WAS LYING IN WAIT FOR ME AT THE GATE OF the school the next day.

"Oh, it's you again," I said as he fell into step beside me. "Are you here to accuse me of more crimes and conspiracies?"

There was finally a chill in the air today, and the sky was overcast and silver. I hunched my shoulders, ducking as much of myself into my school blazer as possible.

Gus was not wearing a school blazer, or any other item of clothing sanctioned by Evergreen Prep. Instead, he was in yet another all-black outfit. I had no idea how he kept getting away with it. If anyone here was a con artist, it was Gus Davenport.

"Did you translate the rest of the codes in the book?" he asked.

I had not, mainly because I didn't feel like dealing with Eddy last night. Plus, I did, in fact, have homework. "What does it matter to you? You think it's fake."

"Maybe I do, maybe I don't," he said smugly. Infuriatingly.

"Well, let me know when you make up your mind." Quickening my steps never helped me escape him, thanks to our relative heights. I longed for the gong, so I could escape him and head into computer science.

"Any more dreams?" he asked now.

"There's no good way for me to answer that," I said to him. "If I say yes, you'll think I'm trying to draw you into some kind of psychic con. If I say no, you'll think I'm playing hard to get as a way to draw you into some kind of psychic con."

"I don't think you're trying to draw me into some kind of psychic con."

"Oh yeah? What changed?"

The answer, by the way, was not necessarily *more* dreams. It was *again* dreams. Again, the same dream of Gus and his parents pleading for help as their souls drained away into oblivion.

Gus shrugged. "I thought about it some more. I thought about what your aunt said, how you've gone to school here for years. Maybe I'm just being oversensitive because of everything."

I wanted to be angry at him. Or at least, angrier. But I couldn't imagine what it was like to lose your parents. Dad was just across the country, and I missed him like crazy.

"That makes sense," I said. "You've been through a lot."

"Yeah," he agreed. "Like—you know—*death*."

Okay, that too. We walked along for a few more paces in blessed silence.

"My sister really wants to meet you," Gus said.

"Oh? Why is that?"

"Well, I told you how she feels about psychics."

I stopped dead and stared at him in disbelief. "You *told* her?" After everything he'd accused me of, he'd told her?

He blinked at me. "Do I look like a person who keeps secrets?"

This was true. He did not. He especially loved telling people about that one time he'd died for two minutes.

"I was out pretty late last night—missed dinner and everything. She wanted to know where I was. So I told her I'd met a nice girl at school who saw dead people in her dreams and was also maybe descended from Edgar Allan Poe. She was especially excited about that last part."

I groaned. I was especially *un*excited about it. "I'm not a psychic."

"Honestly, she'd probably be fine just with the stories about Poe. She's kind of a goth freak."

Now I was curious. "Where was your sister when—when everything happened?"

"With her boyfriend here in Baltimore. They live on their own—or they did before I moved in. She's my half sister, actually."

By some miracle, the gong sounded.

"See you in English class," Gus promised. "Oh, and by the way . . ."

He let the words dangle there for a second, long enough to make sure I'd paused in my escape. Long enough to make sure I was hanging on to his every word.

". . . I found that brooch."

❁ ❁ ❁

Naturally, I got nothing done in computer science that morning. What did he even mean? And why did he even think I'd speak to him after all the stuff he'd accused me of yesterday?

Of course. I had. Spoken to him, I mean.

"Miss Reynolds." Ms. Sakai came by my station. "Did you get anywhere with the cryptography?"

"Sort of," I said. "I was able to decrypt some of the pages, but the stuff inside was still a mystery. It was poems and riddles. I—think I know what some of them meant, but the rest . . ." I trailed off.

Her eyes widened. "Where is the book from?"

"I found it in an old box of junk in my house."

She broke into a smile. "That's really cool! All my old boxes of junk are cables that I don't have any use for."

That sounded way better. I doubted old computer cables came with annoying, poetry-spouting ghosts.

"You know," she added, "there are all kinds of famous, coded old documents in the world. If you really want to go down a rabbit hole one of these days, look up the Voynich manuscript. Scholars have been trying to crack that one for centuries. I hope yours turns out to be something very interesting, and not some old grocery list."

Scholars? "If it was something of value, what do I do with it? Is that something I should sell? Or—" *don't say donate, don't say donate* "—something?"

"I guess it depends on the age. If it's an old military code or something, it might be valuable to collectors or researchers. But

I wouldn't know anything about that. You'd probably have to ask a librarian."

I walked to English class as slowly as humanly possible, just in case Gus was lurking somewhere. I did not want to give him the satisfaction. And all through English class, I successfully ignored him. We were discussing "Annabel Lee" today—one of Poe's most famous poems. Like most of his work, it was about a beautiful dead woman. It was also only published after his death.

Ms. Morris was going through the usual beats. Poe's exquisite rhythm and imagery and the repeated themes that echoed Poe's own life tragedies, like the death of his young mother and young wife.

"Ms. Morris?" Gus's voice came from behind me. "If this was one of Poe's later poems, are we sure that 'Annabel Lee' was supposed to be his wife? It says here 'she was a child and I was a child,' but wasn't Poe all grown up when he married his child bride?"

"Literary license, Mr. Davenport—"

"But if he wrote this in 1949," Gus interrupted her, "then isn't it more likely to be about his fiancée, the childhood sweetheart he was engaged to when he died?"

"I—" Ms. Morris flipped through the book, flummoxed. "His fiancée?"

Everyone knew about Virginia Clemm Poe. His teenage cousin, then later, his dead wife. No one ever talked about the other women.

"Her name was Elmira," Gus supplied. "Sarah Elmira Royster Shelton."

The way he said it was absolutely aimed at me, and I refused to act like I was listening at all.

"How old was she?" Rebecca asked with a smirk. "Twelve?"

"She was his childhood sweetheart," I mumbled before I could stop myself. "She was close to his age."

"What Ellen said," Gus added, his tone one of triumph.

"I suppose that's possible, Mr. Davenport," said Ms. Morris. "Although I assume this woman was still very much alive when he wrote 'Annabel Lee'? What's most likely is that Annabel Lee is a literary invention. Maybe Poe was inspired by this Elmira woman, by his own wife, by his own mother. It could be all three."

"His other girlfriend, Sarah Helen Whitman, also claimed the poem was about her," Gus said.

"His *other* girlfriend! You've certainly been doing your research!" Ms. Morris exclaimed.

"Yes," said Gus. "I have." He poked me between the shoulder blades.

I turned around and glared at him. He grinned.

Somehow, I made it through the rest of class without doing anything that would get me sent back to the principal's office.

But Gus had no intentions of letting it go. When I went to grab my bag after the gong, I found it trapped beneath his sneakered foot. Sneakers were also against the dress code, and yet, I hadn't seen a single teacher ever take Gus to task.

I yanked on the strap, but it didn't budge. "You're on my bag."

"Aren't you even curious?"

"Why you think it's okay to stand on my bag? Yes, I am."

"Noooo." He cleverly twisted to stand up while still grinding the strap of my bag into the hardwood floors. "I mean, about the brooch."

I yanked once more, and this time, it came flying up so hard I nearly lost my balance. Thankfully, almost everyone had already left to go to their next class. On top of everything else, we'd be late to PE if he kept this up.

"I'm not curious about anything until you apologize," I stated, then turned on my heel and walked out.

Somehow, I managed to make it all the way over to the New Building and inside without Gus trying to stop me again. And he kept his distance from me throughout class, though I did catch him looking at me three or four times.

Which I guess means he caught me looking at him too.

By the time class was over I had just about swallowed my pride enough to speak to him, but I didn't see him after changing, or at lunch. In fact, I'd nearly given up entirely by the end of the day.

Which was when I found Gus waiting for me at the bus stop on the road outside the school.

"Why, if it isn't my good friend Ellen Poe," he said with a smile.

"Why, if it isn't—my—" I couldn't think of anything.

He smiled. "Guess you're not as eloquent as your ancestor, huh?"

I rolled my eyes. "Even if he was my ancestor, poetry is not genetic." I turned to face the street, as if he were just another stranger waiting at the bus stop.

Across the street, a large black bird landed on the shoulder of the road and began picking at something stuck to the pavement. It looked up at me, cocked its head, and cawed.

"Dear God," I said. "What is that giant, monster bird?"

Gus looked at it. "Nope. Still a crow."

Darn it.

The bus came and I boarded it. Gus could do whatever he wanted. It was a free country.

And what he apparently wanted to do was get on behind me, plop into the seat across from me, and start talking.

"Come on," he coaxed. "Don't you want to know about the brooch?"

"I told you. I want an apology for thinking I was trying to scam you."

"But Ellen," he said, seriously. "The brooch *is* the apology."

I bit my lip and looked out the window, wondering what things were like for the Ellen in the universe where she'd never shown Gus the journal. Was that Ellen happy right now? Was she, possibly, still laboring under the delusion that Gus honestly wanted to be her friend?

At last, I relented, turning to face him. "Fine."

He beamed and sat forward on the molded plastic seat. "Great. Okay. So, last night, your aunt said that Poe's fiancée's engagement ring was in a museum, so I thought I'd look to see what other jewelry might be connected to him. And guess what I found?"

"A . . . brooch?" Like he'd been saying all day?

"Yes!" he exclaimed. "A pearl brooch that once belonged to none other than Sarah Helen Whitman."

I felt a rush of excitement but quickly tamped it back down.

"And—you'll never believe where it is."

Okay, I'd bite. "Where?"

"The Edgar Allan Poe Collection of the Enoch Pratt Free Public Library." Gus looked so proud of himself. "Right here in Baltimore."

"I know where the Pratt is, thanks."

"I mapped it for us already. We can just walk from the bus station where we changed yesterday. To *the Pratt*," he added carefully, as if that somehow made him a native. Please. He couldn't even say "Baltimore" correctly.

"Why would I do that?"

"To go see it, of course." Gus popped up and joined me on my row. "You're trying to find out if that journal is legit, right? Well, right now, they have the brooch in their collection because it has Poe's hair in it."

That was also like the poem.

"But," Gus added, "they think she got it after he died. Apparently, it was really common to cut dead people's hair off and pass it around as a memento."

"Yeah," I said. "Victorians were goth freaks. Especially Whitman. She used to hold séances and wear coffin-shaped jewelry and try to—" I cut myself off. And try to contact ghosts.

I was definitely not about to mention that to Gus.

"But what if the brooch was not something she had made up to remember him by?" Gus asked. "What if it was a gift from Poe? The one from the poem? Even Poe scholars don't know that. But if you could prove that it's that brooch, then that means the poem in the journal might be genuine."

I shook my head. "But how could we do something like that?"

Gus gave me an incredulous look. "You really aren't great at poetry, are you? The poem says there's a puzzle in the jewelry. All we have to do is solve it."

CHAPTER 13

Celestial Bodies

THE PRATT IS AN ABSOLUTELY MASSIVE MARBLE building in downtown Baltimore, a relic from a time when cities created really beautiful buildings for the public, even in the midst of the Great Depression. The inside is all soaring marble and glass ceilings and fancy metalwork and murals. They have lots of free events here, and Dad and I used to come here all the time to just wander around and read books. Best of all, as the name of the Enoch Pratt Free Public Library indicates, membership here is completely free for any resident of Maryland. You can walk right in and get a library card.

I've had one my whole life.

But until today, I'd never used it to do more than take out books. Still, Gus said that the brooch was part of the library's collection, so once we got inside, we approached the information desk and asked how to speak to someone in special collections.

"What exactly are you looking for?" asked the man behind the desk.

"It's in the Poe collection," Gus said. "It's a pearl brooch with a lock of Poe's hair inside of it." When the guy just stared at us, he added, "It's for an English project," like those were magic words.

"No kidding." The librarian looked very amused. "Let me see if I can get someone to help you. We generally recommend making an appointment for special collections. And, um, adult supervision. But we'll see." He withdrew and made a phone call in hushed tones that I felt hot just thinking about.

I glanced at Gus, who appeared completely unbothered.

"This is never going to happen," I told him.

"Why not?" he asked, seeming genuinely confused. "You have a library card."

After a minute, the librarian returned. "So, the bad news is, we don't provide viewings for items like that, as they are too rare and fragile."

"What's the good news?" I asked.

"Well, there's a Poe exhibit right up the hall this month, and the staff member I talked to said she's pretty sure that brooch is part of the exhibit. It's behind glass, but you'll get a look at it."

"Thanks!" Gus said, but I was disappointed. What were we going to be able to see on the brooch behind a piece of thick glass that Gus hadn't already seen when he found it online?

The exhibit was in a public hallway upstairs, so we headed to the upper level. As always, there were plenty of people taking advantage of the library, but very few were using the hallway as anything other than the passage between the stairs and the bathroom.

Still, Gus was examining the glass cases protecting the exhibit like he was casing the joint.

"Please don't get us arrested," I said.

He pointed. "There it is."

I looked, and he was right. There was a small pearl brooch on a stand, with a sign reading in large script letters *Memento Mori*.

It wasn't an especially flashy piece of jewelry. Just a few rows of tiny seed pearls surrounding a cloudy piece of glass through which I could see what appeared to be a lock of brown hair.

I moved closer to read the accompanying card.

During the nineteenth century, it was common for friends and family members to take hair clippings from the dead before burial as a keepsake. The hair was often incorporated into mourning jewelry or other items. Here, a hollow behind a pearl brooch contains a lock of hair from Edgar Allan Poe that was given to Poe's friend, the poet Sarah Helen Whitman of Rhode Island.

"She was a poet too?" Gus asked me.

"Yes, that's how they met. She wrote him this fawning poem, calling him 'the Raven' and all this stuff. He sent her poems in return. They were super into each other while it lasted—they talked about being soulmates, he apparently proposed in a cemetery, it was all very atmospheric."

If you liked that sort of thing.

"But then they broke up."

I shrugged. "Poe was . . . unstable. He was drinking and taking laudanum."

"What's laudanum?"

"A kind of opium people used to drink. Basically, he was drinking and taking drugs, and Helen's friends and family were really suspicious of him."

"Gee," said Gus. "Wonder why."

"*And* she was a rich widow, and I think the people around her thought it was all too fast and that he was trying to get her money. Remember, he was also maybe talking to those other women too."

Gus was examining the pin from every angle, but it was hard to see the back side, the way it was mounted on the dais.

Now that I was talking about her, all the stories from my childhood came bubbling to the surface. I hadn't really thought of Poe's many girlfriends for years, but I guess that once learned, Reynolds family Poe trivia was like riding a bike. You never really forgot.

"I think she was in love with him forever, even after they broke up," I said. "After he died, she wrote all these defenses of him, she gave all these interviews to biographers. She was really . . . spiritual."

"Spiritual?" He turned back to me, his eyebrows raised.

Oh no, he was going to make me say it. "Well, she believed in ghosts and all that stuff. Séances were super popular in the decades after he died, and she used to hold them at her house. She was into that whole spiritualism movement that got popular in the nineteenth century. Talking to the spirits of the dead and all that."

"Ah," said Gus. "I see." I didn't really like the way he said it, though. *Sarah Helen Whitman* was into séances. Not me.

In many ways, she wasn't all that different from my Reynolds ancestors. Obsessed with their tenuous connection to Edgar Allan Poe, determined to hang on by any means possible. Was it pathetic, or romantic?

Was there a difference?

"She really did think they were soulmates," I went on. "They had the same birthday. January 19."

"That's weird."

"She certainly thought so," I replied. But was it really? There were only three hundred and sixty-five days in the year, and billions of people on the planet, so you do the math. "Oh, and she was actually older than him by six years, so it wasn't another child bride situation like with his wife."

"Am I supposed to find that impressive?" Gus asked.

"Well, people make him out like he's a creep because Virginia was so young, but none of the other women he was ever involved with were teenagers."

Some of them were married, though.

I nodded at the brooch. "So, do you think this is the gift from the poem?"

"Don't you?" Gus looked surprised. "*Three orbits round of tiny moons*—think poetry, Ellen Poe. It's got three rows of pearls."

My eyes widened. "Oh yeah! And our *tresses intertwined*—that would mean that the hair in there is not just Poe's, it's also Whitman's?" Which would mean . . . if we could get experts to test the hair inside there, and they found it belonged to two different people . . .

Who was I kidding? I doubted that the library was going to crack open a precious artifact on the word of a teenage girl.

"But what does the rest of the riddle mean?" Gus asked me. "*Three numbers which—their date divine—a product sacred in our view?*"

"*Three numbers* sounds like another code," I said. "Like a combination lock or something."

Gus nodded in agreement. "You think there's a lock on the back of this pin?"

"Or the pin is the key to another lock?" I suggested. "It could be anything." I peered more closely at the brooch. The protective case around the exhibit was thick, and the glass encasing the hair on the pin was old and cloudy. Unless you looked closely, you couldn't see there was hair under there at all, and there was certainly no way to tell if it was two different people's hair.

The brooch itself was not in particularly good shape either. Some of the tiny pearls were pitted and crumbling, and in the innermost ring, one was an entirely different color.

I certainly didn't see any numbers written down anywhere on the pin. Ugh, how was I supposed to figure this out?

"Three orbits," I murmured. "Three numbers . . . what if the numbers aren't written down? What if we're supposed to count them ourselves?"

Gus looked at me, intrigued.

"Look at this. The first, innermost ring has nineteen regular pearls, and then this one weird silver one."

"So, twenty."

"And the next ring has—" I counted them up "—thirty-nine."

"And the outermost one has forty-five," Gus finished. "Twenty, thirty-nine, forty-five. Does that mean anything to you, Poe expert?"

"Not at all."

"Hello!" said an adult's voice behind us. We turned to see a woman wearing a staff lanyard standing a few feet away. "Are you the two kids who were asking about the special collections?"

"Yes, ma'am," Gus said.

"I'm sorry we can't let you handle the artifacts," she said by way of apology. "They're so rare and fragile. We only take them out for special exhibits like this one. But I thought you might like to visit our Poe room while you're here."

Gus and I exchanged glances. Honestly, we were only here for the brooch. I had enough of Poe-themed rooms in my life.

"We'd love to, ma'am," Gus said quickly, like he noticed my reluctance. "And maybe you can answer some questions for us on the way?"

I noticed his accent got heavier when he turned on the charm.

I took one more look at the little pearl brooch. I wished I really were psychic. I wished I could just look at that brooch and know that Poe's hands had been on it. If his ghost appeared when I held his journal, would he pop out the moment I touched that brooch?

The librarian took us down the hall while Gus peppered her with questions.

"How do we know that hair is actually Poe's?" He was asking the librarian. "Did they do genetic analysis on it or something?"

"You know, I don't know," she replied. "It's part of the collection, though, so I assume it's all been verified. Most of the items in our collection were donated either by descendants of the Poe family or collectors who spent their lives researching the poet."

"Descendants of the Poe family!" Gus exclaimed, as if it were the wildest thing he'd ever heard. "Ellen, did you hear that?"

"Yep," I said, unamused.

The librarian unlocked the door and ushered us inside. "This is the Poe room, which was first dedicated ninety years ago, on his birthday, January 19."

The room itself was very nice—dark, paneled wood, with a purple carpet and long tables. Purple-upholstered armchairs and sofas furnished the room, and there were books lining the built-in shelves. Tall windows were flanked by long curtains, and at one end of the room there was a fireplace over which stood a silver clock and a large portrait of you-know-who himself.

Hey there, Eddy.

It was a beautiful room, don't get me wrong. And one that Poe himself probably would have liked, despite its absence of red velvet furnishings and octagonal marble tables. I bet the Poe who was freezing and starving and selling his most famous poem for nine bucks would be amazed that there was an entire room in this beautiful building dedicated to him.

"What is this room for?" Gus was asking the librarian politely.

"It's just a meeting space. Any library patron can reserve it for free on our website. It gets really busy around this time because of the anniversary of his death coming up and the Poe festival. We've got a group meeting here in an hour, but you guys can look around if you want to."

And then she just left us there.

"Well, that got us nowhere," I said. I started toward the bookshelves, but the books didn't seem to be rare or anything. They were mostly books about Poe—collections of his work, biographies, analyses, and even novels.

Gus sprawled on a couch. "I think this city is Poe-obsessed."

"You just put that together?" I teased. "We call our football team the *Ravens,* for heaven's sake." I walked toward the fireplace.

"They dedicated the room on his birthday," Gus echoed, mockingly. "They throw a festival every year on his death . . . I don't think I know the birthday of any other poet."

"*Their date divine,*" I blurted.

"What?" he said.

"From the poem. *Three numbers which—their date divine . . .*" My heart raced. "Remember I said Helen Whitman and Poe thought they were soulmates because they had the same birthday? There weren't twenty pearls on that first ring on the brooch. There was one silver one and nineteen white ones. One, nineteen. January 19!"

"Okay, but what about the two other rings?" Gus asked. "What do thirty-nine and forty-five mean?"

"1845 was when they first saw each other out walking," I said, "but they didn't get to know each other until later. Poe wrote a poem about it when they finally did meet." But that didn't seem right, and it didn't explain thirty-nine either. His first volume of poetry had been published in 1839, but no one really cared about that.

I kept walking around the room. Weirdly, despite the family obsession with Poe, I'd never actually been inside this room. Or maybe that was the reason. Dad and I loved coming to the library for books and programs. It was an escape from the all-Poe-all-the-time atmosphere of Raven's Rest. Why leave one Poe-themed place only to go sit in another?

I took a closer look at the portrait of Poe above the fireplace. Here, he stood in a black coat and cravat against a brown background. He looked distinguished and wise. He even had some color on his cheeks.

It wasn't a print like the portraits in Raven's Rest. This one was a real oil painting, and the image itself was familiar. This Poe, ironically, looked the most like the Eddy I knew—the one who popped up every time I took out his journal. Of course, tons of people had painted Poe over the years, mostly using the few daguerreotype photographs as references. If this painting had a reference, I'd guess it was most likely the Whitman daguerreotype, which was one of two made in Rhode Island for our girl Helen Whitman.

For someone who had dumped Poe, she sure ended up with a lot of his stuff.

"How old was Poe when he died?" Gus asked from the sofa behind me.

"Forty." I stood on tiptoe to see if the artist had signed the painting or dated it.

"So, in December of 1848, he still would have been thirty-nine."

I paused. "That's right."

"So, January 19 for their birthday, 1845 for when they first saw each other, thirty-nine for how old he was?" Gus said.

I thought about it. "Or January 19 for their shared birthday, thirty-nine for him, and forty-five for her, because she was six years older?"

"That makes more sense," Gus said. "Since it fits into the soulmate part of the poem. How they were intertwined."

"If she really was his soulmate," I said. "They did break up before they got married."

"At least she was the right age for him this time," Gus said.

He could say that again. Six years wasn't too far apart for a couple in their forties, and Helen had even been the older one.

"So now what?"

I had no idea. And I also wasn't getting anywhere with this painting. It didn't seem to be signed or dated. It was probably just something someone had painted for the room, way back in the 1930s. It sat in a pretty gold frame, and when I lowered myself back down, I thought I saw a lump stuck to its underside.

Stay classy, Baltimore. Even in a room this nice, someone saw fit to shove gum under the picture frame. I looked closer. Except it wasn't actually a lump. More like a cylinder.

"Hey, Gus?"

"Yeah?"

"You're taller than me. Come take a look at this."

Gus ambled over and leaned in close. "What are we looking at?" he whispered, practically in my ear.

"That thing, under the frame. What is that?"

"I don't know, the security transponder?"

"This isn't a museum," I said. "They put all the valuable stuff behind glass. Besides, it looks like it's built into the frame of the painting."

I pulled out my phone and turned on the flashlight, aiming the beam behind the frame.

Three tiny black numbers jumped out at me. *1-1-9*.

Of course. It was just the date of the dedication.

I turned to look at Gus, who was still standing entirely too close. Closer to me than he'd been since the first day we met, when we'd banged into each other. Closer than we stood, even in my dreams, when I didn't want to be anywhere near his ghoulish face.

In real life, his face was actually quite nice, and I didn't really mind standing close to him at all. In fact, I very much liked it.

He was looking at me in wonder. I don't think any boy had ever looked at me with that expression before.

"Ellen," he said softly,

"Yeah?" I leaned in a little.

"It's a combination lock."

It is nearly a mon

requesting an in

, I placed it (

swered letters". Thi

seeming discourtesy

answer,

I have now to

you at any tim

adway. You will

the morning befor

Very Respy.

Yr. O

CHAPTER 14

Memento Mori

WAIT, WHAT? MY GAZE SHOT BACK TO THE underside of the frame. In the flashlight's glare, I could see tiny little seams alongside the numbers. It was definitely a tumbler under there—a little three-wheel combination lock, gilded in gold like the rest of the frame, with black printed numbers.

I'd never seen anything like that on a picture frame, and I'd been forced to hang many down in Aunt Marie's coffee shop. "Maybe it's just a counter. So the frame makers could set whatever date they wanted?" But wouldn't it be easier to just print the date on the frame?

"Yeah," Gus said. "Maybe." But he didn't sound convinced either. His hand strayed up toward the frame.

"There are a thousand combinations of a three-wheel lock," I told him.

"How do you know that?" he whispered to me.

"Because it's math," I said. "I may not have gotten the poetry gene, but I understand math."

"Okay, then, genius, if it's not 1-1-9 that opens this lock, what do you suggest?"

"1-0-7?" I said. "That was his death day."

Gus looked at me, worrying his bottom lip between his teeth. "If I get arrested for touching this, will you bail me out?"

"Are you kidding? You're the one with the money, remember?"

"Oh yeah," he said, and the easy smile was back on his face. "Right."

He reached up and slowly turned the numbers to 1-0-7.

Nothing happened.

Okay, fine. That was probably too easy, anyway. Because Gus was right. The people in this town were completely obsessed with Poe's birthday and death day. Maybe not as obsessed as my family, but they knew them.

What other important days existed in Poe's life? I scoured my memory and realized that my Reynolds early childhood education gave me plenty to choose from. He was married on May 16. 5-1-6? Virginia died on January 30. 1-3-0? "The Raven" was published January 29. 1-2-9?

There were a thousand possible combinations. We could be here all day.

"The digits are zero through nine," Gus said. "So we can't actually try twenty, thirty-nine, and forty-five."

"They wouldn't work anyway," I said. "Since no one but us has read the poem. No one but us knows that those numbers were meaningful to Poe."

Although, that wasn't actually true, was it? Poe knew the poem, but Sarah Helen Whitman must have too. Whatever secret numbers he was talking about was a secret the two of them shared.

Whitman had lived a long time after Poe's death, and she spent the rest of her life propping up his legacy to anyone who would listen. Maybe other people knew what these numbers were as well.

I thought for a moment. What was it, exactly, that the poem had said?

Three numbers which—their date divine—
A product sacred in our view . . .

Sacred numbers, huh? I wasn't very religious, and I didn't think Poe had been, either. What numbers were sacred? Three, like the trinity? Twelve, like the apostles? Or maybe he just meant sacred to himself and Helen Whitman. If only I was better at understanding poetry. Though, for a writer, Poe seemed to like math just as much as I did. What other poet wrote about multiplication problems in his poems?

The product of twenty, thirty-nine, and forty-five was going to be a very big number, not one with three digits. But if Poe and Whitman were focused on the date they were both born on—*their date divine*—maybe it wasn't about their ages, but about the difference between the dates?

Like Gus said, maybe Poe liked the fact that he was actually dating someone an appropriate age. One six years older than him.

"Try 1-2-0," I blurted.

"Why?" he asked as he spun the wheels.

I hardly knew. "Because the product of twenty and six years apart may just be . . ." What else was a sacred number than something that combined a little bit of poetry and a little bit of math? ". . . a cosmic key."

As the last digit slipped into place, the tumbler opened and a small, sharp object fell out and plummeted toward our heads.

Two things happened very quickly. Gus's arm shot out to shove me out of the way, while I lunged forward, trying to catch the thing before it smashed on the marble surface of the fireplace hearth.

This move succeeded in saving me from blindness, but it did mean that the thing, whatever it was, stuck me hard in the heel of my palm.

"Ow!" I cried, fumbling to catch it before it continued its descent. My hands closed around the item, and I immediately recognized it for what it was—a pen.

An old-timey fountain pen, with a rusty metallic nib and a long, brown wooden handle.

Speechless, I backed away from the fireplace, staring down at the treasure. I never expected that code to actually *work*. It was so random! A literal one-in-a-thousand chance.

Maybe I was psychic after all.

Gus seemed to have it together better than me. Out of the corner of my eye, I saw him shove the tumblers back into their previous place and reset the lock.

I turned the pen over in my hands. Along one end was engraved in tiny, spidery script:

E. A. Poe, 1875

"What is it?" Gus asked.

"It's . . . a fountain pen."

"Like . . . *Poe's* fountain pen?"

I shook my head. "It has his name on it, but the date is 1875. That was decades after he died. It couldn't have been his."

"Okay." Gus looked around, as if on the lookout for anyone else who might have been lurking in the room all this time. "Put it away, we'll figure it out later."

"Put it *back,* you mean." I offered it to him.

He shoved it back at me. "No, put it *away.* In your pocket, in your bag. Down your shirt, I don't care."

"That's stealing!"

"Stealing is when you take something that belongs to someone else," Gus pointed out. "No one at the library knows that this was here."

"I'm pretty sure that's not how that works," I argued. "Besides, what makes you think no one knows about this pen?"

"Because if they did," he whispered, drawing close as if to shield the pen from sight, "it would be behind a glass case with all the other artifacts." He was still scanning the room.

"That's where it *should* be," I whispered at him. "And what are you doing? There's no one here but us."

"I'm looking for the cameras, you idiot."

Oh, right. Cameras. Of course there were cameras. "It's too late now," I said. "They must have seen us touching the painting. The only thing we can do is tell the librarian what we found and hope we get out of here without getting arrested."

"They won't arrest us," Gus scoffed. "The most that will happen is we'll get kicked out."

Kicked out of the Pratt? Would that mean I lost my library card privileges too? "Look, maybe you never get in trouble for the things you do, but we don't all have that magical ability."

"What's that supposed to mean?"

I rolled my eyes. "I haven't seen you follow the dress code even once."

Gus blinked at me in sheer disgust. "You want to talk about the *dress code* right now?"

Just then, I heard the sound of the door opening and, out of pure instinct, I whipped my hands behind my back.

It was the special collections librarian. "Did you two get what you need? I'm sorry, but we've got to clear the room now for the folks who reserved it."

"We got what we needed, thanks," Gus said, which I thought was basically tempting fate.

But if she'd seen what we were up to on the security camera, wouldn't she have said something else to us?

"All right." She smiled at us. "And if there's something from the special collection you're interested in seeing, just let me know. You can make an appointment. Though that brooch you were after is far too delicate, we have other items that we can arrange viewings for. Clippings from newspapers where Poe published his writing, old letters, even some drafts of his actual manuscripts." She held out a card to me.

Gus swooped in and took it so I didn't have to move my hands. "Thank you—" he checked the card. "Ms. Rice."

We shuffled past her as quickly as possible as I palmed the pen, and when she left us in the hall, I slipped it into my blazer pocket.

Then, we made our way in that quick but orderly fashion they always went on about during fire drills. I cringed as we walked past the big security machines at the front gate, but it was like Gus had said. They didn't know the pen was there, so they had done nothing to protect it.

We hit the steps outside, and Gus held out his hand for a high five. "We did it."

I did not feel remotely cheerful. Technically, I was a thief. No—*actually,* I was a thief.

No matter what Gus said about it.

❁ ❁ ❁

Gus didn't bother with the bus again. He ordered us a ride from an app on his phone, and I sat in stunned silence during the ten-minute drive back down to Fells Point while he regaled me with fun factoids he looked up on his phone about the history of both combination locks and fountain pens.

Very little sunk in, as I was too busy imagining the rest of my life behind bars. I kept looking out the window of the car, bracing myself for the sight of flashing blue lights and the sound of sirens.

Fountain pens, apparently, were invented in the nineteenth century, but Poe probably didn't have one, especially if he was as broke as I was always telling Gus. Combination locks, on the other hand, were way older, and the design apparently hadn't been improved upon much over the ages.

“Weird to think of it, isn’t it?” Gus asked. “Poe would have probably been able to use this lock just the same as we did.”

“News flash,” I replied. “He also used doorknobs and forks like we do too.” It wasn’t like the 1840s were ancient history. And yet, there were all kinds of modern inventions that shocked the ghost who lived in my desk drawer.

The fountain pen was currently burning a hole in my pocket, and my mind whirled with the impossibility of it all. The poem, the brooch, the code. None of it made sense. Why would an 1840s riddle about a piece of jewelry work on a lock hidden in a portrait nearly a hundred years later? Why would the pen say 1875, a date somewhere between those other two?

How had we found it at all?

Soon enough, we arrived in front of Raven’s Rest, and I prepared to get out with my purloined goods.

“See you in school tomorrow?” I asked Gus.

He nodded. “Say hi to your aunt for me. And—Ellen?”

“Yeah?” I paused halfway out the door.

He took a deep breath. “I hope you know I don’t think this is a fake anymore. It’s way too elaborate. It’s the most exciting thing that’s happened to me in my entire life.”

Oh yeah, Gus? Which one?

Upstairs in my room, I looked for a good place to stash the contraband. My still-unpacked suitcase, or maybe a drawer in the desk?

“What do you think, Chip?” I asked the stuffed *crow*.

Chip said nothing, but then I remembered I did have another friend I could summon into this room. One who could talk back.

I got out the journal.

Eddy appeared, but he didn't seem too happy about it. His mustachioed face wore a frown, and he stood by the window, staring glumly out at the dark gathering over the city.

"We went to the library today to see the brooch you gave Helen Whitman."

He turned to face me, his eyes wide in surprise. "It is not to be found!"

"Oh, it is," I said. "They have it at the library, under glass. It's such a precious object that they won't even allow people to touch it. You know why?"

Eddy shook his head.

"Because it's got your hair in it. Only think of that! Do you have any idea how much something like that is worth?" I pointed to the journal at the table. "Which means if I can prove this is yours too, then all my troubles are over."

"Never to suffer would never to have been blessed."

"I know you don't really feel that way." Poe wrote for money all the time. If he'd been rich—if he'd gotten an inheritance from the Allans instead of being disowned—he probably never would have written all the ghoulish horror stories he was so well-known for.

Eddy didn't seem to want to discuss that anymore. He walked over to the journal and reached out, as if to touch it, then looked up at me.

"You really solved it?" he asked.

"Yes—well, Gus and I did. Or we think we did. The brooch was designed to have meaning for you and Helen. Three magic numbers. Is that right?"

Eddy smiled. "I do not mean to say that they are not ingenious—but people think them more ingenious than they are."

"What people?" I asked him. "What other people even knew about it? Other than you and Helen, I mean. Because neither of you were alive in the 1930s, and yet there was a secret compartment in a portrait in the Poe Room at the library that opened to that code."

Poe just stood there, blinking at me, and I realized that he probably had no idea what I was talking about. A whole room devoted to him at a library? A secret compartment that opened with a code? Not even Mr. Cryptography himself could imagine that.

But I had no idea what else it could be. I had not found any evidence of the "Gift" poem among Poe's known works, and literally every note he'd ever scrawled in his life was available to be viewed online, from IOUs he wrote to all the people he borrowed money from to his enlistment papers in the army. Which had made me think that no one knew about this journal at all. No one knew the poem existed, and they didn't realize that the pearl brooch hadn't just been a postmortem receptacle for Poe's hair—it had actually been a gift from the poet himself.

So, then, how did the number code that Poe and Whitman had apparently shared only between them wind up opening a lock on a picture frame from nearly a century later? There were only three possibilities I could think of.

1. It was just a coincidence. A one-in-a-thousand chance.
2. The "Gift" poem was floating around out there somewhere.

3. The person who put that secret compartment in the frame knew about this journal. Maybe they were even a Reynolds.

After all, there were more than a hundred years of Edgar Allan Poe superfans living right in this house. I couldn't have been the only one to know about this journal's existence. And maybe other people knew the code too.

Now, I addressed Eddy. "The code led to a message, which led to a treasure, just like in one of your stories." I reached into the pocket of my blazer, pulled out the fountain pen, and laid it on the desk. "It led to this."

The effect was nearly instantaneous. Eddy's face turned into a mask of horror. He wheeled back from the desk, nearly trembling, his hands pressed to his face in utter terror.

"May God shield and deliver me!" he cried, in a voice of such abject fear that I quickly snatched the pen up again.

"It's a pen," I said to him. "It's just a pen." But when I held it out, he fled across the room, cowering on the other side of my four-poster bed.

I looked down at the object in my hand. It seemed . . . utterly innocent. And how could Eddy have even seen it before? It said 1875 on the handle, which was long after his death.

There was a knock on the door, and Aunt Marie stuck her head in. "Oh good, you're home. I was just about to freak out. Dinner's ready."

"I'll be right down," I said.

She shivered. "It's always so cold in here. Remind me to check the window weather stripping this weekend."

I didn't feel cold at all. Was her feeling of cold the way she experienced Eddy's presence, instead of seeing the ghost standing here with us?

Eddy hadn't moved. His hands covered his face, and he peeked out through his fingers with eyes so wide I could see the whites all the way around.

"Hey, quick question," I asked her. "I know Poe died in 1849, but was the date 1875 significant for any reason?"

Aunt Marie thought about it for a moment. "I believe that's the year they moved his remains to the memorial over at Westminster Hall. He was buried somewhere else on the grounds, but they raised a lot of money to put him and his wife and mother-in-law in a prominent area with a big marble memorial."

I was familiar with the memorial. It was a major tourist attraction in this town.

"They moved him?"

"That's what they say. It wasn't easy, though. Your grandmother used to wonder if they really got the right body. Apparently, it was in a terrible state after all those years underground. They say the coffin splintered into pieces when they tried to get it out of the ground. His bones went everywhere. People were trying to grab souvenirs. There's supposedly a piece of the coffin made into a pen holder over at the Poe House Museum in West Baltimore, but I've never seen it."

"A pen holder?" I choked out.

Aunt Marie lifted her shoulders. "Yeah, well, Poe fans are a little macabre, aren't we?"

Make that *very* macabre.

Eddy practically flickered with distress as she described the horrors visited on his remains. It was almost like something out of one of his stories.

When she left, I glanced down at the little wooden pen in my hands. Was I holding a piece of the coffin of Edgar Allan Poe?

It is nearly a mon
, requesting an in
–, I placed it (g
swered letters". The
seeming discourtesy
answer,

I have now to
you at any time
adway. You will
the morning befor

very Respt.

W. C

CHAPTER 15

Clocks, Crabs, and Other Things with Faces

OVER THE NEXT FEW DAYS, I DEDICATED MYSELF to deciphering the text in the rest of the journal. The volume was slim, and only about two-thirds of the pages had any writing on them at all. Some were stained and moth-eaten, making their content nearly impossible to read, and others dropped the format of coded numbers entirely, opting instead for a cramped, spidery, old-fashioned handwriting that I also found nearly illegible. The numbers, at least, had been nice and orderly.

Did it say something about me that I actually preferred the parts that were in code?

Of what I could make out, the coded sections were snatches of verse. I was able to decipher a few bits of other poems, but there was nothing I recognized or could match up to anything I found online. Poe supposedly wrote "Annabel Lee" in 1849, but there were no lines from that work to be found in the journal.

This was not a point in favor of the journal's authenticity. Still, I tried to comfort myself with the idea that he maybe only used this journal for private poems, the ones he wrote to friends. Or lady friends. Except, one of his more famous poems to a woman, "For Annie," was also published the summer before he died. There was nothing in here that looked like that poem, though.

And nothing for a "Miss Reynolds" either.

I also tried to compare the handwriting on the pages to samples of Edgar Allan Poe's writing that I found online, but all old-fashioned handwriting looked the same level of weird and illegible to me. The little I could make out read like diary entries of some sort, but between the staining and the writing, I could barely understand it at all. Like this bit on the twenty-third page:

. . . here a tree, there a glimpse of water . . . of a chimney . . . fancying . . . ingenious illusions sometimes . . . vanishing . . .

Was that poetry? Did he want it to be? Sometimes, I doubted that I was the proper person for this job.

And then there were the drawings. There were four of the ghostly sketches in all, and each one was more horrible than the last.

The first one was the most like the dream I'd had of Gus—the strange, distorted face of a man, his eyes hollow pits. In another, however, the figure was a woman, though the drawing only showed her head and shoulders. Her hair streamed all around her head, as if underwater, and chains crisscrossed across her chest. The third drawing was even more gruesome, and the man's face was even more cruelly distorted, with his tongue sticking out and a rope wrapped around his neck. And then in the fourth there were several figures, each encased in wreaths of fire.

Though I'd never dreamed of any of these people, I felt like I had seen them before—or people just like them.

If you thought that Eddy would be the slightest bit of help in figuring any of this out, you'd be wrong. Ever since I brought the pen home, he wouldn't speak to me. He just sat in the farthest corner of the room staring in wide-eyed silence at whatever location I had secreted the pen away in before getting out his journal.

Eventually, out of desperation, I wrapped the pen up in a plastic bag and hid it downstairs in the living room, hoping that it would help calm him down.

Instead, Eddy seemed to stare at it through the floor.

Somehow, I'd trapped this poor ghost in his own personal reenactment of "The Tell-Tale Heart"—except instead of being obsessed with his murder victim, he was utterly transfixed by a fountain pen.

I decided that went down in the evidence column for this pen actually being made from his original coffin.

Only I didn't know how to prove any of these things. No historian was going to accept "A ghost told me so" as proper verification. And every day, I watched my aunt list things on eBay and write down paltry numbers in her little balance sheet. Every day, I watched the frown lines on her forehead grow deeper.

That one night at dinner, she'd seemed skeptical that the diary was anything more than just another Poe-themed bit of junk our ancestors had collected. "Even if we wanted to sell this," she'd said. "Where would we start? This isn't like listing old dishware on eBay."

For sale: one diary. In code. Comes with ghost and stolen pen.

Yeah, I could see her point. And I hadn't even told her about the ghost or the pen.

That was where things stood the following week, when Gus invited me to come back with him to his sister's house for dinner. Since it was open mic night at Raven's Rest, I accepted, if for no other reason than to spare myself from another evening spent trying to avoid the sound of excruciating spoken-word poetry floating up between the floorboards.

Plus, Gus said his sister's boyfriend was an art dealer. Maybe he could give me some tips.

Gus's sister, Madeline Davenport, lived in a huge house in Roland Park, a fancy neighborhood on the north side of the city. She and her boyfriend didn't have any kids, so I was honestly surprised by the size of the house when we pulled up. But then again, Aunt Marie used to live alone, and Raven's Rest had like five bedrooms.

I doubted that Madeline Davenport ever considered starting a bed-and-breakfast.

"What does your sister do for a living?" I asked Gus as we stood before the front door while Gus pressed his thumb against the electronic lock.

"Aside from complain?" he replied, ushering me inside.

The interior of Madeline's house was cold and serene, and though the Davenports appeared to possess as many antiques as Aunt Marie did, the scale of the house and the condition of all the furniture made it look more like a magazine spread than a secondhand store. I didn't know exactly what Poe had been thinking when he wrote about his theory of furniture, but I had a feeling he'd be more impressed by the decor of the Davenports than whatever my aunt had cobbled together back at Raven's Rest.

But Gus didn't seem as impressed as I was. He strode quickly through gorgeous, pristine spaces, got us snacks from the mammoth, pristine kitchen, and exited through the majestic glass doors onto an equally majestic back patio, where he sat us down at some wrought-iron tables and turned his face up toward the autumn-gold rays of the afternoon sun.

Once again, I was in the regulation Evergreen Prep uniform, and he was in a black hoodie and jeans. After more than a week of such outfits, I'd given up thinking that his proper clothes were just on backorder or something. Maybe he was in mourning because of his parents' deaths and so got a special dispensation from the school to wear black instead of his uniform.

Did people even go into mourning anymore? I'd obviously been spending too much time reading up on the Victorians in the last few days.

"She'll be home soon," Gus said. "Brace yourself."

"Why did you invite me over if you think it's going to be so awful?" I asked him.

"Oh, I didn't do it for you," he admitted. "Mads has wanted you to come over ever since we met."

"What, I'm your sacrificial offering to her?"

Gus straightened on the bench. "Why would you say that?"

I gave him a skeptical look. ". . . because I was joking? But now you have me worried."

"Oh," he said, completely unconvincingly. "Ha."

I poked him.

"Okay," he admitted. "You are . . . but it's not like *that*."

"I'm your sacrificial offering, but it's not like that," I repeated blankly. "Make it make sense, Gus."

He shrugged. "I just—my sister and I were never actually close before. She's my sister, but we barely ever spoke. She and my dad were estranged."

"Why?"

Gus made a face. "Probably because my mom was only a few years older than her."

"Ah."

"She and my dad had this huge fight when he got married again, and she moved away to Baltimore. And to tell the truth, before their death, I only met her twice my whole life."

"Weird," I said. "That kind of happened to Poe too. After Mrs. Allan died and Mr. Allan remarried, he left Virginia and went to live in Baltimore with his more distant relatives. Mr. Allan cut him off completely."

"Well, I don't know if my dad cut her off, but it wouldn't have mattered anyway because her mom was loaded too, and Madeline had already inherited—" he gestured around him "—all this."

Must be nice.

"So . . . it's weird to be living here now. I don't know her well, and she didn't really intend on getting stuck with some kid, so I'm trying to show her that I'm adjusting to this life fine. That I'm a normal kid with normal friends, and I don't need to be sent off to boarding school or whatever."

I smiled at him. "Aww, you think I'm *normal*."

"I'm trying to *show* her that," he clarified. "I never said it was true."

Still, I saw where he was coming from. Aunt Marie never expected to have to take care of me either, and I was working my butt off to make sure it wasn't harder on her than it had to be. Little things, you know? Like not telling her I was being haunted by the ghost of a dead poet or showing her the antiques I'd been stealing from local libraries.

After our snack, Gus gave me a quick tour of the house, which included a home gym, a sauna, a tennis court, a billiards room, a greenhouse, a wine cellar, and an actual suit of armor.

"That's Rod's," he said, referring to Madeline's boyfriend. "I don't know if he'll be around tonight."

I frowned. I hoped Rod made it. Gus knew I was trying to get verification of the objects we'd gathered, and though I'd been after him to ask his sister's boyfriend about what the proper process was, he seemed reluctant to approach him.

"Rod's going to ask a lot of questions about where it all came from," he warned me.

Anyone was going to ask questions. But I was running out of time. "I'll keep it vague. I just want to know what kind of process we'd be looking at. Like, do we need a lab or something to verify our finds?"

"Well, Rod doesn't have a lab," Gus said. "But he does have four sheiks on speed dial."

Soon enough, Madeline herself arrived, laden with fragrant tote bags filled with fancy restaurant takeout. I wasn't sure what I was expecting from Madeline Davenport, but the tiny, birdlike figure of Gus's sister was not it. I think I was expecting tall and lanky, like Gus, but she didn't even reach his shoulder. She was the kind of thin that came from macrobiotic diets and personal trainers and plastic surgeons, and her dark hair was scraped into a severe bun at the crown of her head.

"August," she instructed her brother, "be a darling and plate these for us while I show our guest into the dining room."

August? I mouthed at him. He shrugged.

The Davenport dining room, I learned, was not all that different from the one at Raven's Rest. It, too, was very dark, with heavy, carved wooden tables and chairs, an ornate chandelier that seemed to give off very little light, and an enormous grandfather clock against one wall—though this one was very much not broken. I could hear it ticking away.

How come all these grown-ups wanted to eat their dinners in the dark? If I ever got a dining room of my own, I'd have windows everywhere and enough light to actually see my food.

"It's so delightful to have guests," Madeline was saying as she lit a pair of long, tapered candles in the center of the table. "We've been basically alone for the last few months, regrouping after such a terrible tragedy."

"I'm so sorry for your loss," I said.

"Thank you, dear." Madeline's long eyelashes fluttered as she lowered her eyes. "It was . . . a terrible accident. I don't know if I'll ever be able to make sense of it. But at least August's life was saved."

Soon enough, Gus brought out dinner, which appeared at first glance to be the red, shiny carapace of a cooked blue crab, mysteriously deprived of its legs, sitting on a bed of greens. Now, I'm a born and bred Baltimorean, and I've never had crabs served like that. But when I lifted the edge of the crab with my fork, I saw there was, thankfully, a large broiled crab cake concealed underneath.

I guess that's how they did it at the kinds of restaurants where they didn't serve things on picnic tables.

"I hope you like crab," Madeline said to me. "August said you're from here."

"Yes, ma'am," I replied. "I love crabs."

"I think August is still learning to appreciate them." She smiled patronizingly at her brother.

He gingerly flipped the crab shell off the cake underneath with the very edge of his fork, like it was on fire. "I like them fine. I'm just not used to eating things with faces."

"All animals have faces, dear," Madeline replied and sipped her wine.

"Not oysters," he said. "Not clams."

"You don't like those either."

Hey, at least this was a crab cake. Imagine if she'd been asking him to pick his own meat. I took a bite, and though the presentation was a little bizarre, it was obvious the chef knew what he was doing.

It was delicious. I hadn't had actual crab cake in months. Crab wasn't exactly in the Raven's Rest budget.

"So, August tells me you live in Fells Point, and that your family has been there for generations," Madeline said.

"Yes."

"Have you tracked your genealogy at all?"

I shot him a look across the table. He was carefully eating around the remains of the crab.

"Well, some, but—"

"You should. You may be eligible to join the Daughters of the American Revolution. All kinds of supporters of the patriot cause can join—not just soldiers or signers of the Declaration of Independence."

If we were eligible, it would be through Poe, whose grandfather had invested his entire fortune in the Revolutionary cause. But Aunt Marie said that people in the family had tried to prove it with no luck.

Of course, that was before the journal . . .

"I—I don't think we have that kind of documentation," I said again.

"Pity," said Madeline. "My mother was a member, and I am too."

"It's a pity our family is *also* eligible to join the United Daughters of the Confederacy, isn't it?" Gus added meaningfully and took a big bite of his crab.

My eyes widened.

"Well," said Madeline. "I didn't join *that* one."

Gus grunted.

"Family history can be so complicated!" I blurted. "My dad and I always thought it was maybe better not to delve too deeply into all that stuff. It can turn into an obsession."

"You don't want to feel a deeper connection to where you came from?" Madeline asked.

"I feel pretty connected already," I said. "Maybe a little *too* connected, you know? Living in the house that's been in my family for over a century." How quickly could I eat this crab and get out of here?

"Imagine that." Madeline's smile did not waver. Honestly, it was beginning to freak me out. "Do you think it's that sense of history that gives you your spiritual power?"

The lump of crab I was attempting to swallow got lost on its way down my throat. "My—what?"

"August tells me you have dreams of the dead. Is your home haunted?"

"I—" I glared at Gus, who was absolutely refusing to meet my eyes. Well, he'd warned me his sister was a sucker for psychics. "That's what my family says."

"But have *you* had encounters with beings from beyond this realm?"

Sure. Who hadn't? "Well . . ." *Edgar Allan Poe likes to hang out in my bedroom.* But it's not like I could say *that*.

"You have!" she exclaimed, clapping her hands together with delight.

"I'm—" I glanced at Gus for help, and when I saw the guilty expression on his face, I put it together.

Back when he'd thought it was all fake, he'd been afraid of me angling to meet his sister. But now that even he was convinced it was real . . .

I had it right. I was a sacrificial offering.

It is nearly a mon
requesting an in
, I placed it (
swered letters". The
seeming discourtesy
answer.

I have now to
you at any time
adway. You will
the morning before

Very Resp.

W. C

CHAPTER 16
The Talking Board

AS SOON AS DINNER WAS OVER, MADELINE RAN OFF to fetch something called a "talking board" while Gus and I cleaned up the remains of the crabs.

Well, the remains of his. I'd practically licked the plate clean.

"How," I asked him in the kitchen, "is talking about my dreams about dead people and my supposedly haunted house supposed to convince your sister that you're making normal friends?"

"Not everyone has the same definition of normal," he said. "She loves that you see ghosts. It's the cheapest psychic she's met in months."

"I'm not psychic!" I insisted to him.

"Neither were the other ones!" He shot back.

I crossed my arms over my chest. "Well, I don't want to play along. I want to go home." Did buses even come all the way out here, or was I dependent on Madeline driving me?

"Oh, please, Ellen," Gus said, and honestly, he sounded a little desperate. "Tell her some ghost stories. I know you have plenty. Save me this month from the con artists."

If only I were a con artist. We could actually use some cash. "You should have had my aunt here. She's the one who does tarot readings on the side." The way she basically did everything in her life on the side—baking, music, running a B&B.

"She doesn't want tarot," Gus said. "She wants ghosts."

"Was she like this before your dad died?"

"I told you, I didn't know her well then. Come on," he wheedled. "Just tell her about the ghost dreams, the way you told me last week. I'll give you all the leftover crab cakes."

"Wait," I said. "There are more crab cakes?"

I hate to admit it, but I'm too much of a Marylander to pass on free seafood.

So that's how I found myself seated once more in the Davenports' dimly lit dining room, while Madeline set out a large plank of glossy wood covered in glittering symbols.

"Obviously, you know how a Ouija board works," she said to me.

I did, having attended my fair share of slumber parties in my life. You know, back when I had friends. But I'd never seen one that looked anything like this.

This was not a cardboard board game with a plastic viewing planchette. Instead, it was heavy and large, with letters printed in glowing, metallic ink in a strange zigzag pattern. There was a diamond-shaped metal piece that slid over the surface of the "talking board," and as it paused on different colors, they lit up.

It was a pretty cool Ouija board. Oracle board. Talking board. Whatever.

"Did you know that Ouija boards were invented right here in Baltimore?" Madeline said. She turned off all the lights so the room was lit only by the candles. "I had such a hard time tracking down one of the originals, but I think it will have far more spiritual power than some children's toy. This one is from the 1930s."

I wondered if she'd gotten it in an online auction, from some other desperate family selling off the contents of their basement.

"You know, ma'am," I tried, "I don't think ghosts are actually interested in devices like this. From what I've—" *experienced myself* "—heard, you don't need séances or accessories. Either they show up and talk to you, or they don't."

And sometimes they did even if you didn't want them to. In iambic pentameter too.

"It's possible you're uniquely talented in that way," Madeline said to me, that placid smile looking a bit tight around the edges. "We can't all be so lucky."

Sure. Lucky.

In the darkness, we all placed our hands on the planchette. And you know, it was funny, but I was suddenly wildly curious to know what Eddy would think of this whole procedure. How would the king of the ghoulish horror story take this ham-fisted approach to talking to the dead? He'd acted both angry and fascinated by my computer decryption program. I wonder what he'd make of this shimmering, electric means of contacting spirits from the beyond.

“We seek to commune with the voices of those who have departed this life on Earth,” intoned Madeline. Oh, so she was getting right to it. “Tonight, we have brought a special, new friend of August’s—a soul who can peer through the veil herself and tell of the spectacular visions which await us in the realms beyond.”

First of all, they were *not* spectacular. Not one of the dead people I’d seen in my dreams seemed happy to be there. And Eddy never seemed to want to talk about death at all. He’d been horrified by the sight of what was maybe a piece of his own coffin.

Secondly, describing me as “peering through the veil” made me feel a bit like a Peeping Tom.

Across the table, my eyes met Gus’s. He looked bored.

Slowly, beneath our fingertips, the planchette began to move in lazy circles.

“Who visits us this night?” Madeline asked the air.

The planchette kept moving in circles.

“Fun fact,” said Gus, “scientists think that it’s really us answering questions on a board like this. That we’re subconsciously moving the planchette and predicting the answers that we think the rest of the people want to hear.”

He gave me a look across the table.

I shook my head slightly. *Tell her about your ghost dreams,* he’d said in the kitchen. Did he want *me* to push the planchette?

Beneath our fingers, the board stopped on a letter, which sparked in the darkness.

E

It moved again.

D

Madeline called out each of the letters in turn.

Wait, *was* I doing this? I willed my fingers to stop. I closed my eyes.

The planchette jerked back and forth.

"Ed?" Madeline called out.

I opened my eyes in time to see the planchette roll to *Yes*.

She looked at me. "Ed was our father's name."

"It was *not*," Gus insisted. "No one ever called him Ed."

"My *mother* did," she snapped back.

The siblings stared daggers at each other. I did not think this was a good time to point out that the ghost I regularly spoke to also went by a variation of that name.

The planchette began moving again. The letters sparked up in the darkness.

W-A-R

I decided Poe would like this. It would appeal to the code-making side of him. He died before the whole séance movement got started, but occasionally he'd write stories about speaking to the dead. In one story, a dying man was hypnotized and held conversations with people. In another, they reanimated a mummy like it was Frankenstein and had a chat with him.

N-I-N-G

"Warning," said Madeline.

D-A-N-G-E-R

"Danger," she reported, as if neither Gus nor I were capable of reading the letters ourselves.

Y-O-U-A-R-E-N-O-T-S-A-F-E-W-H-E-R-E-Y-O-U-A-R-E

The planchette kept moving, faster and faster, as if now the spirit had got the hang of pushing it around.

E-V-I-L-I-S-C-O-M-I-N-G

The lights on the board flashed and flickered. Across from me, I watched them light up Gus's face from below, making him look pale and gaunt in the gloom.

Just like the ghostly version of him in my dreams.

I gasped and pulled my hands off the planchette.

The candles both went out, plunging the room into complete darkness.

"Ellen!" Gus cried. "Are you okay?" He came around the table, his face in deep shadow, and I shot out of my chair and stumbled backward.

Weeks of the same horrid dream came rushing back on me all at once. The stifling darkness, the reaching hands, the twisted, unearthly faces . . . and then they were there. They were all there. It wasn't the real Gus coming toward me through the shadows, it was his cursed spirit.

"Stay away from me!" I shouted, backing up so fast I tripped over my feet. I stumbled against what I thought was the wall, but I felt it give beneath my weight. As I hit the floor, there was an enormous, eardrum-shattering crash.

All of a sudden, all the lights came on. "What's going on in here?" came a man's voice.

I was sprawled across the floor and—next to me—lay the remains of the grandfather clock. It was smashed to pieces on the hardwood floor. It's kind of a miracle it didn't crush me.

"Oh, Rod!" Madeline cried and ran over to him.

The man standing in the threshold was nearly my father's age, but he was dressed in a perfectly tailored business suit and had a swoop of dark hair gelled to fall just so over his head, with shaved sides. His shoes, closest to me, were very shiny. His face, much farther away, was very grim.

Before Madeline reached him, Rod put out his hand. "Madeline, you're not holding another séance, are you?"

"We took out the talking board," she explained. "And you'll never guess—it really worked."

"Of course it worked. We're unconsciously pushing it." Gus knelt at my side. "Are you okay? What happened? You freaked out."

"I'm sorry. I'm so sorry." Oh God, the clock. It must be worth thousands!

I was so dead.

"Who is this?" Rod asked.

"Ellen Reynolds. She's a friend from school."

"She's a psychic, Rod," Madeline cooed. "She's been dreaming of my father."

"Of course she has," he said, his eyes narrowed at me. "They always do."

Gus took my hands in his and pulled me to my feet. "Careful, there's glass."

"I'm fine."

He squeezed my hands, then only dropped the one. But even Gus's very solid and very much alive presence was doing nothing to quell my anxiety. The memory of the vision loomed as large as if I'd just woken up from the nightmare again. Those things—those frightening things—had appeared in front of my waking eyes.

And now I had a whole different nightmare to deal with.

"Do you have any idea how much that clock was worth, young lady?" Rod spat at me.

"It's insured," Gus said, moving to stand between us. He looked at his sister for confirmation. "Right?"

"Leave her alone, Rod," said Madeline.

He turned to her. "I thought we talked about this. No more of these dime-store scam artists. They're just trying to take you for everything you're worth. We have to start being more careful."

"But I feel like my father is trying to contact me!" she insisted. "I can feel it. And this girl is not like the others. She didn't cost us anything."

"She just broke a ten-thousand-dollar clock."

I felt like I was about to throw up a whole crab cake. Ten thousand dollars?

"If I could just talk to him again, I know I could understand what happened."

"He ignored you when he was alive," Rod said, "What makes you think he'd want to talk to you now? You're better off without him, trust me."

Only I was standing close enough to Gus to hear his small, sharp intake of breath.

I tugged on his hand. "Hey, uh, let's go outside."

He nodded and led me through the kitchen and out onto the front walk. The night had turned dim and cool, but the driveway landscape of Madeline's house had an artful lighting design, with bright spotlights shining up beneath every manicured bush and tree. I bet the nesting birds hated it, but I was grateful for the illumination.

Not that lights had ever kept ghosts away. Still, Eddy had always been different than the monsters in my dreams. And those things had always stayed in my dreams . . . until now.

I was also thankful for the cool night air, and we both stood for several long moments, doing nothing but breathing and listening to the final trill of autumn insects.

My heartbeat started slowing to a regular pace.

I looked back at the house, dark and still. From out here, it didn't look like there were any lights or life inside at all.

I thought about Gus returning to this place, day after day, night after night. Not even Raven's Rest felt as haunted to me as this home did. It was huge, it was fancy, and it was cold and lifeless too.

Poe once wrote a story—one of his most famous—called "The Fall of the House of Usher." In it, a man goes to visit a friend and his friend's sister at their crumbling mansion, and terrible things befall everyone inside. Death had come for that family—for the very house they lived in—and nothing could stop it.

I shivered and looked at Gus. He'd already been through so much—losing his parents, even dying himself for a few minutes. And now he practically lived with strangers. I understood now why he kept getting on the bus with me, why he wanted me to come over. I wouldn't want to be here alone with his sister either.

And especially not his sister's insufferable boyfriend.

"I guess tonight is not a good time to ask him about the pen or the journal, huh?" I said, half joking.

But Gus had dropped all pretense at humor. "Never would be a good time, but now is definitely one of the worst ones. You should probably just go home." He took out his phone and began punching in a request for a ride service.

He was always making jokes, even about the most horrible things in his life. Was this the real boy, under the sly grin and cool disregard for all the rules? He buzzed with some kind of dark energy, like those wires on the talking board, ready to let out a shower of sparks.

"I'm really sorry, Gus," I said softly.

"Not as sorry as I am." He shoved his hands in the pockets of his hoodie. "It's not usually like that, you know. The—uh—board."

That wasn't what I meant. I was sorry about the talking board, for sure, and also about the clock. But I was really sorry about Rod and Madeline, and the way they both spoke about Gus's father. I took a deep, shuddering breath. This boy had been through so much. And now the only family in the world he had left was forcing him to relive it every chance she got.

"What's it usually like?"

"Oh, you know. *We're at peace, sending you love, we're in a better place*—the usual. I guess that's what I get for telling you to give her a ghost story."

"Wait—you think *I* was doing that?"

"It certainly wasn't my father!" He ran a hand through his hair and strode a few steps away. "And I don't care what Madeline said. Edward was his middle name. No one called him Ed, not even her mother."

But what if it wasn't Ed at all? What if it was Eddy? The journal was locked away in my room, but what if it was me who was haunted? What if I really was a psychic, like Madeline thought?

What if those things I saw in Madeline's dining room tonight could come and get me, even in my waking hours?

Eddy was one thing. He never scared me. Those . . . creatures were something else entirely. I'd put up with an annoying ghost spouting poetry at me forever if it meant never seeing those horrible things again.

"If it was me, then it was subconscious, like you said," I told him.

But was it even possible to create entire sentences like that? Without realizing it? I had no idea my subconscious mind could spell so well. Whenever I'd played with Ouija boards before, at sleepover parties and stuff, I hadn't thought too hard about what was going on behind the scenes. Maybe we were unknowingly pushing the planchette. Or maybe we were contacting a ghost. It never seemed to matter much.

But this was different. It mattered a lot to Madeline . . . and maybe too much to Gus.

"*You are in danger. Evil is coming.* What was all that?" he asked me accusingly.

I bit my lip. The truth was, I had no idea. Whatever Gus had wanted from me tonight, he'd clearly gotten more than he bargained for. I didn't think I had anything to do with the message the talking board had sent, but then again, I was the only one in the room who had ever admitted to seeing dead people. Maybe I was to blame, after all?

And as scary as the words on the board had been, they were nothing compared to the knowledge that my nightmares could still come after me when I was awake.

CHAPTER 17
Family Curses

IT WASN'T UNTIL I WAS SITTING IN THE CAR, HALFWAY home to Raven's Rest, that I realized I'd forgotten the crab cakes in Gus's kitchen. All that, and I didn't even get extra seafood out of it.

Then again, if I wasn't held responsible for breaking that grandfather clock, I'd count myself lucky. How many crab cakes was that thing worth? A thousand?

The open mic night was still going strong on the ground floor, so I sneaked upstairs to my room, turning on every last light as I went. I took a shower, changed into my pajamas, and—even though I'd probably had enough of dead people to last me forever—I took the journal out of my desk drawer.

But Eddy did not appear.

I spun around my room. I checked behind the curtains. I looked under the bed.

"Eddy?"

Nothing.

How very curious.

I sat down on the bed and folded my legs up underneath me. Cattarina hopped up beside me and curled up on the purple coverlet. I scratched behind her ears and flipped through the journal again. Each time I saw a page with one of the drawings on it, a chill went down my spine. I dreaded closing my eyes tonight, dreaded seeing Gus's ghostly face.

Warning. Danger.

But the danger was over for Gus. He'd survived the terrible accident that took his parents' life. His living situation with his sister was not exactly great, but he didn't seem to have any other options. That I understood well.

But what if the warning wasn't for Gus at all? The board had identified the spirit talking through us as Ed.

I didn't need the ghost of Edgar Allan Poe telling me that I wasn't safe in my current situation. Aunt Marie had about half a dozen past-due notices that made it abundantly clear without the help of a Ouija board.

I turned the page where the fiery figures were sketched and heard the telltale crackle of the aged paper crumbling. My fingers froze on the paper.

I should be using gloves or something on this. I shouldn't be looking through it at all. I'd long ago photographed all the pages, in case they started disintegrating on me, and also so I could try increasing the contrast on the photos and making out words that had faded with time.

But with Eddy only coming out with the journal, I'd relied too much on its physical form. And now I was paying the price.

This time, when the page cracked, I saw that it had been stuck to another. With care, I tried to peel them apart, revealing scraps of writing heavily smeared and damaged by time.

Hardly more than one word out of every three was legible on the page. I tried to read it, but as always, I didn't get far.

. . . the papers this morning . . . street . . . all four . . . to a crisp in their beds . . . Sunday last at Temperance Hall . . . Dear God . . . did not want to believe . . . that I had known before . . . must not . . . it dulls the dreams, but bedevils . . . cannot escape . . . curse.

I was afraid to touch the journal again, so I took out my phone and carefully photographed the words. Gently closing it back up and placing it on the desk, I vowed not to touch it again without gloves on. If nothing else, I was probably ruining the market value.

Then I flipped through my photos of the journal pages until I found the one I was looking for, of the four figures covered in flames.

. . . to a crisp.

Burned to a crisp, maybe?

When I dreamed of Gus and his family, I saw them choking. And they'd suffocated—or a kind of suffocation. They'd died because they could not breathe. Maybe the drawings in this journal revealed other dreams about real-life deaths. Eddy had seen these figures dying in a fire—and they actually had.

Did Eddy have the same kind of dreams I did? Were these drawings in his journal the visions he'd seen every time he closed his eyes, and did they correspond to the real-life, horrific deaths of people from his time?

The Ouija board had been right. I was in danger. I was cursed, just like my famous ancestor.

My eyes began to burn with unshed tears. I didn't want to believe it. Edgar Allan Poe had been crazy. He'd been a drunk. But was this why? Was he just willing to do whatever it took to stop the nightmares?

In the months before Poe's death, he'd tried to stop drinking. He'd joined the Temperance Movement, which was like a nineteenth-century political party for recovering alcoholics and other people who thought alcohol should be banned.

Sunday last at Temperance Hall . . .

Poe had been trying to save himself by avoiding drinking. But maybe there was more to it than that. There'd been a reason he was drinking too much in the first place.

It dulls the dreams, but bedevils . . .

Bedevils what, Eddy? Every other aspect of your life? Your ability to hold a job? To keep friends? To separate reality from your horrible nightmares?

I didn't want to end up like Poe, insane and desperate, dead by forty. I didn't want to have pages and pages of nightmares to fill up a journal with.

In my hand, my phone began to ring, and when I saw the caller ID pop up, I nearly burst into tears with relief.

It was my father.

❁ ❁ ❁

Dad didn't call me often, ever since he'd started his new job. His hours were apparently long and irregular, and he never knew when he'd be available to talk. But I was so glad he could make it work tonight. I really needed a friendly ear. Aunt Marie was great and all, but it just wasn't the same.

"Daddy!" I cried into the phone.

"Hey, sweetie," he replied. "How are things?"

So awful, I can't even think straight. I'm having nothing but nightmares, we're about to lose the house, I'm being haunted by Edgar Allan Poe, I stole a priceless artifact from the Pratt, and I just destroyed a ten-thousand-dollar grandfather clock that belongs to a weirdo who thinks I'm psychic.

"Well," I began, "I'm definitely getting straight As in English class this quarter. We're studying Poe." I'd have to ease him into all the rest of it.

"That's great!" There was a lot of noise on the other end of the line, as if Dad was outside in public or something. Maybe he was still at the work site.

"How's work? When will the job be over? Do you think you'll be home by Thanksgiving?"

"Oh, more like Christmas," he said, so offhand I felt sick. "Or maybe the New Year."

"That long?"

"Well, construction, baby. It always takes longer than you think. Why, do you miss me?"

"*So* much. And I miss living in our own place." The New Year? Would Aunt Marie even be able to keep Raven's Rest that long?

"For sure. It's going to be great. In fact, I've got some great ideas for that. I want us to get more than just some other crummy apartment. You need a real house."

Right now, I'd settle for anything without a stuffed crow in it. "No, I don't. I just want you home."

"Some friends and I have a plan to go out to Vegas on our days off, make some real money."

My insides squeezed even harder. "Oh."

"And this won't be like last time either. I have perfected my system."

Dad thought he had a system for winning at cards. But here's the thing about gambling. If your system doesn't work, you lose everything. If your system *does* work, the casinos catch on and you still lose everything. I can't say whether Dad's system is for real, but we don't live in our own place anymore, and he's working construction across the country, so you tell me.

"Dad, no."

This was not the correct thing to say.

When he spoke again, his voice had a hard edge to it. "Listen, kiddo, it's my money. I know what I'm doing. With my new methodology it's totally foolproof—because if there's a flaw, I'll be able to catch it before too much is gone."

Like me, Dad's really good at math. And over the years, there have been plenty of mathematicians who have figured out tricks to win card games. Most of those guys end up banned from casinos. Sometimes, they end up in even bigger trouble. If that were Dad's problem, we'd at least get the benefit of his initial winnings.

But like all the other Reynolds family business ventures, his gambling career had yet to pay out.

"Besides, don't you see?" he said to me. "The construction job is taking forever. If I can get a big score now, it means I'll get home to you even sooner. You be on the lookout for a house you want. Something nice and big so we can get that dog you're always talking about."

Cattarina lifted her head and meowed at me in protest. But I didn't think she had to worry. That house and that dog seemed farther away than ever.

"And I know I'm on the right track. After all this time, I finally feel like I know what I'm doing. Don't you ever just have a feeling, honey?"

Sure. I had a feeling all the time. Mostly, it was dread.

❁ ❁ ❁

Much later, I wandered back downstairs for a snack and found Aunt Marie sitting in the kitchen, her elbow resting on the counter, her chin resting in her hand.

Eddy sat beside her in nearly the same pose.

"Ellen, you're up. I hope I didn't wake you!"

"No," I said. I doubted I'd sleep tonight, between the nightmares and—now—worrying about my father. School tomorrow promised to be a blast.

"Tonight was—" she sighed happily "—quite possibly the best open mic night we've ever had. The performers were on fire. It was . . . amazing."

“Really?” I poured myself a glass of water and sat down at the other end of the counter.

Aunt Marie gave the chair with Eddy in it a weird look, as if wondering why I wasn’t sitting closer.

“Yeah, I don’t know what it was. There was a real creative spirit in the room tonight.”

“A creative spirit.” I looked at Eddy, whose expression appeared both pained and blissful, if such a thing were possible.

He let out a great sigh, which looked especially funny on an entity who could not breathe. “Beauty of whatever kind, in its supreme development, invariably excites the sensitive soul to tears.”

“You can’t be serious,” I said to him. Poe was one of the harshest literary critics of his age. He hated everyone. He’d accused Longfellow of plagiarism. People called him the “Tomahawk Man” because he did such a hatchet job on every book he was given to review.

There was no way he liked the Raven’s Rest open mic night.

“Of course I am,” Aunt Marie exclaimed. “Look, I know you don’t think much of the people who come to these things, and Lord knows I do my best to be supportive of them, week after week. But tonight was different, honestly. There was an energy there.”

“I think you just need to get out more,” I said, still mainly to Poe. “You’ve been deprived.”

“Yes,” he agreed. “Was I left to perish of starvation in this subterranean world of darkness?”

Okay, no need to be dramatic. It was a desk drawer. And it couldn't have been any worse than however long he and the journal had spent in that crate.

When I had him alone again, I definitely planned to ask how it was that he was wandering around without the journal. I'd taken it as a given this past week that he only came out when I was handling it. If that wasn't actually the case, then we needed to set some new boundaries—particularly when it came to me doing normal things in my bedroom, like sleeping or changing my clothes.

Still, it's not like I begrudged him the chance to take in a little Baltimore nightlife. My first choice would not be an open mic night, but then again, I wasn't a world-famous poet.

Time for a change of subject. "Dad called," I told Aunt Marie.

She smiled. "How is he?"

I shrugged. "He says he and his friends are going to go to Vegas for the weekend to make a big score."

"Is that so?" Her tone was mild, but her smile turned tight around the corners. There's this thing that grown-ups do where they are too polite to tell you that your plan is complete nonsense, but they know it is anyway. Aunt Marie was doing that thing when it came to Dad's gambling. But that was okay. I already knew.

And I couldn't blame her if she was as upset as I was, inside. She didn't have the cash to support me and save Raven's Rest at the same time. And I hadn't even told her about the grandfather clock yet.

But how could I tell her now? She was so happy. She'd just had an actual successful event in her weird little art space. Maybe, for once in this family's miserable history, one of our business ventures could actually work out. How could I deny her that?

Enough was enough. I'd been sitting on two sources of serious income for too long now. The pen and the journal had to be worth some money. I just had to prove it.

Aunt Marie needed to keep Raven's Rest. And I needed to figure out how.

CHAPTER 18

Busted

GUS WAS NOT AT SCHOOL THE FOLLOWING DAY, and I wondered if he was skipping after getting about as much sleep as I did. Since I was too afraid of the nightmares that came whenever I shut my eyes, I pounded caffeine all night and devoted myself to researching how to go about getting rare historical artifacts verified and auctioned off. Unfortunately, it seemed like a pretty lengthy process, which is, I guess, why Aunt Marie was just going with eBay for most of the junk in the townhouse.

By English class, the hours were catching up with me, and I sleepwalked through our impromptu essay on themes and motifs of Gothic fiction, then fell asleep entirely in art history. There, snoozing on the desktop, drool soaking into the handout sheet on the sculptor Bernini, I had my most restful sleep in weeks and dreamed of absolutely nothing. It was so peaceful, in fact, that I took another nap in study hall and was awoken by the monitor, who sternly told me that I was needed in the principal's office.

This, I felt, was a bridge too far. So I'd fallen asleep in class! Was that an offense worth a visit to the principal? How come Gus could get away with never donning a stitch of Evergreen Prep's uniform, but I couldn't doze off in study hall? It was unfair.

Armed with arguments like these, I entered Ms. Engle's office ready to defend my position and stopped dead.

For there, seated at the desk across from the principal, was the very helpful special collections librarian from the Pratt.

Oh. Oh no.

"Miss Reynolds," Ms. Engle said. "There's someone here to see you."

I fumbled for the woman's name, but it had been Gus who'd taken her card. She'd been so nice to us at the library. She'd showed us to the brooch, let us sneak into the Poe room, told us to contact her if we'd needed anything—and we'd repaid her kind helpfulness by stealing a priceless artifact right out from under her nose.

"Hi there, Ellen," the librarian said brightly to me. "Ms. Rice, from the Enoch Pratt Free Public Library. We met last week."

I nodded, my mouth dry. Where was Gus when I needed him? He was always the one who got me out of trouble. He was the one who came up with the bright ideas.

He's the one who opened the lock, lady, not me.

"Ms. Rice has been telling me that you and Mr. Davenport are working on a special project about Edgar Allan Poe," said the principal.

"Well," I managed to say in a tone so weak I wasn't sure it would carry across the carpet. "We're doing a Poe unit in English class."

Ms. Engle gave me the most skeptical look in the entire world. "Ms. Rice says you two took the initiative to visit the special collections at the Pratt."

I mean, it wasn't *not* assigned? It was a free country. It was a free library, for that matter. Right there in the name and everything.

"I was so delighted to see students their age taking advantage of the resources we have," Ms. Rice added, as if trying to be helpful to me, which didn't make sense at all if she was about to have me arrested, "but I seem to have misplaced their contact information when it came time to tell them their request was ready. Luckily, I remembered your school uniform and thought I might be able to track you down here."

My uniform! Well, Gus had that advantage over me. In the future, I needed to remember to dress more generically when stealing priceless artifacts. Not that I'd realized that was what we were going to do.

Not that I ever—*ever*—planned to do it again.

I glanced over at Ms. Engle's desk and saw a printout of a security camera showing Gus and me standing in the Poe room at the library, right next to the fireplace mantel. In the photo, we were very close together. It didn't actually look like we were in the middle of stealing anything.

To be honest, it kind of looked like we were kissing.

But now was very much not the time to think about things like that. It wasn't just my scholarship that hung in the balance here. It was my whole life.

Ms. Rice turned to the principal. "Thanks so much for your help, ma'am. Is there a quiet place where Ellen and I can chat about her research?"

"Of course. The library will be free this hour. Ellen can show you the way."

I felt a bit like a condemned prisoner on her way to the gallows as I led Ms. Rice up the stairs and into the library. The library at Evergreen was one of its most impressive locales, featuring heavily in all the brochures and on the website. This building had once been the home of some robber baron, and back then, rich people prided themselves on their book collections instead of their spaceships.

Around us, carved bookshelves soared to the ceiling, which was painted with murals of muses and other mythological figures. Most of the books in the original collection were kept on the very top shelves, behind plexiglass plates so kids wouldn't become curious and try to touch them.

I'm sure this librarian knew exactly how that went.

Ms. Rice clucked her tongue. "And this is where you go to school . . ."

"You work at the Pratt," I blurted. "It's really pretty there too."

"True," Ms. Rice admitted. "But I don't think most kids in America get to go to schools that look like this." She gestured to a pair of cozy reading chairs by the window. "Shall we chat?"

I sat down and braced myself.

"I think you know why I'm here," she began.

Of course I did. I just didn't know why it was her and not a sea of cops.

"The object in your possession is not yours to keep. It's part of—a larger collection."

Wait—was she just *asking* for it back? Was I not actually in trouble?

"What's it doing hiding in a picture frame in the library, then?"

"Ah," said Ms. Rice. "So, you have questions too."

Too? *Too?* None of this made any sense. I narrowed my eyes at her. "What are your questions?"

"Simple: How did you know it was there?"

"We didn't." I shook my head. "We just—we saw the lock and opened it."

"Luck?" She cocked her head. "That's unlikely."

Tell me about it. It was one in a thousand. I looked at her. "Is it Poe's coffin?"

She sat back, surprised. "You really had no idea it was there, did you?" She studied me carefully, then began to nod. "And that's why you haven't progressed, either . . ."

I had no idea what she was talking about. *Progressed?*

Ms. Rice looked exactly like what you'd expect a research librarian to be. She was middle-aged, and her hair had streaks of gray in it. She wore a pair of sensible black pants, a berry-colored blouse, and a black cardigan. She was the kind of person my dad had taught me to ask for help if I got lost on the bus.

But I was terrified of her. I wished Gus were here. He'd know what to say to her. He'd pull out his easy smile and his drawled-out *ma'am*s and weasel our way out of this, just like he'd done to the principal on the day we'd met.

And then I had an even worse thought. Is that why Gus wasn't here? Had they already taken him into custody? But no, that was impossible—she said she recognized me by my uniform.

Of course, everything else she'd said to Ms. Engle was a lie as well.

"Where is Gus?" I asked her.

"I'm told he's absent today," said Ms. Rice, serenely. "Ellen, you aren't in trouble. Not yet, anyway."

I really would have loved to believe her.

"After all, this is all my doing, in a way," she went on. "I heard you talking about the brooch, and I thought perhaps you were someone you are not."

Another riddle. Where was Poe when you needed him?

On the day we found the pen, I couldn't stop thinking about how random it was that the code in Poe's poem about the brooch had opened the lock on the painting. But maybe it wasn't random at all.

"You took us to the Poe room because you heard us talking about the code."

Her eyes widened. "You really don't know anything at all, do you?"

That was probably true, but the pieces were starting to come together.

"You're not here just because you want the pen back," I said carefully.

"Well, yes, we do want the pen back. But not *just*. We want to know how you found it. Nothing like that has ever happened before."

Yes, it was also a shock to me that precious artifacts from library special collections would be kept in secret coded compartments in a picture frame. Seemed unsecure, especially if a couple of teenagers could crack the code.

"And, to be honest, we'd like to know a little bit more about you too, Ellen *Poe* Reynolds. You're quite as fascinating a discovery all on your own."

I didn't like the way she said that. It made me sound like I should be behind glass too.

And I was starting to wonder exactly who she meant by "we." It didn't sound like she was talking about her special collections department anymore.

"Do you like puzzles?" she asked me abruptly

"Like . . . jigsaw puzzles?"

"Like codes. Like escape rooms. Like treasure hunts."

I definitely liked the sound of treasure. "Depends on the prize."

She laughed. "Fair enough." She sat back against the seat. "I'm intrigued by you, Ellen Poe Reynolds. Intrigued enough to let it slide that you've already cheated and skipped several steps. So, I'm willing to give you a chance."

"A chance—to not get arrested?"

She gave a slight nod, then added, "A chance at solving the puzzle."

"What's the—"

"You must know by now that I can't tell you *that*. It's part of the puzzle. And no more help from your little boyfriend. This is not a group project."

"He's not my boyfriend," I said automatically.

"Nevertheless."

I didn't like this at all. This was exactly the kind of game that I was no good at. The kind where I didn't know the rules.

It was the numbers versus poetry thing all over again. Numbers made sense because they were always exactly the same, but not poetry. Sometimes in poetry, words didn't even mean what they were supposed to, and the rhymes were different all the time. When you finished a math problem, you were supposed to feel right, complete. When you finished a poem, you were supposed to feel surprised, knocked off your axis.

Some people were good with both, like Poe. I was definitely not.

"Is Gus supposed to do it on his own too?"

"August Davenport is not a part of this."

Oh yes, he was. He'd tracked down the brooch in the library in the first place. I'd never have been able to figure out what the dumb poem was getting at without his help.

This was exactly what I was talking about. How was I supposed to play her stupid games if none of the rules made sense?

"Why not?" I asked. "He opened the lock on the frame. For all you know, he has the pen right now."

"For all I know," she repeated meaningfully. "You might be surprised what it is I know, Ellen Poe."

"Stop calling me that," I said. I didn't like it at all out of her mouth. It didn't sound the same as when Gus used it. "Would you call *him* Edgar Allan?"

She laughed, as if she found this whole conversation adorable. "Where did you come from?"

"Fells Point."

She laughed again. "I'm taking a risk here, but I think you'll be very interesting."

"I have no idea what that means," I said, then added, "ma'am."

And maybe that's why Gus said things like that all the time. Because it was a magic charm of some sort, an incantation that made adults stop laughing at you and talk straight.

"Okay," she said. "Here's the deal. You have one week to make some progress—and, before you ask—you'll know when you make it. One week. And if you haven't, then you return the pen to me in the library and forget any of this ever happened."

It was like she'd burned a big pile of cash right in front of me. "I was going to try and sell it."

She tsked at me. "Selling stolen property is a very serious crime, Ellen Poe."

"Well," I replied, "isn't stealing it in the first place a crime too?"

"You're absolutely right," she said. "So for now, we're going to say you borrowed it. After all, you got it from the library."

And now I knew exactly when it was due.

It is nearly a mon

requesting an in

, I placed it (

swered letters". The

seeming discourtesy

answer,

I have now to

you at any time

dway. You will

the morning befor

Very Respy.

H. C

CHAPTER 19

Handwriting Lessons

GUS HAD NOT RESPONDED TO ANY OF MY THREE texts by the time I got home that afternoon, and I figured sending more would look pathetic. But I did not know where else to turn. I hadn't even told Aunt Marie about the grandfather clock. How could I tell her that I'd barely avoided being arrested that afternoon, and that I was concealing valuable stolen—or *borrowed*—property in her living room?

At Raven's Rest, I retrieved the pen from where I'd hidden it and brought it back up to my bedroom. If Eddy didn't like it there, that was his problem. I had work to do.

Down in the kitchen, I'd grabbed a pair of disposable latex gloves from under the sink and put them on before removing the pen from the bag. It wasn't that I was afraid of fingerprints or anything—both Gus's and my prints were all over this. But if a professional librarian wanted it back, she probably cared what condition it was in. I'd destroyed enough expensive items this week.

I sat down at my desk, removed the pen from the plastic bag, and examined it carefully. The handle of the pen was made of a single piece of oblong wood, carved into a simple tapered cylinder shape and finely polished, with no decorations or other embellishments aside from the engraving, which was black in color and said nothing more than *E. A. Poe 1875.*

The year he'd been dug up. Or whatever the fancy name for it was. Disinterred.

Next, I looked closely at the nib. It was gold in color, but I didn't know enough about metals to know if it was actually gold or some other material that just looked gold, like brass or something. It was the usual shape of a pen nib, with two swooping sides that ended at a sharp point and a little hole in the center. There were some little swirls engraved in the surface of the nib, but whether that was to help direct the ink down to the point or just for decoration, I had no idea.

I also had no idea where the ink was supposed to go. When you looked at the pen from the nib end, it looked like it was a single, solid piece of wood.

Which made sense. If I had a piece of the coffin of Edgar Allan Poe, I probably wouldn't carve it up any more than absolutely necessary. As it was, there seemed to be little more than a tiny slit cut into the tip of the wood, into which the edge of the metal piece had been inserted.

Ms. Rice had said it was a puzzle. She'd talked about making progress. But puzzles had pieces to take apart.

I was deeply terrified about trying to take this thing apart. It was over a hundred years old. What if I broke it?

I gingerly squeezed the pen nib in my hands and tried to wiggle it. It immediately shifted under my fingers, so I gave it a good yank, and it came free completely.

The part that had been inside the wood was metallic silver in color and engraved with the faded profile of a man's face, along with the words "Washington Medallion Pen."

The man's face looked nothing like Poe's. If I were to venture a guess, I'd suppose it was meant to look like George Washington and was the "medallion" in the name.

If Gus were here, I bet he'd tell me all kinds of fun factoids about old pens. I wondered if the nib meant anything at all or was just some manufactured piece.

Was I missing a part? What else came along with a pen?

Paper? Ink?

Oh no—they didn't expect me to use this thing for writing, did they? My handwriting was terrible. I barely even knew how to write in cursive. I'd been typing nearly all my homework since about fourth grade.

And maybe people had pots of ink lying around in the 1800s, but I sure didn't. If I broke open one of my ballpoint pens, could I even get enough out of the tiny chamber to dip this pen into?

Then I remembered that Aunt Marie had an entire art space downstairs. Maybe there was ink down there.

Downstairs, I found Aunt Marie shutting up the pastry stand for the afternoon and counting out stacks of cash and coins.

"Hey, hon," she said to me. "How was school?"

"I wasn't arrested," I said, which was at least honest.

She chuckled. "Banner day, then."

"How were sales?"

"Not bad. Between the muffins and last night's take after the open mic, we may just keep the lights on another month or two."

That was a relief. Especially since I wasn't going to be selling that pen anytime soon.

"Hey, do you have any ink?"

She looked at me. "Like, printer toner?"

Would that even work? "Like, ink for a pen."

"What kind of pen?"

I mimed dipping a pen in an inkwell. "An old-fashioned pen. It's—" Was I lying about projects for school too often? Would people start asking me to see all these supposed projects?

Maybe I was better off with the truth, or at least a version of it. "I found an old pen, and I wanted to see if I could write with it."

"Ah." She thought for a second. "Let me look around. We had a calligraphy class here not too long ago, and I might have some left." Aunt Marie went into the storeroom and emerged with a small vial of ink. "I hope you have good luck with it. If I remember from the class, it's a lot harder than it looks. Make sure you have some paper towels or something ready for the splatters."

The splatters? Suddenly, the idea of dipping a piece of Edgar Allan Poe's coffin in ink sounded like more than I wanted to handle.

"It's hard to get into the flow too," Aunt Marie was saying now. "You have to stop and dip your nib every few letters. Can you imagine how exhausting that would be? I sometimes wonder how people like Poe ever got anything written that way."

Back upstairs, armed with paper towels, I stared at the pen and ink for several long moments.

Was I really going to do this?

And if I was, did I have any paper?

I opened my desk drawers, looking for something to write on, and found some old sheets of paper. I also saw the journal. I set it on the edge of the desk, hopefully far enough away that it would not be in danger from any random ink splatters.

Maybe Eddy could give me some penmanship tips.

But when the ghost appeared, he seemed—as ever—fascinated only with the pen.

"You're the father of the detective story," I told him. "You tell me how to solve this puzzle."

But he just stared.

I wished Madeline Davenport could see what I saw. That would end her obsession with wanting to contact the spirits of the dead real quick. Ghosts weren't interesting to talk to. They were actually pretty useless.

I didn't know what he was so frightened of. He was dead. His problems were over. I was the one in big trouble.

I picked up the pen and cleaned the nib with a bit of paper towel.

Okay. Do it. Just . . . dip the priceless antique into ink. Carefully.

My hand shook. "What kind of puzzle is this?" I begged the silent ghost. "Or is it more like a test? First I stole it, now they want to see if I'm willing to ruin it?"

And Eddy, miraculously, responded. "Nothing is more clear than that every plot, worth the name, must be elaborated to its denouement before anything be attempted with the pen."

"You're right." I nodded vigorously. "I need to know what it is I'm doing before I try it. I need to watch instruction videos online. I don't even know how far to dip it in the ink. And do I let it drip for a bit before writing? And how often do I have to re-dip? And what do I do after I'm done writing? I can't put it down. The ink will get all over. Did you guys use pen holders or something?"

Wait, pen holder? Why did that sound familiar?

Behind me, Eddy shook his head, sadly. "The very atmosphere was redolent of death. The peculiar smell of the coffin sickened me. And in that coffin was all that remained."

The coffin. This pen was made of Poe's original coffin. Aunt Marie had said other pieces of it had been taken and made into objects too. Objects like pen holders.

Perhaps I needed to collect them all.

❁ ❁ ❁

This time, it was me who approached Gus after English class, where he weirdly chose to sit on the other side of the room.

"Hey," I said, as he packed up his stuff. "Where have you been? You haven't been answering any of my texts."

He shrugged. "Yeah, I've kind of been busy."

"Busy doing what?" I asked. "Not shopping for your school uniform, I see."

"Very funny." He slung his bag over his shoulder and ambled off.

"Hey!" I turned and tried to catch up with him, but it wasn't as easy in reverse. I'm pretty sure Gus was taking the stairs four at a time.

What in the world?

In P.E. I watched him score fourteen points for my team while I studiously avoided ever being passed to and wondered where it had all gone wrong. Yes, dinner at the Davenports had been a terrible disaster, but the clock was an accident, and Gus had seemed like he was on my side about the whole thing.

"Reynolds, think fast!" yelled some kid as a basketball flew at my face.

I put up my hands, but right before it reached me, a long arm came out of nowhere and slapped it away.

Gus stood there, glaring at me as the ball bounced into the bleachers and the rest of our team went scrambling for it. "Can you?" he asked. "Think fast?"

"It depends if you're talking about reflexes or actual cognition," I replied. "I'm certainly not great at basketball."

"Or generally not tripping over your own feet."

The clock! "Gus, I'm so sorry about that—"

"Don't worry about it. I worked it out with Rod. Honestly, he's more upset about the séance, and that was on us, not you."

"Was it—really worth ten thousand dollars?"

Gus gave a nod.

Oh dear lord. "And was it . . . insured?"

He looked down.

I felt ill.

Gus must have noticed me turning green. "I said don't worry about it. Madeline and I inherited a ton of money from our parents, so it's no big deal. And Madeline said she was going to look into her home insurance policy."

But he was still obviously mad at me, and I couldn't blame him. I could barely stomach owing someone ten dollars, let alone ten thousand.

The basketball game continued, but I couldn't even pretend to care anymore. This was not the kind of game I even liked. There was another one I'd much rather be playing, and, somewhere along the way, it had started to matter to me that Gus was involved as well. Ms. Rice had told me to leave him out of it going forward, but that felt wrong.

My old friends—they didn't know about the Poe stuff. My dad didn't know about the journal. No one knew everything except Gus.

How weird was that?

Gus kept his distance from me for the rest of the school day. Well, either that or they'd finally had enough and dress-coded him into solitary confinement.

But as I exited my last class, I found him sitting under the maple tree on the green, watching me walk toward the bus. And just then, I realized that I didn't care what Ms. Rice had said. I wanted him to be a part of it.

We might be the two founding members of the Outcasts Club, but that was all the more reason we had to stick together.

"Listen," I said when I reached him, "we need to talk about the pen—"

"Do you think I'm a monster?" he asked, not looking up at me.

"What?"

"I think I might be a monster," he said. "You said that in your dreams, I look like a monster. And the other night, in the dark, you were afraid of me." He shuddered. "Maybe when you die, you come back kind of wrong. I definitely feel wrong. Like nothing matters anymore. I should care, right? About alienating my friends, or my sister. I should care about school—God knows I should care more about money. But I just don't."

I sat down beside him. Forget about Poe and the puzzle for a minute. This was way bigger. "You've been through something terrible. I don't think you're supposed to feel normal again for a long time after that."

Gus was silent for a moment, and I wondered if I'd said the wrong thing. Maybe I was just supposed to reassure him that I did not, in fact, think he was a monster.

And he definitely didn't look like one.

He finally spoke up again. "Is it weird that all Madeline wants to do is talk to our dad? They never talked when he was alive. Shouldn't *I* be the one who wants to talk to them?"

"I don't think you not wanting to consult with psychics has anything to do with not wanting to talk to your dad," I said gently. "You don't want to talk to a psychic *pretending* to be your dad. That's a totally different thing."

Or maybe it wasn't. After all, a psychic pretending to be your father could lie to you as easily as your own father could. Did ghost parents lie too?

He grunted. "Do you think—do you think there are any psychics who really can talk to ghosts?"

How in the world was I supposed to answer that? Gus's dead parents had been showing up in my dreams for a month, and they'd never said a word.

“I’m not sure that talking to ghosts is all it’s cracked up to be,” I said at last. “It’s probably just as annoying as talking to living people.”

And at last, Gus smiled again. “You know that’s not exactly a denial, right, Ellen Poe?”

Yep. I sure did.

CHAPTER 20

Cramped Quarters

THE EDGAR ALLAN POE HOUSE IN BALTIMORE WAS one of several homes across the northeast that hold that title. Poe didn't have a real, permanent home in his lifetime. He wasn't some rich landowner or robber baron with a huge mansion and a fancy library that would later be turned into a school for spoiled rich kids.

No, Poe lived in a series of sad, small, rented houses and apartments, and though some of them now serve as museums, there was always a long period of time between when Poe resided there and when anyone thought to preserve the place.

The Poe House in Baltimore, for example, had a steady stream of residents in it until the twentieth century. It's now one of the only nineteenth-century buildings still remaining on its block. The rest of the area was redeveloped as a public housing project in the early twentieth century, which was actually named the Poe Homes, after the famous writer.

This city will never miss a chance to remind you of Edgar Allan Poe.

Poe lived here with his grandmother in the 1830s, soon after being disowned by his foster father. Also in the tiny house with him were his aunt and his cousin (and soon-to-be wife) Virginia. He wasn't a famous writer at the time, though he did write and publish many short stories and poems while living here.

Just as with the Poe room at the Pratt, I'd never been to his house before. But when I asked Aunt Marie if she'd take me on Saturday, she was all too eager for our little excursion.

"Maybe I can get some ideas for the B&B," she said. "Or maybe they'll even let me put up a flyer advertising it."

"Maybe they can give you a job," I replied. No one knew more about Poe than Aunt Marie.

She made a face. "Actually, let's keep on the down-low. I don't think there's anyone still there who remembers I've got a lifetime ban, but you can never be too sure."

Thus forewarned, I packed up Eddy's journal in my bag, put the pen in a pocket of my coat, and we set off for West Baltimore. The weather was blustery and cool. As we walked the few blocks from the bus stop to the museum, I saw a gathering of large, black birds. They were big, sure, but not *that* big.

"Oh, look," Aunt Marie said. "Ravens!"

I didn't have the heart to tell her.

The Poe House is so tiny that only a few people can go in at a time. Still, when I'd told Gus all about my visit with Ms. Rice, he'd insisted on coming as well, in case there were more puzzles to solve.

"She was very clear that you weren't supposed to be working on this too," I'd explained.

Gus didn't like that at all. "Then she didn't watch the security video very closely," he argued. "I'm as much to blame for taking that pen as you are."

That's what I thought too. But Ms. Rice had been weird. She acted like she knew things about me that even I didn't know.

Gus didn't like that part either. "You're playing a game, and she hasn't told you all the rules. She hasn't told you what you'll get if you win, or what happens if you lose."

"She did tell me that I could bring the pen back and pretend that none of this ever happened," I offered. But then what about Raven's Rest?

He thought about this. "Nope," he said finally. "I'm coming with you. People who make games with stupid rules should not be surprised when those rules are broken."

No wonder he'd never known the polyester wonder of a school uniform.

I'd given in. We were clearly very different people.

Because of the size of the Poe House, you're supposed to wait outside for your entry window to start, and then the guides let in a handful of visitors every fifteen minutes. Gus was supposed to meet us there, but when a black luxury car pulled up to the curb, he wasn't the only Davenport to get out. He'd brought along Madeline, much to my dismay; Rod was seated behind the wheel.

He leaned over and spoke to Gus through the open window. "You can't seriously expect me to park on this street, can you?"

I will be honest with you. Rod, with his fancy car, did not look like the kind of person who'd ever been to West Baltimore in his life.

Gus glanced up and down the block, taking in the run-down houses, boarded-up windows, and murder of crows. "Looks like free parking," he said with a shrug. I bit back a smile.

Gus made the introductions while Rod was across the road locking down his car. Madeline looked overjoyed to meet my aunt.

"Are you psychic too?" she asked eagerly.

A few of the other people gathered on the curb for the tour gave us a funny look. So much for the down-low.

"Yes," Aunt Marie replied casually, "but I'm not currently practicing."

Soon enough, a man came out of the house. He was younger than both Aunt Marie and Madeline Davenport and wore a black sweater over a button-down white shirt and black tie. He had on thick, black-rimmed glasses and checked in all our tickets.

"My name is Charles Neilson," he told the assembled group, "and I'll be running your tour today at the Edgar Allan Poe House. The home is very small, and there are sections that only one person can view at a time, so I'll appreciate your patience as we move around. Before we go inside, does anyone have any questions?"

"Yeah," said Rod, as he joined the assembled crowd. "Is it okay to park here?"

Gus sidled up to me on the sidewalk. "Sorry about this. They insisted."

“They insisted?”

“Yes. Madeline because she hasn’t yet given up hope you’ll help her contact Dad, and Rod because he thinks you’re a bad influence and he’d like to ‘temper’ it.” Gus’s finger quotes dripped with disdain.

“*I’m* a bad influence?” I repeated. “I never stole anything in my life before I met you.”

“Borrowed,” he replied, pretending to be offended. “*Borrowed.* You’re going to give it back, remember?”

“Depends on what we find inside.”

He looked at me in surprise. “Whoa, Ellen Poe. I’m impressed.”

“See?” I teased. “Bad influence.”

The house made Raven’s Rest look like a mansion, and that was saying something. An overcrowded gift shop barely bigger than a bathroom stall held a few pieces of china said to have once been owned by Poe’s foster family, the Allans, and then a door led to what they described as the kitchen during Poe’s time. We were instructed to ascend the narrow, curving stairs one by one to the second floor, where there would be more information and rooms.

Gus maneuvered us to the front of the group, so we were among the first to make the journey up the steep set of stairs. The rooms up here were just as tiny and cramped. The walls were covered in photos and informational plaques about the Poe family and what their lives were like when they lived here. There was hardly any furniture in either of the rooms, but they were so small I couldn’t imagine what furniture could even fit inside them.

Five people had slept here? Where?

In the smaller of the two second-floor bedrooms, there were a few pieces of furniture behind large plexiglass cases. More artifacts behind glass. One was a simple wooden chair with a card proclaiming it was thought to have once been owned by the Poes in this house. That was, I suppose, a fancy way of saying "Edgar Allan Poe sat here."

The other was a wooden box the accompanying card identified as a writing desk said to have been used by Edgar Allan Poe while he was a student at the University of Virginia. The object was about the size of a toolbox and opened in a similar fashion, revealing a tray with a flat surface on which to write and several drawers to hold paper and writing implements. I searched the case for anything that looked like a pen holder but saw nothing.

"Excuse me, sir," Gus asked the tour guide when he made it into our room. "We heard something about there being a pen holder at this museum that was actually made from Edgar Allan Poe's coffin? Where would that be located?"

The man blinked in confusion behind his glasses. "Edgar Allan Poe's coffin! Now that's a new one. Don't believe everything you read online, kids."

"We didn't read it online," I said. "There's plenty of documentation that when Poe was exhumed in 1875 and moved to his new burial spot, his coffin splintered into pieces and people took those as souvenirs and made them into various objects."

"Is that so?" He narrowed his eyes at me. "You've certainly done your research, young lady."

"What is a pen holder, anyway?" Gus asked him.

“I have no idea,” said Mr. Neilson. “I use a mug, personally.” He took two steps across the room to the door in the far corner. “Now, up this last set of stairs is the garret room, which would have been used as a bedroom in Poe’s time. Unfortunately, it’s an extremely tight fit and off-limits to visitors, so you can only stand at the top of the stairs and peek inside. The staircase is narrow, though. Only one person up at a time. Would you care to look?”

“After you, Ellen Poe,” Gus said, waving me forward.

I shot him a look, but if Mr. Neilson noticed the name, he made no indication.

I started up the stairs, which quickly turned a corner and became so narrow that my little cross-body bag dragged along the wall as I ascended. I pulled the bag around to my front, gripping the journal through the fabric.

Up, up, I went, toward the narrow opening at the top, which was closed off with a pane of plexiglass about eighteen inches high, so you were forced to stop at the top of the stairs. But as I reached the top, I gasped.

There was already a man in the room.

Somehow, I caught myself before I screamed or fell, and a second later, I let out a sigh of relief.

It was only Eddy.

Eddy was just slightly taller than me, but he still filled the tiny garret room, with its sharply sloping roofline that peaked in the center. Gus would never manage to fit in here without stooping. There was a single window along one sloping wall, and

Eddy stood at it, looking out over what I imagined was a very different city than he'd seen the last time he stood in this room.

Eddy beckoned to me.

"No," I said. "Look, there's plexiglass." The ghost might not know what plastic was, but certainly he could see there was a barrier keeping me out.

Unlike the other rooms in the house, this one was actually furnished. A narrow bed was pushed against one wall, with a wooden chair beside it. There was a black coat and a pair of boots sitting there too, very similar to the ones Eddy himself wore. And on the trunk pushed against the base of the bed there was a pewter pitcher, a book, a quill pen, and a large, stuffed black bird.

A very large stuffed black bird.

"Now *that's* a raven," I said.

Eddy looked around, as if seeing the furnishings for the first time. The serene expression on his face turned to one of horror. I watched him pale, watched his eyes become round and his cheeks hollow out as his mouth drooped open.

Oh no, not again.

"Eddy, it's okay," I whispered.

He didn't move. Just stiffly raised his arm and pointed at the trunk.

I followed the line of his finger toward the quill pen, which was standing straight up in . . .

A gray, wooden pen holder.

I didn't let myself think, just quickly stepped over the plexiglass and over to the trunk. I maybe had seconds.

Up close, I could see that the quill was resting in a small stand carved from wood that appeared to match the pen in my pocket. Quickly, I ditched the feather and replaced it with the coffin pen.

It was a perfect fit. The color, the grain of the wood—everything matched exactly.

I was delighted. Eddy was horrified.

But nothing happened. No gong sounded, no trapdoor opened. I stood in the center of the tiny room, and I stared at the two little artifacts, sitting on a book on a trunk in the pale light of a gray autumn day.

Was this progress? Was this what Ms. Rice had been wanting me to do?

And if so, now what?

I looked at Poe for help, but if he hadn't liked one piece of his coffin, he really didn't like two together.

"By each spot the most unholy," he intoned. "In each nook most melancholy . . ."

More poetry. I couldn't escape it.

"Not helpful right now!" I hissed at him. I knelt in front of the trunk, taking in the pen and holder from all angles. Maybe there was another combination lock here? Maybe I was supposed to take both pieces?

Wait. There was something written on the holder. I craned my head to examine it, but all I saw was a similar engraving to the one that had been on the pen: *E. A. Poe.*

"You must not—you shall not behold this!" Eddy begged me. I looked up to see him kneeling beside me. And even though I thought I was used to having a ghost so near, in this tiny room, it was still a little much.

"Eddy, I have to know. I have to figure out the puzzle."

"Some person equally your enemy and mine has been its author," he said. "They are a heartless, unnatural, venomous, dishonorable set."

Gee, Eddy, tell me how you really feel!

"They might be all those awful things," I said to him. "But to be fair, I did steal their pen." I reached out to rotate the pen holder and, on the back, I saw another engraving.

January 20, 1875.

"No!" Eddy cried. But it was too late.

"What are you doing?" came a voice from nearby. "Get out of there at once!"

Mr. Neilson, the tour guide, stood at the top of the stairs.

CHAPTER 21

Forbidden Things

WHAT HAPPENED NEXT CAME SO FAST AND IN such a rush that it's hard to even recall how it all went down. The short version is, my aunt Marie is no longer the only Reynolds to have received a lifetime ban from the Poe House and Museum in Baltimore.

The long version is an even bigger mess.

The second I heard Mr. Neilson's voice, I got startled and toppled over, right into the spot where Eddy had been standing. For a moment, the world went topsy-turvy and I heard the ghost's voice, much closer and more loudly than I'd ever heard it before.

From a wild weird clime that lieth, sublime, out of space—out of time.

And all of a sudden, everything was different.

The light was no longer the cool, silvery glow of an overcast morning, but warm and golden. The paint on the floorboards vanished, and a small table appeared under the window, its top angled toward me. A writing desk. I stood and walked over to it, as though in a dream. Pages sat on top of the writing desk, covered in a close black script. Through the window I saw—not the tops of houses and the city skyline—but trees and rolling green fields, a Baltimore countryside of yesteryear.

And on the windowsill, just beyond the panes, a giant black bird. It stared at me through the glass, tapping, tapping. Gently rapping.

A hand gripped my shoulder hard and yanked me forcefully out of the room.

Mr. Neilson pulled me bodily down the stairs and by the time I was on the second floor, everything was back as it had always been. Now. In the twenty-first century.

"—very clear you are *not* to enter—don't you think we have cameras?"

I couldn't think enough to speak. I saw the faces of Gus and Aunt Marie, their eyes wide and worried. I saw Madeline and Rod, peering out from the second bedroom as Mr. Neilson rushed us both down the stairs he'd just finished telling the group were only built for one. The other tourists flattened their bodies against the walls to give us room to pass.

We careened through the tiny rooms, through the minuscule maze of a gift shop, and back out the door onto the street.

Outside, the weather was cold and gray again. Outside, the city was just as it had been before.

Mr. Neilson let go of me at last, and I nearly dropped to the ground without his support.

"Ellen!" Aunt Marie burst out after me. "Take your hands off her this instant or I'll call the police!"

"I'm the one who is going to call the police," Mr. Neilson said. I noticed he was holding my bag—the one with Eddy's journal in it. "She was trespassing in forbidden areas of the museum and touching things!"

"Give me back my bag!" I shouted.

"Once I'm done searching it to see if she took anything." He opened it up and began rooting around inside, but I hadn't brought anything except the journal, my keys and phone, some lip gloss, and my wallet.

And the pen, which was still up there on the third floor.

Oh no. I'd left it!

I glanced up at the house, but the garret window was not on this side of the building.

The others had begun to exit the building as well. We'd drawn quite a crowd.

What had just happened? What had just happened to me?

"Ellen!" Gus pushed past a few of the onlookers. "Are you okay?"

"What were you thinking?" Mr. Neilson shouted at me. He shoved the bag into Aunt Marie's arms, clearly satisfied I hadn't stolen anything. Like a stuffed raven would fit in my purse anyway. "There are very clear signs everywhere saying do not cross that barrier. Did you think we just *wouldn't notice*?"

For a moment, I'd been with Poe. With Eddy, way back when.

Or at least, I thought I had.

"What do you have to say for yourself, young lady?"

"I—I saw a raven."

"It's part of the exhibit, you fool." He turned to Aunt Marie. "She is permanently banned from this museum. You both are."

"What else is new?" said Aunt Marie.

"You're lucky I don't have you arrested!" He turned to the others. "I'm so sorry for the disruption, folks. It's very important that you respect the history and age of this home. And keep your children in line," he added, giving me and Aunt Marie a dirty look. "Your tickets will be refunded, and the house will be closed for the next thirty minutes as we review it for any damages or missing artifacts."

And with one last withering glare in my direction, he walked back up the front steps and shut the door behind him.

There were a ton of people staring at me right now, and I wanted to crawl out of my skin.

Aunt Marie put her arms around me. Her expression was firm, but grim. "Come on," she said softly. "Let's go home."

I felt tears welling up in my eyes, burning like my lungs. "He's not going to find anything missing," I wept. "But I left the pen! I left the pen!"

"We can get you a new pen," she said softly.

"No! You don't understand!"

"What happened?" Gus drew close, the concern obvious in his voice. "Did you find the pen holder?"

I nodded miserably and buried my face in Aunt Marie's shoulder. "It fit the pen. But it's still up there."

"What are you talking about?" came a far harsher voice. I looked over Aunt Marie's shoulder to see Rod descending on us.

"Ma'am, your daughter is completely out of control. She causes disasters wherever she goes."

"She's my niece, and she was just manhandled by that total—"

"She shouldn't be allowed out of your sight!"

"Did you find any clues?" Gus asked me, as Rod and Aunt Marie got into it a few feet away.

I shook my head. I had absolutely no idea. "There was a pen holder. It—it matched. But nothing happened. There were no more clues. There was nothing on it but a date."

And it wasn't even the right date. The pen holder said *January 20, 1875,* but his coffin wasn't even dug up at that point.

"What were you saying about a raven?"

"Come on, August, leave these people alone," Rod was saying to him. Gus ignored him.

"I—saw a raven out the window." Also, I may have traveled back in time with a ghost.

Suddenly, Madeline was standing on my other side. "Do you think it was a messenger?" she asked. "Ravens are messengers from the land of the dead! Just like in the poem, you know. You could have been getting a message from Edgar Allan Poe himself."

That was silly. If Eddy wanted to say anything to me, he would just go ahead and say it. Probably in rhyme.

"This is absolute nonsense," Rod insisted. "This girl is not psychic, Mads, she's clearly mentally disturbed."

Maybe he was right. Maybe I was crazy. After all, it was no longer merely dreams we were talking about, but full, waking hallucinations.

I was seeing other times, other places. I was talking to ghosts. Those things were generally agreed upon to be very, very bad.

"She's not crazy!" shouted Gus, which is not the kind of thing I'd usually appreciate a person shouting about me, especially on a crowded public street. "Leave her alone!"

"No, *you* leave her alone!" Rod snapped back. "You are not to have anything to do with this girl ever again."

"Oh yeah?" Gus said to him. "I don't recall anyone dying and making *you* my guardian."

Rod merely straightened, which still didn't make him as tall as Gus, and turned to Madeline. "Mads?"

Madeline folded her hands before her. "I think—I think that Rod may be right, August. I don't deny that your friend has some kind of strange talent, but she's obviously unstable."

Unstable! I was the only one here who wasn't shouting.

"Ellen," Aunt Marie said in a voice of steel. "We're going *home*."

"We'll drive you," Gus insisted.

"We absolutely will not," Rod said, and, clamping a hand down on Gus's shoulder, steered him firmly away.

The other tourists had dispersed by now, leaving our tiny group alone on the sidewalk. Nearby, I saw a few passersby standing on the street corner watching the commotion. This was probably way more drama than they were used to seeing outside the local dead poet's museum. Aunt Marie and I watched Gus and his family get back in Rod's fancy car and drive away, and then we slowly began our walk back to the bus stop.

As we rounded the corner, I finally got a glimpse of the garret window of the Poe House, and through the glass I saw a shadow moving.

I wondered whose it was.

❁ ❁ ❁

Aunt Marie said very little on the journey home, and as soon as we arrived at Raven's Rest, she took me right upstairs and told me to put on my PJs and get in bed, as if I had the flu and not a bad case of criminal behavior and possibly lunacy.

Still, I did as I was told because I couldn't face anything else.

Cattarina once again took pity on me, hopping up on the bed and laying down nearby the moment I was settled under the covers.

A few moments later, Aunt Marie arrived with a tray on which she'd put a mug of soup and another of apple cider.

I looked at it and my stomach turned over. There was no way I could eat.

Aunt Marie nodded in understanding and put the tray aside. Then she sat on the edge of the bed and stroked Cattarina, who purred in appreciation and rolled closer to her.

Jerk cat.

"I think," said Aunt Marie gently, "that it's time you tell me what's been going on."

So I did. I started with the journal, and how Eddy had appeared on the bus, and again at school, and over and over at home. I told her about the codes, and the poems, and the brooch, and the lock. I told her about the pen, and the visit I'd gotten at school from the Pratt librarian. I told her about the awful dinner at Gus's sister's house, and the electric Ouija board and the grandfather clock, and the visions that appeared every time I'd been closing my eyes.

"And I didn't even get the extra crab cakes," I sobbed. I had no idea how long I'd been crying like that. "I know that's not the important part," I said between sniffles.

Aunt Marie handed me the tissue box. "Oh, hon, of course it's important. It's *crab cakes*."

She could crack all the jokes she wanted, but I was not going to laugh.

"I know we've talked about your dreams, but I didn't realize they were causing you this much distress."

Then I told her about the drawings in the journal, and how they matched up so well with what I was seeing, and how maybe Poe had been seeing the deaths around him too.

"May I see this journal?" she asked.

I nodded. "It's in my bag. I had it today." Maybe that was the whole problem. If I hadn't brought Eddy with me to the Poe House, none of this would have happened.

Aunt Marie retrieved the journal, and Eddy appeared in the room, standing stiffly against the far wall and watching us with wary eyes. I rolled away from him. I couldn't even look at him.

"Is he . . . here?" she asked me.

I nodded miserably.

"Thought so," she said. "I felt the chill." She opened the journal and flipped through a few pages, then closed it up again and put it on the desk. Eddy went nowhere. "I'm so sorry you've been carrying this all on your own. I've been so busy with my own stuff, I probably haven't been paying you as much attention as you needed."

"Am I going crazy?" I asked her.

Aunt Marie hesitated for a long moment. "I'm not a doctor, hon. I can't answer that. But that's also not how mental illness works. You don't 'go crazy' like it's a one-way trip. It's the same as any other condition people have, like diabetes or eczema. Sometimes it's better and sometimes it's worse."

"But you think I'm mentally ill." My voice broke on the words.

"I think you're having thoughts and feelings that are a struggle for you, and I think you're seeing things that are making it hard for you to live your normal life. And that's something we need to get you help with. But you aren't the first person in our family to have these issues."

"I'm not?" Was she talking about Poe again? He'd had all those bouts of hallucinations too. He'd complained to friends and families in his letter about his periods of depression and mania. He'd even written stories in which the narrators were psychopaths. "The Tell-Tale Heart" was about a murderer who hallucinated that he heard the heart of his victim beating under the floorboards. "The Black Cat" featured an animal abuser who killed his pet cat, imagined it came back to life to haunt him, and ended up hitting his own wife in the head with an axe when he tried to kill it again.

Well, maybe that's what it was about. The guy in that story wasn't exactly stable. And neither, apparently, was I.

Aunt Marie gave me a pained smile. "Ellen, it's not a freak accident that I can't stick to a job for longer than six months. And there's a reason you're living with me and not your father right now."

Realization washed over me. She wasn't talking about Poe. She was talking about *us*. The Reynolds family. "Dad too?"

"We can talk about your father later." She glanced at the journal. "Is—*he*—still around?"

I looked at Eddy, lurking awkwardly in the corner. "Uh-huh."

"Is he bothering you?"

"Annoying me, more like," I said. "But not always. Sometimes I like having him around."

"Yeah?"

"Like when he went to your open mic night. I think he really liked it."

"Wait . . . he went to open mic night?" Aunt Marie looked truly delighted by this. "I knew we had something special going on that evening."

It helped, somehow, that Aunt Marie wasn't totally horrified by the thought of Eddy. Like it wasn't the absolute worst thing in the world that I was seeing someone who wasn't there.

"It's not like the dreams of the other dead people," I explained to her. "I don't find him scary. I just—I don't always know what he wants."

She sighed. "I told you my grandmother used to claim to see him too. She always told it like a ghost story, but I kind of put it under the heading of imaginary friend."

“Is there such a thing as an imaginary enemy?” I asked her. “Because he’s kind of ruining my life.”

Eddy’s head shot up at that, and his somber expression turned to one of disappointment and pain. “Heaven knows that I would shrink from wounding or grieving you!”

“Too little, too late,” I told him.

Aunt Marie’s eyes widened at my words and the way I directed them across the room.

My stomach sank.

“I see,” she said.

I groaned and pulled the covers over my head. Cattarina meowed in protest, but I no longer cared. The cat would abandon me the first chance she got anyway. Just like everyone else.

“Will I have to go stay in a hospital?”

“I don’t know.” I felt her hands covering my own through the sheet. “I think that’s usually for people who are going to hurt someone, or themselves, or people who don’t want to find out what’s going on in their head.”

I peeked out again. “That’s definitely not me. All I want is to figure this out.”

“Me too,” said Aunt Marie. “Let’s get started.”

It is nearly a mon

, requesting an in

, I placed it (

swered letters". The

seeming discourtesy

answer,

I have now to

you at any time

adway. You will

the morning befor

Very Resp.

Yr. O

CHAPTER 22

Secrets, Suffering, and Soccer Balls

I DIDN'T HAVE TO GO TO THE HOSPITAL, AND THE medicine the doctor gave me helped me sleep for twelve hours straight without any dreams at all. It was total bliss. When I woke up, the journal was nowhere to be seen, and Aunt Marie had even brought up a bunch of new lamps for my bedroom. Mood lighting was one thing, but I guess the doctor told her it was time to de-Poe the place for the time being.

She even removed Chip. I kinda missed him.

I appreciated the efforts she was making, though, especially as I knew how little she was able to afford them.

I spent the whole week home from school "recentering" myself, and despite being in Raven's Rest and without my dad, it almost felt like old times. There were no ghosts, either in my waking life or when I was asleep. Since the doctor's note excused me from my English class assignments, and I was far too embarrassed to contact anyone I knew, I had very little to do. I read books, watched movies, and helped Aunt Marie with the baking and listing some old knickknacks on the online auction site.

She said my piecrusts were really coming along.

I wrote an apology letter to Mr. Neilson at the Poe House and Museum and another to Ms. Rice at the Pratt, explaining to her where she could retrieve her pen. Whatever "progress" she was hoping I was making had not come to pass, but it was out of my hands now. Literally.

I asked Aunt Marie if I should write another letter to Madeline Davenport, but she said if anything, Madeline owed me an apology for the whole Ouija board thing.

Dad and Aunt Marie apparently talked on the phone that first day when I was still sleeping, and he sent his love, but when I tried to call him later in the week it just went to voicemail. Day after day, he seemed to only check in late at night, long after I'd gone to bed. I guess that was due to the time change out in Nevada.

By the following Monday, I was more than ready to get back to my usual routine. Aunt Marie offered to ride with me up to school, but I told her I could manage it on my own. She'd missed enough work trying to take care of me. Besides, I had Mr. Sousa, the bus driver, to look after me.

The last week had transitioned the city into the peak of fall, with trees turning bright yellow and orange seemingly overnight. Even Evergreen Prep seemed hardly worthy of the name, with leaves of every hue drifting overhead and blanketing the lawns in a cascade of brilliant color.

In computer science, you'd barely know I'd missed a week, as I slotted right into the zone with our new programming challenge. Ms. Sakai mentioned that she was glad to have me back, but none of the other kids even noticed I'd been gone.

I was bracing myself for English, though. I debated whether it was better to get there early and suffer the sting of each person walking in and being surprised to see me or try to get there late and get all the shock over with at once.

In the end, I attempted to slip in with others, which worked pretty well until I got to my usual seat and saw Gus right behind it instead of across the room. He sat up straight, his eyes widening when he saw me. I nodded, hoping I looked casual, and sat down in front of him.

Across from me, Rebecca looked over, her expression softer than I'd seen all year. "Hi, Ellen," she whispered.

Oh no. Pity from Rebecca? I dreaded to imagine whatever story was going around about what had happened to me.

We'd started a new unit, this time on mystery fiction. Arthur Conan Doyle and Agatha Christie. I somehow managed to avoid volunteering that it was Poe who had truly invented the modern detective story with his tales of murder in Paris and the amateur sleuth who used logic to solve seemingly impossible crimes.

One of those stories even included an orangutan.

After class, I took my time packing up, keeping my focus on my books and papers and not on anyone who may or may not have been staring at me. It worked, mostly. When I finally raised my head, the room was practically empty. Even Gus was gone.

But Rebecca Lambert was still standing next to my row.

"Ellen," she said, "I know we haven't really gotten along this year—"

That was one way to put it.

"But after what happened last summer, I was really mad at you."

"Yeah, you've made that abundantly clear."

"I wanted to apologize," she said now.

I squeezed my eyes shut. I wanted to dive through the floor. What in the world were they saying about me that Rebecca Lambert of all people was trying to be nice?

"We—we thought you flaked. You weren't answering your texts, we couldn't cover the costs without you, and the whole trip kind of fell apart."

Ugh, that sucked. I hadn't realized that. It wasn't as bad as getting evicted, probably, but no wonder they'd been so mad. I stared down very hard at my bag. Did she want me to apologize or something?

"But—" Rebecca swallowed so loudly I could actually hear it. "I heard last week that—"

"Please do not tell me what you *heard*." I hoped it didn't sound too much like begging. The thought of the kids at this school spending the last week gossiping about me felt like bugs crawling all over my skin.

She took a deep breath. "I was going to say, I heard that you aren't living with your dad anymore, and I was thinking maybe there was more going on last summer than I realized."

Surprised, I glanced up. Rebecca was pale, and she was twisting her fingers together in front of her body. "When I was in middle school, my mom—" she stopped. Her eyes got glassy. "Well, anyway . . . If I've been mean to you this year, I'm genuinely sorry. I hope we can be friends again."

For a moment, I couldn't say anything at all. I just stared at Rebecca. Part of me wanted to tell her that I didn't need her pity. But was it pity? Or was it something else?

Ever since we got kicked out of our place and I'd had to move into Raven's Rest, I'd been in hiding. When the other girls acted standoffish at the start of school, I'd accepted their scorn as something I deserved—not because I'd bailed on the beach trip, but because I figured they'd never understand a girl who'd been evicted from her apartment.

But if the trip fell apart without my paltry contribution, maybe I was assuming too much about my classmates. And maybe if I'd been honest with them from the start, Rebecca would have taken it better. Maybe she would have even understood.

"I hope we can too," I managed to choke out.

She let out a huge sigh. "Oh, good. Also—"

Oh no. I hoped she wasn't about to tell me that there was some huge rumor in school that I was a hallucinating psychopath.

She was not. It was way worse.

"Are you dating Gus Davenport?"

Oh God, get me out of here.

❁ ❁ ❁

After that little interaction, I was not feeling up to PE, so I told the nurse I was tired, and given my doctor's note, they agreed that it would be a good idea to let me sit quietly in the library for all of PE. I read the introduction to the Sherlock Holmes book, which included this little gem from Sir Arthur Conan Doyle himself:

> *It is the irony of fate that Edgar Allan Poe should have died in poverty, for if every man who wrote a story which was indirectly inspired by Poe were to pay a tithe towards a monument, it would be such as would dwarf the Pyramids. Where was the detective story until Poe breathed the breath of life into it?*

There was no escape.

At lunch, I skipped the usual collection of picnic tables and went off by myself to sit under the silver maples, although the ground was cold through the fabric of both my sweatpants and my school skirt, and the leaves were damp where they'd fallen among the roots. I brushed them aside, looking for the driest area on which to perch.

"Welcome back," came a familiar voice from above.

I looked up to see Gus standing by the trunk of the tree, his hands shoved deep into the pockets of his ever present black hoodie. Another whole week, and he was still sans uniform.

"I'm pretty sure you're not supposed to be talking to me."

"Since when do I ever do what I'm supposed to?" He crouched down beside me. "How have you been?"

Nuts? "Not great," I admitted. "But, you know, improving."

"Well, that's something," he said. "Still dreaming of me?"

"Nope." I stole a look at him from under my lashes and he appeared almost disappointed. "But that's a good thing, you know, Gus. They were nightmares."

He nodded, slowly. "I wish you only had good dreams. Of me or otherwise."

I looked away again. We sat in silence for a moment and listened to the wind in the dying leaves. I saw Rebecca and the other girls in my class sitting at their usual picnic table, and imagined they were drawing their own conclusions about Gus and me, regardless of the denial I'd given Rebecca after English class.

I wish I had good dreams about Gus. I wish I was able to have good dreams at all.

"I'm sorry that I dragged you into all that mess with my sister," he said at last. "I didn't think about how hard it would be on you."

"It isn't exactly easy on you either," I replied. "You've been through a lot. You shouldn't have to listen to her trying to resurrect your father all the time. Are you talking to anyone about it? Like . . . doctors, not psychics? Because Aunt Marie had me talk to a doctor last week, and it was super helpful."

"Therapy's the one thing Madeline does not believe in," Gus said, with humor that came across as kind of hollow. "Maybe your aunt can give her some tips."

After what had gone down at the Poe House, I was sure there was plenty Aunt Marie would have to say to Gus's sister, none of it pleasant.

"I'm less worried about myself at the moment than I am about her, actually," Gus said. "I've spent all this time thinking there was something wrong with me because she seemed so much more upset about Dad's death than I was. But maybe she's just falling apart. She and Rod have been fighting—a lot. I don't think he was prepared to have a teenager living with him, even for two more years."

"I'm sorry." At least when my father couldn't take care of me, I had Aunt Marie to fall back on. Gus's sister was not on her level. "But you know, there's not a wrong way to feel about what happened to you and your family. Different people grieve in different ways."

"Oh, there's a wrong way," Gus said with a crooked smile. "Robbing libraries, manipulating new friends . . ."

". . . Refusing to adhere to the dress code?"

"You're never going to drop that, are you?"

Out on the lawn, the other students were playing with a soccer ball, chasing it through the intermittent carpet of fallen leaves.

"What's the gossip about me?" I asked. "Are they saying I ran stark raving mad through the streets of Baltimore?"

"Why would they say that?" Gus said. "I'm the only one who saw what happened, and I haven't said a thing."

I gave him a curious look. "But after English class, Rebecca was saying all this stuff to me about how I must have been through a lot—"

Gus snorted air through his nose. "Rebecca's nosy. Someone was saying something last week about checking on you at your father's old place, and I said you lived in Fells Point with your aunt now. I guess she filled in a bunch of details all on her own."

She certainly had. And now I knew why she thought Gus and I were a thing, as well.

"But," Gus dropped back to a full sitting position, as though making himself comfortable for the long haul, "if you wanted to finally enlighten me as to what was going down last week, I'm all ears."

During my week at home, I'd wondered why he hadn't texted. I thought maybe he was mad or that Madeline had forbidden it. But now I thought it was possible he was just giving me time. Gus more than anyone would know I might need it.

I dropped my face in my hands, letting the ends of my hair shield me from this embarrassment.

"Ellen," he said softly, quite close. "It's okay."

I remembered how he'd tried to protect me—with the principal, in the library, at his sister's, even after Mr. Neilson had thrown me out of the Poe House. No matter what else had happened, Gus had wanted to help.

"I was hallucinating," I said into my hands. "I . . . have been hallucinating. You saw it at your house. But it's been happening a lot. About Poe, especially. And when I went up there—alone—when I was standing somewhere I shouldn't have been—it was all too much. For a minute, I thought I was back in the 1800s. That I was Poe, standing at his writing desk, getting that first bolt of inspiration to write 'The Raven.'"

Gus stared at me in silence for a few seconds. "Wow," he said at last. "I have to say, if I was going to choose a hallucination, that would probably be high on the list."

I couldn't help but laugh at that.

"I'm serious. That's so much cooler than me as a dying ghost or whatever."

He wasn't wrong. There was something kind of grand about that last vision. That thrill of recognition, that snick when I saw the raven at the window, and I knew that Eddy had taken the first steps into literary stardom.

But even before that, I'd never minded my visions of Eddy. Sure, he was a bit on the cringey, dramatic side, and I'd never get used to him quoting obscure poetry at me. But he'd acted like my friend. He'd never scared me. Even that brief little trip with him into the past had been cool.

It wasn't like the nightmares. It wasn't like the other dead people.

Weird how the mind worked.

"I don't want to have the hallucinations anymore," I said. "They were distracting me. They were making it hard to sleep. I just want to move on."

He nodded in agreement. "And what about the journal? What about the pen?"

"Aunt Marie put the journal away since it was—triggering some of the hallucinations. And the pen is gone—left up in the garret in the Poe House. I wrote to Ms. Rice to tell her what happened, and I haven't heard anything since, but I guess she can go get it there. I doubt that Neilson guy would have thrown it away."

"You said you found the matching pen holder. Was there a secret compartment on it anywhere? A message written down?"

I shook my head. "Just his name and a date, like on the pen. Probably the date it was made."

"What was the date?"

I thought for a moment. So much else had happened since that moment. What *was* the date on that pen holder?

"Never mind," Gus said at once. "It's probably a bad idea to keep going there. It's over now."

"Yes," I agreed firmly. "It's all over."

But of course it was not.

It is nearly a mon

, requesting an in

, I placed it (

swered letters". Thi

seeming discourtesy

answer,

I have now to

you at any time

dway. You will

the morning befor

Very Respy.

W. C

CHAPTER 23
Cemeteries and School Dances

UNDER NORMAL CIRCUMSTANCES, YOU WOULD never catch me dead at any school dances, which Dad used to claim were "rank displays of heteronormative conformity and capitalist excess," but neither of us had heard from him in over three weeks, so who cared what he thought?

Besides, Aunt Marie said that this semester had been hard enough as it was, and that if I was going to the Evergreen Prep fall formal, we were going to splurge on something nice for me to wear. Splurge, in our case, meant a trip to a secondhand shop, but it was a very hip secondhand shop where we found a vintage party dress that fit me like a glove.

I didn't even mind that it was a deep, jewel-toned Baltimore Ravens purple.

The bodice of the dress was velvet, with capped sleeves and a sweetheart neckline. The skirt was full and made of polka-dot netting. It even had pockets! When I tried it on in the shop and looked in the mirror, I didn't feel like a girl who'd spent the last few months battling nightmares, a possible psychotic break, and serious financial doom.

I felt—dare I say it? Normal.

At school, half of the kids were talking about nothing but the formal, and the other half were doing anything to avoid talking about it. I'd started eating lunch with Rebecca and the other girls again, and from what I could tell everyone was just going on their own or in a big group. But all the conversations about salon visits and blowouts made me feel more than a little uncomfortable. Would I stick out like a sore thumb at the dance?

Today, I claimed I had homework to do and disappeared to the library during lunch. And that's where Gus found me, hiding in the stacks with a manga and trying not to think about how much a professional makeup session would cost.

"Hey," he said, plopping down in the armchair across from me. "You're not going to that stupid shindig on Friday, are you?"

I bit my lip and turned a page in my book.

"Oh, man, you *are*?" He groaned and tossed his head back. "No! Ellen Poe, you *traitor*."

"Ix-nay on the Oe-pay," I said lightly, and turned another page.

"I thought we were too cool for that stuff."

I looked up, regarding him through the slanting sun rays coming through the library windows. They turned his longish hair into pure gold and highlighted every faded mark and frayed cuff of his beat-up hoodie. I wondered what Gus would look like at a school dance. Would he dress up for a change? Would he dance?

"I think the correct take is that we're cool enough to do it and not suffer any long-term emotional damage."

"I've already suffered long-term emotional damage," he reminded me. "I'm an orphan, and I *died*."

"All the more reason you need to get out there and go to something cheesy like a high school dance," I told him. "It's good to feel normal, trust me on this. Besides, what's going to happen? You die again?"

Famous last words.

❁ ❁ ❁

Westminster Hall in downtown Baltimore used to be a church back in the old days, but now it was an event space. It still looked like a church inside thanks to the peaked, Gothic stained-glass windows and the huge organ dominating one end of the hall. It looked even more like a church outside, though, especially because it was surrounded by a historic graveyard where lay buried all kinds of famous people from Baltimore history.

Including—of course—Mr. Edgar Allan Poe.

Poe had not one but two different gravestones in the yard at Westminster Hall's burial ground. There was the giant marble monument that they put up in his honor in 1875, and a separate stone in the back marking where he was buried for the first twenty-five years after his death. The big monument was right out in front where everyone could see it, since it still brought people to visit a century and a half later. There were

Revolutionary War heroes and town founders in the back, but no one really cared about them so much.

I did my best to ignore all that as Aunt Marie pulled up outside of the picturesque building on the evening of the Evergreen Prep fall formal. The weather was cold and clear, and the trees on the street had dropped all their leaves, stretching out skeletal fingers that glowed in the light of the streetlamps in contrast to the indigo night sky.

For the occasion, Aunt Marie had borrowed a car from the neighbors so I didn't have to ride the bus or walk the extra blocks in my dress. She'd made the plans before she found out that I had put on a pair of high-top sneakers under my gown, but I still thought it was a good idea because then I didn't have to lug around a coat.

Inside, everything was decorated with garlands of fall leaves, candlelit pumpkins, and baskets filled with berries, pine cones, and gourds. Autumnal lighting shot beams of crimson, orange, and gold up along the walls and stained-glass windows. It was a cool effect and probably much easier to live with than the deep red paint in our dining room. I should mention it to Aunt Marie.

I said hi to a few kids I knew and made a circuit around the hall, checking out the photo booth, selfie wall, and snack table and grabbing a soda, even though I knew I'd have to touch up my lipstick afterward. The rich kids at the school may have gotten their hair and makeup professionally applied, but Aunt Marie and I did the best we could with online tutorials and stuff from her bathroom drawer. My short brown bob had been curled into bouncy waves around my face, and she'd given me a rather impressive smoky eye that we'd paired with a violet lip to match my dress. It was kind of goth, but after a month of ghosts, I was into it.

I was also really nervous. No matter how chill I'd acted about the whole thing in front of Gus the other day, this was actually my first Evergreen Prep fall formal too.

He'd said he would come. He'd better come.

Ten minutes and half a soda later, I was feeling pretty sheepish. I'd avoided making plans to actually go to the dance with any of the other girls because I couldn't afford their pre-dance salon excursions and professional photo sessions. But now they all seemed to be congregating in groups without me. I'd sidled over to the outside of different knots of people, but there never seemed to be a good way to get in on the conversation.

I'd finished off my soda and was seriously considering going back for a cup of hot apple cider when I heard someone say my name.

"Ask Ellen Reynolds, she'd *definitely* know."

My head shot up, and I looked around to see Rebecca, standing in a sand-colored satin minidress and surrounded by a gaggle of other girls in nearly identical styles. She was pointing my way. I looked down at my tea-length, full-skirted gown. Once again, I had not gotten the memo. Now I understood why they wanted us to wear uniforms at school.

They came over to me as one.

"Hey, Ellen!" Rebecca called. We'd been hanging out a fair amount again, but I wouldn't say we were friends-friends. She knew I lived in Fells Point, but I hadn't exactly had her over to visit or anything. The fashionable address and the bizarre reality gave two entirely different impressions. "Help us settle a debate."

"Okay," I said warily.

"I *love* your dress," said a girl from my art history class, Ciara. "Is it vintage?"

I nodded, relieved. Maybe this wouldn't be so bad.

Rebecca had enough of clothing talk. "We heard a rumor that it's not really Edgar Allan Poe buried out there under the monument."

Then again, maybe not.

"That when they dug him up, they took someone else's bones," Rebecca said. "You seemed to know everything about Poe when we were studying him in English class. Is this true?"

"I know they dug him up," I said. Boy, did I ever. I'd touched a piece of his actual coffin. "And I know that when they did, his cousin was there, who had been present at his original burial, and also the same man who managed the graveyard when he died too. So, I think they probably knew where he was buried, and that it was really him. Even all those years later."

"Wouldn't they have known just from his gravestone?" asked another girl.

"He didn't have a gravestone," I said before I could stop myself. "His cousin had bought him one, but it was destroyed before they could place it, and they never bought another one. That's why there was such a big push to put up the memorial instead."

Rebecca shook her head in disbelief. "How do you know all this stuff? You sound like a tour guide."

I wondered how much tour guides got paid.

"Have you guys heard about the Poe Toaster?" Ciara said now. "They say that for a hundred years, some anonymous person has been regularly leaving gifts of roses and half bottles of liquor on Poe's memorial in the middle of the night."

"Eww," said Rebecca. "Like a bum?"

"Yes, a bum who leaves people roses, Beck," Ciara said with a laugh. "No. The story goes he appears in the middle of the night, like some strange person is out there toasting Poe. Or *persons,*" she added, waggling her eyebrows. "Because it's been going on for a *century.*"

Since 1949, actually. Not that I still had those dates in my head. Poe died in 1849. He was reburied in 1875. And 1949, the centennial of his death, supposedly marked the beginning of that tradition.

Jeez, maybe I *should* be a tour guide?

I also thought it had ended a good decade ago, but who wanted to ruin the other girls' fun?

"*We* should go toast Poe!" someone cried, and everyone thought this was a marvelous idea. Except me, of course.

Still, I was swept along with the others as they all went and collected cups of hot apple cider and beelined for the door of the hall.

Where we were stopped in our tracks by the principal, Ms. Engle. Thank goodness.

"Where do you think you're going, girls?"

"We want to toast Poe in the graveyard!" Ciara announced, holding aloft her paper cup.

Ms. Engle shook her head. "Sorry, we aren't allowing reentry. For safety reasons. If you leave the hall, that's it for the dance."

A wave of whining overtook the assembled group, and we dispersed back onto the dance floor in dismay.

Well, all dismayed except me. What did I have to toast Poe for? He didn't need another drink, anyway.

After an interlude in which I actually managed thirty-five whole seconds of dancing before the dumb DJ picked a song no one could dance to, Ciara sidled up to me.

"Hey, we found a back way out. Wanna come?"

I mean, what was I supposed to do, just stand there like an idiot with no one to talk to? Gus hadn't shown up, and the DJ was playing bad music. I barely even had a choice.

Ciara's back route turned out to be a fire exit by the ladies' room that led down to the basement.

Here's the thing, though: Westminster Hall didn't really have a basement. What it had was this dark, dank, hollowed-out area under the floorboards that was barely big enough to stand up in, and was made up of a dirt floor and a ton of giant cement blocks the size of cars. I was glad I'd opted out of heels as I watched the other girls pick and trip their way through the rocky underbelly. Above us, the muffled beat of music and the shuffling of teenage partiers felt miles away, instead of mere feet. It was cold down here—colder even than it had been out on the street, in the wind. The smell was stale and dusty, an odor that I recognized from the basement of Raven's Rest. It was the smell of history.

And dark. The only light came from the streetlights shining in from arched openings around the perimeter of the building, but as we came close to the nearest one, we realized that it was covered in bars, probably meant to keep people out but not altogether convenient for us in that moment.

"We need a light," someone said in the darkness, and then a wave of cell phone flashlights burst into life.

Which was when we discovered that we were already standing in a graveyard. All around us were crumbling headstones. The giant blocks? Mausoleums. The smell? I wasn't sure I wanted to know.

There was squealing, and a few muffled screams, as the other girls clapped their hands over their mouths, realizing that if we screamed any louder, the chaperones upstairs would surely hear, even over the sound of the music.

"Oh yeah," Rebecca said. "There are catacombs down here. I forgot!" Her eyes danced with merriment, and I suddenly got the sense that she hadn't completely forgotten.

Maybe she should be the one who was the tour guide.

"I found a door!" Ciara announced, pulling with all her might on a large piece of sheet metal. It gave with a metallic twang, scraping along the dirt to let in a wedge of light. One by one, the five of us squeezed through and outside into the side yard of the church.

There were gravestones and mausoleums out here too, but we'd expected that. Here also was light from the building itself, from the hospital across the road, and from the streetlamps beyond the iron fence. To our right, the tall, white marble monument to Edgar Allan Poe stood in the corner of the grounds, right by the front gate.

I gulped in breaths of fresh—or at least fresher—air. "There it is," I said, pointing.

The Edgar Allan Poe memorial monument is a large, rectangular column topped with the usual decorations of arches and carved oak leaves. On one side is a carving that's supposed to resemble his face, though—trust me—it doesn't. On the other three are listed the names and birth and death dates of Poe, his wife, Virginia, and his mother-in-law, Maria Clemm, who are all buried alongside him.

We gathered around this monument, still clutching our little paper cups of now-cooled cider. Ciara pulled a flask out of her clutch and added dollops of something fiery to anyone's cups who wanted "a real toast."

I figured I was probably breaking enough rules just by being here and decided to leave mine plain. We circled the monument, our cups at the ready.

"To Edgar Allan Poe!" Rebecca cried, raising her cup up high. "You were kind of a creep, but Baltimore loves you anyway."

"To Edgar Allan Poe!" the others echoed, toasting the memorial.

"Edgar Poe," I repeated, and drank. I was standing alongside the west side of the monument, farthest away from the building, so as to be shielded from the chaperones' view. It was the side of the monument that commemorated the poet himself. In front of me, the weathered stone read:

EDGAR ALLAN POE

BORN
JANUARY 20, 1809
DIED
OCTOBER 7, 1849

I stared at it for a long moment, like I was in a trance. The numbers rattled around in my brain, looking for something to connect to.

"He wasn't born on January 20," I said to no one in particular.

He was born on January 19. I knew that. Gus knew that. Everyone knew that.

So why did the stone say January 20?

It is nearly a mon
, requesting an in
, I placed it (
swered letters". Th
seeming discourtes
answer,

I have now to
you at any time
adway. You will
the morning befor
Very Respy.
Yr. C

CHAPTER 24

The Catacombs

OKAY!" REBECCA WAS ANNOUNCING TO THE GROUP. "Now let's go toast his other gravestone. Just in case his body never got moved, okay?"

There was a loud cheer, but I didn't join in. I was too busy staring at the numbers carved into the rock.

The last time I'd seen the date January 20 was on the pen holder in the Poe House. It hadn't made any sense to me then. His coffin wasn't even dug up on January 20, 1875, so that couldn't have been when the pen was made. But this monument had been dedicated in that year. And the same wrong day had been carved into its face.

Why?

"Ellen?" Gus's voice cut through both my whirling thoughts and the chatter from the other girls. I glanced up from studying the stone to see him approaching through the graveyard, and for a second, all I could think was *he cleans up nice.*

He was still in black, of course, but it was a much sharper look than I'd ever seen him in before. Black dress shirt, black pants, and even a black tie with a pattern of shiny black fleur-de-lis on it. His blond hair was combed nicely, and he may even have gotten it trimmed.

"I've been looking for you," he said.

There was a chorus of *oohs* from the other girls.

"How did you get out of the hall?" Rebecca asked him. "Engle's been a total jailer."

"I asked her nicely?" he said with a shrug. He came toward me. "You look great."

More *oohs*. I was glad it was dark out because I was positive I'd turned scarlet from head to toe. I was super glad he noticed, but did he have to notice in *front* of people?

"Well," said Rebecca, completely ignoring the vibe, "we're off to toast Edgar Allan Poe's *real* grave. Wanna come?"

"We'll . . . catch up," I said quickly, which earned me the longest repeat on the *oohs* yet. I rolled my eyes, mostly for show, but also, it was not remotely what they thought.

Well, not much.

After the others had scurried around the back side of the building, Gus gave me a smug look and leaned his forearm casually against the marble above my head. "Fancy meeting you here," he said mockingly. "I thought you were on a break from our man Poe."

"The date's wrong," I said without preamble. After all, it was cold out here, and my arms were bare.

"What?"

"The date. On the monument, is wrong—look." I dragged him around the pedestal. "It says he was born on January 20."

"Oh, that's wrong," said Gus.

"Yeah."

"He was born on January 19," he said.

"Yeah," I repeated.

"Everyone knows that—who has been through your little gauntlet, at least."

"Shut up!" I pointed at the bad date. "The pen holder in the Poe House also said January 20. January 20, 1875."

"It did?"

"Yeah. I didn't understand why at the time. I thought it was a mistake. But now I think it was a clue. Like with the brooch. This monument went up in 1875. And it's the only place that would connect Poe with the date January 20."

Gus was silent for a moment. "I thought you weren't supposed to be doing stuff like this anymore."

Technically, I wasn't. But it wasn't like I'd been seeking it out. I'd been doing normal teenager-at-a-dance stuff, and it practically jumped out and bit me.

Then, at once, his eyes got really wide. "Wait. What was the code that unlocked the portrait compartment?"

"1-2-0," I said, then gasped. "Like January 20!" I couldn't believe it.

"You got it," Gus said.

"Why didn't I put that together before?" I asked, amazed and sheepish all at once.

"Right? You're the numbers girl." He started feeling around the edges of the stone.

"What are you looking for?" I asked him as he finished the Poe side and began examining Virginia.

"Another combination lock."

He came around to the front, where the large black medallion of Poe's face carved in relief took pride of place. He pulled out his phone and shone the flashlight on it, as I looked over my shoulder and back at the hall to make sure no one noticed us here.

"Look," he said. In the marble, around the outside of the medallion, was a tiny *20* etched into the stone.

"Graffiti?" I suggested. This gravestone had been sitting out on a Baltimore street for a hundred and fifty years. It was a miracle it wasn't covered with junk.

Gus slid the beam of his flashlight down along the edge of the medallion until he found a tiny little divot in the rim. I peered closer. It looked like little more than a notch. But it wasn't.

"It's a 1," I whispered. The 20th of January.

1-2-0

The same cosmic key.

Gus looked at me, then put his palm flat against the medallion, covering Poe's silly, carved face. He twisted, and the whole thing began to rotate like the top of a jar. When the 1 lined up with the 20, we both heard a click.

The medallion face swung open, revealing a crevice of darkness.

Gus shone his flashlight inside, and I noticed a small engraving on the surface of the stone.

Roses that grew in an enchanted garden,
Where no wind dared stir, unless on tiptoe.

And in front of the words sat a tiny figurine, carved of dark stone—a trio of roses in a bundle. It looked out of place, like something that belonged on your grandmother's bookshelf instead of locked away in a world-famous monument.

Before I could think better of it, I reached in and snatched the figurine, and Gus pushed the door back closed.

Quickly, I pulled him back around into the shadows of the rear of the monument. My breath was coming in gasps.

"I can't believe it," I said. "I can't believe we found something else."

"I can't believe we *stole* something else," Gus said, "but, you know. You do you."

I leaned back against the stone, clutching the tiny roses to my chest. It was still freezing out here, but I felt hot all over.

"It really is a game," I whispered excitedly. "That's what Ms. Rice was trying to tell me. We stumbled on a treasure hunt. A *Poe* treasure hunt."

"Did Poe have treasure to hunt?" Gus asked. "I thought he was broke."

"I don't think he set it up," I said. "All this stuff is from long after his death. When he'd become so famous the city was building monuments to him and stuff." Roses. What Poe story was about roses? I'd figure it out. I squeezed the roses against my chest and sighed in excitement.

Gus smiled down at me. "It is good to have you back."

I looked up at him and frowned. "Back?"

"Don't get me wrong," he said softly. "I'm so glad you're having an easier time sleeping. And that you're happy. And . . . *healthy.* I am. But I kind of missed the Ellen who was nonstop Poe trivia and scavenger hunts. I kind of missed Ellen Poe."

I missed her too. The rush of solving his codes and figuring out his secret messages. Whoever had put together these clues would have to know Poe every bit as well as I did.

Maybe they were a Reynolds too.

Gus's face was very close, back here, in the shadows of the burial ground. Closer than he'd been in weeks, since that moment in the library where I first thought he might kiss me.

He was staring at me, still, his smile smaller now, but somehow all the more real. I didn't have to say a word. I just tilted my chin up a few more inches, and he leaned down to press his mouth against mine.

For three whole seconds, the kiss was everything I'd been hoping it would be—soft and sweet, and full of promise. Then Gus pulled back from me. I blinked slowly up at him, my vision clearing, and nearly screamed.

Because before me stood his horrifying ghost, and behind him, the ghoulish spirits of his parents.

❁ ❁ ❁

Too scared to think, I ducked out from under Gus's arm and sprinted away down the path, ignoring his shouts coming from behind me. To the left, I saw the metal basement door we'd come through, and I plunged into the darkness of the catacombs again. My shoulder slammed against the sharp edge of a mausoleum, and I'm pretty sure I ripped my skirt on a gravestone, but I didn't stop sprinting until I reached the stairs.

Up I went, as if the hounds of hell were chasing me, and then I was back in the hall, with the loud, pulsing dance music and the golden lights. All at once, I felt foolish and crazy, and exposed. One tiny slipup with Poe, and I was back to having hallucinations.

How could I keep living in my aunt's house if that was the case? How could I keep living in *Baltimore*?

Before me stood the door to the ladies' room. A refuge. I pushed it open and nearly tumbled inside. The stalls were not in use, and miraculously, no one was fixing their makeup in the mirror. I walked over to the sinks. Despite the cold weather outside, I felt hot all over. I could probably thank my mad dash through the catacombs for that.

Miraculously, I still held the tiny rose figurine we'd taken from inside the monument. I stuck it in my pocket, uncertain of what else to do with it. Clearly, I had no business partaking in Poe scavenger hunts. I was a crazy person.

I closed my eyes for a moment.

Well, for sure Gus thought I was crazy now. Who kissed a boy and then dashed off like that?

I took a deep breath and opened my eyes again.

All the lights were off, and the ghosts were standing before me. I opened my mouth to scream, but no sound came out, and I realized I was back in the dream.

They weren't all there. It was just his parents this time, their bizarre, distorted faces streaming away, their eyes on fire, their hands reaching out to me, begging, pleading . . . but for what?

What do you want? I asked them without words. Why did they keep appearing to me? They were dead!

Go away! I shouted in my head, and the vision vanished like the bad dream it was. I was standing in the bathroom again, alone. And I was never going to shut my eyes again.

I spun around and headed for the door, but as I began to open it, I heard Gus's voice.

"Ellen!" he shouted.

I stopped dead. I absolutely could not face him right now. Seconds later, I saw his tall form in the corridor and shrank back into the shadows in the bathroom vestibule.

"Ellen," he was saying to someone. "Have you seen her?"

"I—I think she went down there, into the catacombs."

"What?" He sounded skeptical.

"Are you sure you know what you're doing, August?" Now I recognized the voice. It was Rod. *What was he doing at the dance? Was he a chaperone?* "That girl is not well."

"She's fine. I just—I just scared her. I'm going to find her."

Rod's voice dripped with disdain. "If you must."

I flattened myself against the wall, my face burning with humiliation. He hadn't been the one to scare me. He'd been wonderful. It was those awful ghosts.

I hated to think of Gus wandering around down there looking for me. But there was no way I could walk outside the bathroom with his horrible sister's boyfriend standing there waiting to judge me.

"Rod! Did you find him?" I peeked through the crack in the door again and saw Madeline, alongside Ms. Engle. This was getting worse and worse. "The principal said she saw him run back here. Did you know he wasn't supposed to leave the party?"

"He's looking for that Reynolds girl," Rod said now. "She's dangerously unstable, in my opinion. I don't know how she hasn't been suspended by now."

"Calm down, sir. Ellen Reynolds is not a danger to herself or others." Well, at least Engle was defending me. "She's been having a difficult semester due to a complicated situation at home—"

"And what is this about her threatening him on his first day of school?" Rod went on. "Why are we only hearing about this now—"

"It was a misunderstanding—" Engle said, to my relief.

"And look at the way she trashed my house! Madeline, are you going to let these people keep making excuses for her until something terrible happens?"

I stifled a gasp. What if Rod was right, and Aunt Marie and the others were wrong? Maybe it wasn't good for other people to be around me.

There's a reason you're not living with your father right now . . .

"I'll send a teacher out to sweep the graveyard," the principal was saying. "That usually brings in all the lovebirds."

"Go with her," Rod advised Madeline. "I'll look around back here."

That's when I realized that he hadn't told either of them he sent Gus into the catacombs after me. In fact, he'd heavily implied that he had no idea where Gus had gone. And no sooner had I put this together than I saw Rod yank open the door to the fire exit and disappear down the stairs.

I froze to the spot, my mind whirling. Why would he lie?

As if in a trance, I opened the door to the bathroom and stood staring as the fire exit door down to the catacombs slowly drifted closed. Behind it stood the ghost of Gus's mother, wavering like a dying flame. Her figure was almost unrecognizable now. Her face was as gaunt as a skull, her eyes like two black pits. She stared at me, reaching out, like I could help her. As if I could do anything.

"But you're already dead," I sobbed.

And then, in a flash more powerful and terrifying than all the nightmares that had come before it, I knew. I knew what the ghosts had been trying to tell me all along.

She was dead. Gus's *father* was dead. But Gus had survived. The freak deadly accident that should have killed his entire family—Gus had survived. He'd survived to live with his weird sister and her mean, lying boyfriend and his giant inheritance . . .

And maybe, just maybe, he'd never been supposed to.

The ghost's terrifying eyes stared deep into my soul.

Danger. You are not safe where you are. Evil is coming.

The talking board had spelled out that warning, then Rod had been the one to walk into the room.

"Gus!" I said out loud. I hadn't been the one the ghosts were trying to talk to that night. The message had been for Gus the whole time.

He'd always been the one the spirits were trying to help.

With a final, silent scream, the ghost drained away to nothingness.

I bolted out of the bathroom and across the hallway to the fire exit. I pulled the door open and ran down the stairs, back into the dank, frigid darkness of the catacombs. As soon as my feet hit the earthen floor, I heard Gus shouting for me.

"Ellen!"

A few yards in front of me, I saw Rod, crouched behind a stone. He had a long piece of metal in his hands. My answering call died in my throat.

It all happened so fast.

I drew breath to scream, Gus turned the corner and saw me, and Rod jumped out from the shadows, his arms raised to strike.

"Rod, no!" came another scream, and Madeline Davenport dashed in front of her brother, just as Rod brought the pipe down on her head.

It is nearly a mon

, requesting an in

, I placed it (

swered letters". The

seeming discourtesy

answer.

I have now to

you at any time

dway. You will

the morning befor

Very Respy.

Yr. Co

CHAPTER 25

Family Business

I ALWAYS THOUGHT IT WAS WEIRD IN TELEVISION SHOWS where the cops give victims and witnesses blankets and stuff after a tragedy. Turns out that when you watch people's skulls get cracked open right in front of your eyes, it makes you feel unbelievably cold.

My teeth couldn't stop chattering, no matter how many scratchy wool blankets they put around me or cups of hot cider they gave me to drink. Gus had been taken away—somewhere. Maybe he went with Madeline in the ambulance?

Even now, after all the cops had come and the kids had gone home and the detectives had talked to me and the medics had told Aunt Marie that "I was just in shock," I could not make sense of any of it.

In the days that followed, as the story spread on local, then national news, it hardly seemed any more real.

Madeline Davenport remained in a coma for nearly a week, and so the story that dominated the news cycle was the one that came with Rod Compagnare's confession. You probably heard most of it, though they kept a big part out of the news because—well, I'm a minor.

I had to get the rest of it filled in for me by the detectives on the case—as filtered through Aunt Marie, who wouldn't stop hounding the investigators to "make sure that maniac never saw the light of day again."

According to Rod, the whole thing was his idea, and his idea alone. Madeline hated her father and his new family, and she resented that their estrangement meant she wouldn't be getting any of her father's money. She'd already spent most of her inheritance from her mother, and the two of them were feeling desperate for funds. Rod, apparently, was desperate enough to commit murder.

He had set upon the idea of poisoning the Davenports with carbon monoxide, which he figured would be ruled an accident. The news stories never explained how he did it, though, kind of like they don't explain how people built bombs.

The problem was, when Gus survived the attack, they were left with no inheritance and a teenager to care for. It would be too coincidental to suffocate him again, so Rod had no idea how to get rid of him and not draw suspicion . . . until I came along.

Between the séance drama and my "outburst" at the Poe House, Rod had decided that Gus could possibly be "killed by his crazy girlfriend." He just needed to hang around Gus and me and wait until I caused another scene. He even figured that forbidding Gus from seeing me would make him want to sneak around so that the two of us would be more likely to be alone together.

I couldn't decide which part I hated more: that Rod thought he could manipulate Gus into having romantic feelings for me, or that he may have actually been right.

Gus never did what people told him to do, from dress codes to homework. Had he searched me out that night—had he kissed me by the Poe memorial—because Rod and Madeline told him to stay away?

But after giving it some thought, I concluded that the part I was angriest about is that Rod was the one who kept saying I was crazy and unstable. Aunt Marie and Ms. Engle didn't believe it, but that night, as I was hiding behind the bathroom door listening to him, he almost convinced me.

And in the end, it didn't matter anyway, because Rod forgot one thing. Madeline really *was* worried about her brother. Regardless of what had happened between her and her dad, Gus was her brother and she loved him. She'd been searching for him in the churchyard. And she stopped Rod just in time.

When I heard that, I couldn't help but remember Rod's paralyzed stupefaction, down in the catacombs, when he realized what he had done. Whatever else he was capable of, I don't believe he'd wanted to hurt Madeline.

I sometimes wondered if Madeline suspected that her boyfriend was responsible for her father's and stepmother's deaths. If the reason she was so obsessed with speaking to the spirits of the dead was that she wanted to know the truth.

But those spirits weren't speaking to Madeline. They were asking for help from me.

I have not had a single vision of ghosts since the night of the attack. The message they were trying to send me was delivered. It's finally over.

I hope.

❁ ❁ ❁

I finished placing the pumpkin pies in their boxes and stacked them up for Aunt Marie's last delivery round of the day. She was on a real roll lately—her Thanksgiving demand had grown nearly four times as big this year, ever since she put out order forms alongside the counter of the shop downstairs. We'd had to rush to try to get all the pies baked in time for the holiday, but at least this year she had a few extra hands. She'd even rented a van.

It had been more than a month since the tragedy at Westminster Hall, and things had nearly calmed down completely. We had now had a long-term, paying guest at Raven's Rest: Gus Davenport. He was staying in the Pit and the Pendulum room, which I thought was a terrible choice, but he said he liked the black carpet.

And no, he has not kissed me again, because that would be *super* weird, especially now. I mentioned he was just across the hall, right?

I couldn't believe Aunt Marie offered to be his temporary guardian while Madeline recovered, but he had no other family, and as soon as Madeline was conscious enough to sign an affidavit saying it was okay, it worked out. Gus still had all his lawyers from when his parents died, which also helped. According to Aunt Marie, the authorities are still working out whether they believe Rod's story, or if they think Madeline was somehow involved.

Since my opinion on this involves talking to ghosts, I haven't volunteered my thoughts on the subject.

Gus would be home later this evening. He may not have had a chance to be in the school play this term, but Aunt Marie talked him into auditioning for the Fells Point community theater *Christmas Carol* this season, and they cast him as the Ghost of Christmas Yet to Come. He's thrilled—mostly because he gets to wear all black.

He still hasn't bought a school uniform. I've decided that the school administration is never saying a word.

The doorbell rang, and I figured it was Aunt Marie, forgetting her keys again. But when I answered, I found Ms. Rice standing on the stoop, her hands politely folded behind her back.

"Hello, Ellen Poe," she said with a smile. "May I come in? Say yes, if you know what's good for you."

If Ms. Rice was surprised by the purple splendor of our Raven-themed entryway, she made little note of it; she just followed me up the stairs and into the living room.

There, she took in the silver wallpaper, velvet drapes, and octagonal table. "'The Philosophy of Furniture?'" she asked, having a seat on one of the damask couches. That was the essay Poe had written on how to furnish a room.

I followed in behind her. "Yes, how did you—"

"That's a deep cut," she said pleasantly. "You'll find, Ellen Poe, that I can figure out a lot of things."

"It's just Ellen."

"I don't think it is." She laughed, but there was no humor behind it. Once again, she was dressed in the world's most boring office attire. Her hair was pulled back in a plain clip. She wore no makeup and little jewelry.

And she was the most intimidating person I'd ever seen.

"I've been doing some research on you since we last met," she said. "You, and your family. The *Reynoldses*." She drew it out some, like it was a dirty word. "Do you know that he was calling for someone named Reynolds as he died?"

I did not need to ask her who she meant by *he*. Instead, I sank into the couch opposite, clasping my arms around my knees. I should not have let her in. I should have said, *My aunt is not home, can you come back another time?*

It was too late now.

"I do," I said. "That's basically my family's entire claim to fame. They think—"

"I know what they think," she spat. "But it's impossible. We know all the women that Poe was involved with before his death."

Hey, she'd get no argument from me. I'd never wanted to be related to Edgar Allan Poe.

"There were . . . several of them," I volunteered, awkwardly. Maybe there was another one that people weren't entirely aware of.

"He wrote poems about them," she argued. "He wrote poems *for* them. He wrote them long, involved love letters, and they spent the rest of their lives defending him against his enemies."

"That's great," I said. What was she getting at? "Like . . . Annie Richmond? Or Sarah Helen Whitman?"

"Exactly."

The silence stretched between us. I had no idea what this woman wanted.

"You—uh . . . did you get your pen back?"

"Ages ago," said Ms. Rice, with a wave of her hand. "But I'm here to ask you why you haven't progressed. We've been very patient, given everything that you're going through. But there should be progress."

Oh right, the roses. Honestly, I had not thought about them in weeks. With the support payments from the Davenport estate and Aunt Marie's business improvements, we'd been able to pay all our bills. Treasure hunts had gone on the back burner. I'd had midterms to think about.

"I'm so sorry." I stood. "Do you need those back too?" If it was a game and I was keeping the pieces, it might mean no one else would get to play.

Ms. Rice held up her hand. "That's not what I want."

I paused, halfway to the door.

"Ellen," Ms. Rice said. "I'm with—well, let's just say I represent a group of people. For a long time—longer than you can imagine—we've been keeping the real legacy of Edgar Poe alive in this city. And beyond. The game you're playing is how we identify people who are worthy."

"But I already lost," I said. "I lost the pen in the Poe House. I wrote you—"

"Then you found the roses." She gave me a knowing look. "A strange move for a person who wanted to quit."

She had me there. "Maybe you ought to tell me the purpose of this game. I don't even know what it is I'm playing, or why." Or with whom. If only Gus were here!

"It's—complicated," said Ms. Rice. "You didn't start where most people would, so you're missing a lot of answers. That's why I was so surprised when you found the pen. I have no idea how you've gotten as far as you have. Some of the people in my group think that it should matter. That if you found any piece of the puzzle, you should still be allowed to play. That all paths lead to the same prize. Others . . . do not."

I bet I could guess exactly which side of the table Ms. Rice was on.

"It would help," she went on, "if we knew where you were coming from with this. You seem to have secret information that no one outside our group has had in over a hundred and fifty years. Will this game even work the same with you, and—whatever secret store of information you seem to possess? I don't know."

"I—I just know a lot about Poe," I confessed, shrugging. "My family is completely obsessed with him. I mean—look at this place."

She made a face. "Yes. It certainly is . . . a place." She regarded me for a long moment. "For example, how did you know the combination, in the portrait?"

"I—" Honestly, it was mostly a hunch. "It was because of the pearls in the brooch. The, um, math—"

She appeared unconvinced. "And how did you figure that?"

I opened my mouth to answer, then paused.

The poem! It was in the poem in Eddy's journal. Aunt Marie had taken it away from me after that awful day in the Poe House, but she'd put it away on the shelf in here, with all the other Poe-raphernalia, as she called it. She said she liked to take it down in the evenings and "vibe" with his ghost. She never said she could see him, like me, but that didn't seem to bother her any.

In fact, she probably preferred it.

She also took the journal to all the open mic nights she'd held, and every last one of them had been a smashing success.

I guess it made sense. Poe had made more money as an orator in his life than he ever had writing.

I stood up and crossed the room to the bookshelf.

But as soon as I arrived by the wall, Eddy was there. In the room. I hadn't seen him in weeks.

He shook his head at me, silently.

Ms. Rice was no fool. "Is it a book? Do you have access to unpublished writings of Edgar Poe? Show me."

I swallowed and looked at Eddy. His face was set and solemn. "I fear what will happen in the future," he said. "Not for what happens, but for the result of what happens."

"You know, Ms. Rice, I think you should come back when my aunt's home. This is her house, and—" I flailed "—I just don't feel comfortable."

“If you have a book like that,” she said. “It could be worth a lot of money.”

Didn’t I know it! I’d spent weeks imagining just how much.

“But here’s your problem,” Ms. Rice said now. “Proving it. Poe has *such* a distinctive style, but it’s been copied *so* many times over the years. I’ve heard there are even AI poetry bots who can do it now. It would be so hard to authenticate. Trust me—I’m a research librarian.”

She laughed again, but it rang false and hollow.

“But you and I know it’s real, because we know that you already found something real inside it. Something private. Secret.” She nodded at me, as if we were co-conspirators. Which I guess, in a way, we were. “You don’t have to suffer through months and years of expensive verification to get value out of it, Ellen Poe. I will offer you a hundred thousand dollars for that book, today.”

I let out a bark of laughter. “You’re joking.”

“Two hundred thousand,” she said so fast that I almost fell over.

That was not what I meant at all, but I’d take it.

Only . . . would I?

I thought of what Gus said all those weeks ago, about his passing theory that Aunt Marie and I were con artists trying to sell him a fake book for cheap right away with the promise that he’d make a killing on it by selling it to true experts later. An actual book by Edgar Allan Poe would be worth more than two hundred thousand dollars.

Besides, she was a librarian. No way she had that cash lying around.

I looked over at Eddy, who was standing in the middle of the floor between us, looking at me with such abject pleading in his big, dark eyes that I was surprised.

"How can you be so cruel?" he asked me. "My wretchedness is more than I can bear."

"I—" I clasped my hands together. "I really think you should talk to my aunt when she gets back."

"I'm talking to you, Ellen Poe," said Ms. Rice. "You solved the puzzles. You know what is at stake. Consider this as well. I am a research librarian, and one of the world experts on Poe collections. If you do not accept my offer now, you may find it difficult to get an authentication without my assistance. And I *will not* assist you."

And here I'd always loved the Pratt!

"You don't have two hundred grand," I said softly. Eddy looked appalled.

Ms. Rice smiled softly. "I assure you I can get it. I can get you twice that."

A chill stole over my skin. I knew I should wait for my aunt. The journal wasn't even mine. Not technically.

But two hundred thousand dollars? That would change everything. My dad could come home. We could get a place to live. Raven's Rest would be safe for the rest of my life.

Then I thought about the journal, locked away all those years. About poor Eddy, and how much he'd wanted me to solve his code, how excited he'd been to attend Aunt Marie's performances, how scared he'd been of the idea that I'd send him away.

I thought about the messages I had yet to decipher, the strange drawings that were so much like my own visions, the mystery of his death that may still be hidden in the pages.

Downstairs, the door to Raven's Rest opened.

"I'm home!" Gus called, his voice popping my thoughts like a bubble. I heard his feet on the stairs—four at a time, as usual. He appeared on the landing and his smile faded as he took in the tense scene.

"Oh, Ms. Rice," he said brightly. "From the Pratt, right? So nice to see you again, ma'am."

I looked at Eddy. My own Eddy. The most annoying ghost in the world. Could I really give him up? Banish all of it, forever?

"Hey, Gus," I said. "Can you hang here with Ms. Rice a minute? I have to get her something from my room." And I didn't want her casing the shelves while I was gone.

"Sure thing." He sat down in a chair in front of the octagonal table and gave the librarian a pleasant smile.

Her expression was harder to read. Relief, sure, and happiness, but something more. Something grasping. Her eyes seemed to glitter as she watched me.

Eddy, too, was watching, but his eyes were pleading with me, as desperate as Ms. Rice's.

I ran up the stairs, away from both of them.

In my bedroom, I retrieved the little trio of roses. They were carved in a distinct triangle of stems, their flower ends revealing bud, bloom, and full blossom, but they bore no other identifying marks. It was a puzzle I hadn't found time to work on.

And now I never would.

Back in the parlor I found Gus asking Ms. Rice tiresomely intricate questions about how to get a library card. She was unamused.

"I think it's time for you to go, Ms. Rice," I said. "Here, I have what you came for."

I held out the stone roses.

She looked at the figurine in my hand, then up at my face, her eyes cold and harsh. "You're sure about this?"

Two hundred thousand dollars. Two hundred grand! I could feel Eddy's eyes on me. I could feel Gus's eyes on me too, for that matter. Poor boy had no idea what was going on.

My hand with the roses in it trembled, but my voice remained steady.

"Yes."

She snatched the roses out of my hand and stormed off. We followed her down the stairs, just to make sure she left.

At the door, Gus stood beside me, watching her stomp down the cobblestone street. "What was that all about? Isn't that our next clue in the Poe game?"

"Yes," I said. "But it was a good trade."

I turned around and saw Eddy lurking in the shadows of the hall.

"What did you trade her for?" Gus asked.

Eddy smiled and I smiled right back.

"I don't know," I said. "But I'm going to find out."

The End

Ellen Poe Will Return...

AUTHOR'S NOTE

ALMOST ALL OF THE STORIES IN THIS BOOK ABOUT Edgar Allan Poe are absolutely true . . . or true to the best efforts of current Poe scholarship. Though many things about Poe's life—and particularly his death—remain a mystery, few authors have been as closely studied and documented. Even houses that Poe barely lived in are preserved as architecture of historical significance: everywhere from his cottage in the Bronx, New York, to his family's tiny townhouse in Baltimore, Maryland. There are still groups that study the codes Poe produced, and some scholars believe there are secret codes in his works that have never been solved.

And the things that "Eddy" the ghost says in this book are all quotes from Poe's actual writings: his stories, poems, essays, and even his letters. I didn't want to put words in the poor man's mouth.

It would actually be quicker to tell you the things I made up for the story. For instance, although Poe was known to complain about having hallucinations and suffering from what we'd now recognize as bouts of mental illness, he never claimed to see ghosts. Ghosts, in general, do not appear often in Poe's writings.

He was interested in far more ghoulish topics, like people coming back from the dead, and horrible crimes like murder. Poe knew he was writing scary stories and did it on purpose.

The journal in Raven's Rest is fictional, and so is nearly all the writing inside it, though the poems are based on real secret message poems that Poe wrote to his various lady friends.

There really is a pearl brooch similar to the one in the book that contains a lock of Poe's hair, but it is located in Indiana, not Baltimore, and is said to have belonged to Poe's friend Annie Richmond, and not Sarah Helen Whitman. Poe was indeed exhumed in 1875, and there are several stories about people making artifacts from pieces of his coffin. The Poe Room at the Pratt and the Poe House in Baltimore look exactly as I described them, but the combination lock on the portrait and the wooden pen holder are fictional. And though I invented a fictional secret compartment at the Poe memorial at Westminster Hall, every other utterly wild story about his various burials there, as well as the typo on his monument and his secret loyal visitor, are one hundred percent real.

We don't know exactly what happened to Poe in the days before his death, though there are plenty of theories. And although it is true that Poe kept calling for someone named "Reynolds" in his final hours, no one knows who he meant, and it is unlikely that he was talking about a woman he was romantically involved with. The real Edgar Allan Poe had no descendants, nor did his siblings, but there are still several people who can claim ancestry in Poe's extended family alive today.

Poe was possibly engaged at the time of his death to a rich widow named Sarah Elmira Shelton in Richmond, Virginia, whom he had been in love with as a young man many decades earlier. He'd also been previously engaged to another rich widow, a fellow poet in Providence, Rhode Island, by the name of Sarah Helen Whitman.

After his untimely death, it is true that Helen Whitman mourned him, wrote biographies of him, corresponded with many people about him and their relationship, and got deeply involved with the budding spiritualism movement, holding many séances herself. Whether she was trying to contact her ex-boyfriend (or started a secret society in order to do so) is an exercise in imagination.

The names of the characters in this book are in honor of Poe's friends, enemies, relations, and (in several critical cases) characters. And yes, this includes the cat. See if you can spot them all.

Despite the actions of Ellen and Gus, I highly recommend you do not try to touch, manipulate, or steal items, or enter off-limits areas in public places like museums and libraries. Not only are you sure to get into far more trouble than Ellen ever did, but also—the ghosts don't want you to.

FIND OUT WHAT'S
IN STORE FOR ELLEN IN

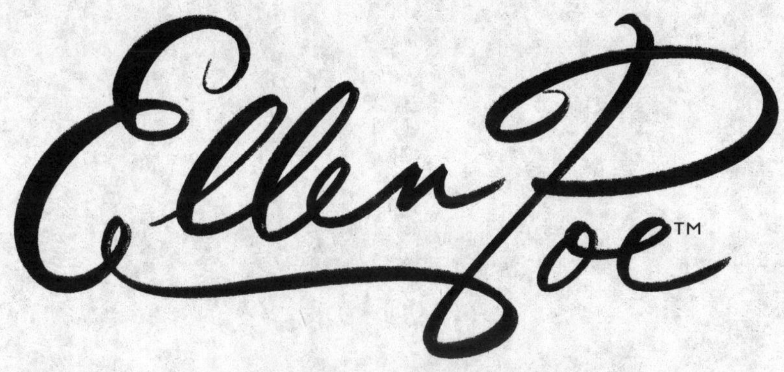

FOR EVERMORE

❁ ❁ Book 2 ❁ ❁

It is nearly a mon
, requesting an in
, I placed it (
swered letters". Th
seeming discourtesy
answer.
I have now to
you at any time
adway. You will
the morning befor
Very Resp.
W. C

EXCERPT FROM

Ellen Poe for Evermore

GUS TURNED THE STAGE OVER TO A MAN WITH A pair of bongo drums, and Rebecca beelined to him with a cup of cappuccino.

Flirting was fun, right?

I cleared my throat and scrubbed harder at a nonexistent smudge on the side of the drinks cooler.

Eddy put his non-corporeal hands over his non-corporeal ears and groaned. "I heard all things in the heaven and in the earth. I heard many things in hell. But anything was better than this agony!"

"Oh, come on," I said to him. "It's not so bad."

But Eddy just parted his fingers and stared at me with a single baleful eye.

Work got busy after that, so I stopped paying attention to both the performers and the ghost. And maybe Eddy got distracted too. That was sort of the whole point of this, wasn't it? He came down here and listened to people and their spoken-word compositions, adding a little supernatural juice to the whole endeavor.

I hate to say it, but I'm not a huge fan of poetry. Yes, I see the irony. I'm maybe the only person on Earth with a direct line to the ghost of one of history's most well-known poets, and I could not care less.

I wondered, sometimes, if there were other people like me. Was there some psychic accountant or something in London who was just as tired of Will Shakespeare whining in her ear? What about an actual poetry fan saddled with the spirit of Albert Einstein or something?

Although I'm not qualified to judge the poetry at these events, I can't argue with the results. Before Eddy and his journal showed up, Aunt Marie had a tough time gathering more than a handful of people to her open mics. Now it was standing room only, and even talent scouts had started coming. Do they believe in the ghost story? Doubtful, but they know there's a powerful vibe here, and that the performances coming out of these evenings are a cut above.

One guy who read an excerpt of his book onstage got a literary agent two weeks later, and last month, a stand-up comedian's clip went viral on social media, and he was flown out to LA to do a late-night show segment. They aren't all winners, of course, but there are some diamonds in the rough here.

And the money earned on these nights is finally paying the family's bills, for the first time in what feels like forever. So, I can't really protest against the bongo drums, or the lipstick marks, or even the ghost and his myriad opinions about meter and rhyme.

I had just replenished the big coffee bowls we used for lattes when Rebecca waved at me from the other side of the counter.

"The lady at table twelve asked for you specifically," she said to me when she came over, clearly annoyed to be losing out on the tips. But joke's on her. My service was so bad that I never got tips anyway.

"What, like, to serve her? Did you tell her my aunt has me confined behind the counter?"

Rebecca just shrugged and looked over her shoulder at the table in question.

My gaze followed and when I saw who was sitting there, I stiffened.

I'd met Ms. Sara Rice three times. The first time, I was in the Enoch Pratt Free Public Library amidst what I supposed was some kind of accidental library heist, because I wound up walking out of there with an antique fountain pen carved from a piece of Edgar Allan Poe's coffin.

The second time was when she tracked me down at my high school and told me that my actions meant I'd unknowingly entered some kind of high-stakes, Poe-themed treasure hunt.

The third time was when she came to my house, kicked me out of said treasure hunt, and offered me more money than I'd ever seen in my entire life in exchange for Eddy's journal.

I turned her down, mostly because Eddy begged me to.

And now, months later, she was sitting here on open mic night. The crowd at Raven's Rest was always diverse but tended to be a bit younger and funkier than the middle-aged librarian with her simple pantsuits, tasteful jewelry, and conservative low ponytail.

Was this research librarian secretly a poet, come to ply her skills on the Raven's Rest stage? Or had she, too, heard the rumors about Poe's spiritual presence and come to find out if they were true? After all, the only thing I knew about this woman was that she loved her some Edgar Allan Poe. She once hinted heavily to me that she was part of some secret society that venerated him.

Maybe if I'd kept playing her little treasure-hunting game last fall, I'd be part of it too.

But to be perfectly honest, I already spent too much time with the dude.

I came out from behind the counter and started over to table twelve, but I hadn't gone three steps across the painted cement floor when Eddy's ghost swooped up before me, stopping me dead in my tracks.

"It is always desirable to know who are our enemies, and what are the nature of their attacks," he said in warning, holding his hands up.

"Well, that's what I'm trying to do," I said under my breath, shifting right. Eddy also dodged. "I'm going to go ask her what she wants."

Now, ghosts are not made of matter, as hopefully everyone—even people who don't converse with them daily—knows well. Technically, I could just keep walking right through him. It's just that the last time I did that, it didn't go so well.

I dodged left and he blocked me again.

This was a big problem, because I was the only one who could see the ghost, so to everyone else in the room, I just looked like a person who was stopped in the middle of the floor, talking to myself. And I couldn't even count on the current performer to distract the crowd.

"Out of my way," I hissed under my breath. "There's no harm in finding out what she has to say."

"Not only lies, but deliberately and willfully lies," he scoffed.

I was not going to fight with a ghost in the middle of the coffee shop. I tried one more time to get around him. Near the stage, I thought I saw Gus looking at me strangely.

Great.

"Move," I growled at the ghost.

Poe did not move.

So, what choice did I have, really?

I stepped forward into his space, as if the ghost and I were about to dance.

The world changed, and right away I knew I'd made a huge mistake.

ABOUT THE AUTHOR

DIANA PETERFREUND has published sixteen novels for adults, teens, and kids. Her works have been named to the New York Public Library's Books for the Teen Age list, the Capitol Choices reading list, the Texas Lone Star Reading List, and the Sunshine State Young Readers Awards list, as well as Amazon's Best Books of the Year list. In addition, she's written dozens of short stories and a variety of nonfiction essays about popular children's literature. Diana lives in Maryland with her family.